Sherlock Holmes
On Stage

Sir Arthur Conan Doyle
and William Gillette

THEBES PUBLISHING

Introduction

Long before he became a staple of TV, movie and radio schedules, Sherlock Holmes found fame away from the pages of Sir Arthur Conan Doyle's novels and short stories in another medium – the theatre. For decades, going to see a play or a show at a theatre was the equivalent of a contemporary visit to the cinema. Theatre was the main entertainment of the masses… where better for Sherlock Holmes to begin expanding his legend?

Contained within this volume are the scripts of two major theatrical productions from a hundred years ago, along with two smaller, lesser known pieces. Each of them was important in its own way in expanding the legend of Sherlock Holmes and were an important early part of Holmes' metamorphosis from literary fad to being an instantly recognizable part of Britain's – and the world's – collective culture.

While the Holmes of Sherlock Holmes: A Drama In Four Acts may not stick to our current idea of Holmes, it's worth wondering if Holmes' legacy would be as world famous as it is now without these productions. Certainly his legend would have reached a far smaller audience in those early days.

So relax and enjoy these early scripts… the game's afoot.

Sir Arthur Conan Doyle

Sherlock Holmes
A Drama in Four Acts

Sir Arthur Conan Doyle
and William Gillette
1899

Cast of Characters
In the order of their appearance

Madge Larrabee
Alfred Bassick
John Forman
Billy
James Larrabee
Doctor Watson
Terese
Jim Craigin
Mrs Faulkner
Thomas Leary
Sidney Prince
"Lightfoot" Mctague
Alice Faulkner
Mrs Smeedley
Sherlock Holmes
Parsons
Professor Moriarty
Count von Stalburg
John
Sir Edward Leighton

ACT I

Drawing-room at the LARRABEES. Evening.

The scene represents the drawing-room at Edelweiss Lodge, an old house, gloomy and decayed, situated in a lonely district in a little-frequented part of London.

The furniture is old and decayed, with the exception of the piano — a baby-grand. The desk is very solid. The ceiling is heavily beamed. Many places out of repair in the walls and ceilings. Carvings broken here and there.

The music stops an instant before rise of curtain. A short pause after curtain is up. Curtain rises in darkness — lights come up. MADGE LARRABEE is discovered anxiously waiting. A strikingly handsome woman, but with a somewhat hard face. Black hair. Richly dressed.

Enter FORMAN with evening paper. He is a quiet perfectly trained servant. He is met by MADGE who takes the paper from him quickly.

| FORMAN | (Speaks always very quietly.)
Pardon, ma'am, but one of the maids wishes to speak with you. |

MADGE is scanning the paper eagerly and sinks on to seat at the foot of the piano.

MADGE:	(Not looking from paper.) I can't spare the time now.
FORMAN:	Very well, ma'am. (Turns to go.)
MADGE:	(Without looking up from paper.) Which maid was it?
FORMAN:	(Turning towards MADGE again.) Térèse, ma'am.
MADGE:	(Looking up. Very slight surprise in her tone.) Térêse!
FORMAN:	Yes, ma'am.

MADGE: Have you any idea what she wants?

FORMAN: Not the least, ma'am.

MADGE: She must tell you. I'm very busy, and can't see her unless I know.

FORMAN: I'll say so, ma'am.

Turns and goes out, carefully and quietly closing the door after him — immediately coming in again and watching MADGE, who is busy with paper. Finds what she has been looking for and starts eagerly to read it. As if not seeing the print well, she leans near light and resumes reading with the greatest avidity. FORMAN quietly shuts door. He stands at the door looking at MADGE as she reads the paper. This is prolonged somewhat, so that it may be seen that he is not waiting for her to finish from mere politeness. His eyes are upon her sharply and intensely, yet he does not assume any expression otherwise. She finishes and angrily rises, casting the paper violently down on the piano. She turns and goes near the large heavy desk. Pauses there. Then turns away angrily. Sees FORMAN, calms herself at once. Just as MADGE turns, FORMAN seems to be coming into room.

FORMAN: I could get nothing from her, ma'am. She insists that she must speak to you herself.

MADGE: Tell her to wait till to-morrow.

FORMAN: I asked her to do that, ma'am, and she said that she would not be here to-morrow.

MADGE turns toward FORMAN with some surprise.

MADGE: What does she mean by that?

FORMAN: Pardon me for mentioning it, ma'am, but she is a bit singular, as I take it.

MADGE: Tell her to come here—

FORMAN bows and turns to go. MADGE goes toward the piano, near where the paper lies. She sees it. Stops with hand on piano.

MADGE: Oh —Judson!

FORMAN stops and comes down. Everything quiet, subdued, cat-like in his methods.

MADGE: How did you happen to imagine that I would be interested in this marriage announcement? (Takes up paper and sits in seat below the piano.)

FORMAN: I could 'ardly help it, ma'am.

MADGE turns and looks hard at him an instant. FORMAN stands deferentially.

MADGE: I suppose you have overheard certain references to the matter — between myself and my brother?

FORMAN: I 'ave, ma'am, but I would never have referred to it in the least if I did not think it might be of some importance to you ma'am to know it.

MADGE: Oh no — of no special importance! We know the parties concerned and are naturally interested in the event. Of course, you do not imagine there is anything more. (She does not look at him as she says this.)

FORMAN: (Not looking at MADGE —eyes front.) Certainly not, ma'am. Anyway if I did imagine there was something more I'm sure you'd find it to your interest ma'am to remember my faithful services in helpin' to keep it quiet.

MADGE: (After slight pause, during which she looks steadily in front.) Judson, what sort of a fool are you?

FORMAN turns to her with feigned astonishment.

13

MADGE:	(Speaks with sharp, caustic utterances, almost between her teeth. Turns to him.) Do you imagine I would take a house, and bring this girl and her mother here and keep up the establishment for nearly two years without protecting myself against the chance of petty blackmail by my own servants?
FORMAN:	(Protestingly.) Ah—ma'am—you misunderstand me — I —
MADGE	(rising—throws paper on to the piano) I understand too well! And now I beg you to understand me. I have had a trifle of experience in the selection of my servants and can recognize certain things when I see them! It was quite evident from your behaviour you had been in something yourself and it didn't take me long to get it out of you. You are a self-confessed forger.
FORMAN:	(Quick movement of apprehension.) No! (Apprehensive look around.) Don't speak out like that! (Recovers a little.) It — it was in confidence — I told you in confidence ma'am.
MADGE:	Well, I'm telling you in confidence that at the first sign of any underhand conduct on your part this little episode of yours will —
FORMAN	(Hurriedly—to prevent her from speaking it.) Yes, yes! I — will bear it in mind, ma'am. I will bear it in mind!
MADGE	(After a sharp look at him as if satisfying herself that he is now reduced to proper condition.) Very well … Now, as to the maid — Térèse —

FORMAN inclines head for instruction.

MADGE: Do you think of anything which might explain
                her assertion that she will not be here to-
                morrow?

FORMAN: (His eyes turned away from MADGE.
                Speaking in low tones, and behaviour subdued
                as if completely humiliated.)
                It has occurred to me, ma'am, since you first
                asked me regarding the matter, that she may
                have taken exceptions to some occurrences
                which she thinks she 'as seen going on in this
                'ouse.

MADGE: I'll raise her wages if I find it necessary; tell
                her so. If it isn't money that she wants — I'll
                see her myself.

FORMAN: Very well, ma'am.
                (He turns and goes out quietly.)

MADGE stands motionless a moment. There is a sound of a heavy
door opening and closing. MADGE gives a quick motion of listening.
Hurries to look off. Enter JIM LARRABEE, through archway, in some
excitement. He is a tall, heavily-built man, with a hard face. Full of
determination and a strong character. He is well dressed, and attractive
in some respects. A fine looking man. Dark hair and eyes, but the hard
sinister look of a criminal.

MADGE: Didn't you find him? I

LARRABEE: No.
                (Goes to the heavy desk and throws open the
                wooden doors of lower part, showing the iron
                and combination lock of a safe or strong-box.
                Gives knob a turn or two nervously, and works
                at it.)

MADGE follows, watching him.

LARRABEE: He wasn't there!
                (Rises from desk.)
                We'll have to get a lock smith in.

MADGE: (Quickly.)
No, no! We can't do that! It isn't safe!

LARRABEE: We've got to do something, haven't we?
(Stoops down quickly before door of safe again, and nervously tries it.)
I wish to God I knew a bit about these things.
(Business at safe.)
There's no time to waste, either! They've put Holmes on the case!

MADGE: Sherlock Holmes?

LARRABEE: Yes.
(At safe, trying knob.)

MADGE: How do you know?

LARRABEE: I heard it at Leary's. They keep track of him down there, and every time he's put on something they give notice round.

MADGE: What could he do?

LARRABEE: (Rises and faces her.)
I don't know — but he'll make some move — he never waits long! It may be any minute!
(Moves about restlessly but stops when MADGE speaks.)

MADGE: Can't you think of someone else — as we can't find Sid?

LARRABEE: He may turn up yet. I left word with Billy Rounds, and he's on the hunt for him.
(Between his teeth.)
Oh! it's damnable. After holding on for two good years just for this and now the time comes and she's blocked us!
(Goes to and looks off and up stairway. Looks at MADGE. Goes to her.)
Look here! I'll just get at her for a minute.
(CONT/)

(Starting to go out.)
I have an idea I can change her mind.

MADGE: (Quickly.)
                Yes — but wait, Jim.

LARRABEE stops and turns to her.

MADGE: (She goes near him.)
                What's the use of hurting the girl? We've tried
                all that!

LARRABEE: Well, I'll try something else!
                (Turns and goes to archway.)

MADGE: (Quick, half whisper.)
                Jim!
                (LARRABEE turns, MADGE approaches
                him.)
                Remember — nothing that'll show! No marks!
                We might get into trouble.

LARRABEE: (Going doggedly.)
                I'll look out for that.

LARRABEE goes out, running upstairs in haste. As MADGE looks
after him with a trifle of anxiety standing in archway, enter TERESE.
She is a quiet-looking French maid with a pleasant face. She stands
near the door. MADGE turns into the room and sees her. Stands an
instant. She seats herself in the arm-chair.

MADGE: Come here.

TERESE comes down a little way—with slight hesitation.

Madge: What is it?

TERESE: Meester Judson said I vas to come.

MADGE: I told Judson to arrange with you himself.

TERESE: He could not, madame. I do not veesh longer to
                remain.

MADGE: What is it? You must give me some reason!

TERESE: It is zat I wish to go.

MADGE: You've been here months, and have made no
                  complaint.

TERESE: Ah, madame — it is not so before! It is now
                  beginning zat I do not like.

MADGE: (Rising.)
                  What? What is it you do not like?

TERESE: (With some little spirit but low voice.)
                  I do not like eet, madame — eet — here — zis
                  place — what you do — ze young lady you
                  have up zere! I cannot remain to see!
                  (Indicating above.)
                  Eet ees not well! I cannot remain to see!

MADGE: You know nothing about it! The young lady is
                  ill. She is not right here —
                  (Touching forehead.)
                  She is a great trouble to us, but we take every
                  care of her, and treat her with the utmost
                  kindness and —

A piercing scream, as if muffled by something, heard in distant part of
house above.

Music on scream. Very pianissimo. Agitato.

Pause. Both motionless. TERESE does not assume a horrified
expression; she simply stands motionless. After quite a pause, MRS.
FAULKNER comes down stairway rapidly, a white-haired lady,
dressed in an old black gown.

MRS. FAULKNER: My child! my child! They're hurting my child!

MRS. FAULKNER stands just within archway, looking vacantly,
helplessly, at MADGE. MADGE turns, sees her and goes quickly to
her.

MADGE: (Between her teeth.)
        What are you doing here? Didn't I tell you
        never to come down!

The old lady simply stares vacantly, but a vague expression of trouble
is upon her face.

MADGE: Come with me!
        (Taking MRS. FAULKNER by the arm and
        drawing her towards stairs.)

The old lady hangs back in a frightened way.

MADGE: Come, I say!
        (The scream again—more muffled—from
        above. Sudden change. Tenderly.)
        Don't be alarmed, dear, your poor daughter's
        head is bad to-day. She'll be better soon!
        (Turns to TERESE.)
        Terèse — come to me in the morning.
        (To old lady.)
        Come along, dear.
        (Then angrily in low threatening voice.)
        Do you hear me? Come!

She takes MRS. FAULKNER off with some force up the stairs.
TERESE stands looking after them. Enter FORMAN quietly. He looks
a moment toward where MADGE has just taken the old lady off.
TERESE is looking also the same way. FORMAN goes down to
TERESE. They look at one another an instant in silence. Then he
speaks to her in a low voice. Just before FORMAN speaks the music
stops.

FORMAN: She's made it quite satisfactory, I suppose.

TERESE looks at FORMAN.

FORMAN: You will not leave her — now?

TERESE: Leave her now? More zan evaire before! Do
        you hear young lady? What is eet they make to
        her?

19

FORMAN: (Low voice.)
It may be she is ill.

TERESE: Indeed, I think it is so zat zey make her eel! I
weel not remain to see!
(Turning a little.)
I can find another place; eet eez not so
difficult.

FORMAN: Not so difficult if you know where to go!

TERESE: Ah—zhat eez it!

FORMAN: I have one address —

TERESE: (Turns to him quickly.)
Bien — you know one?

FORMAN nods.

TERESE: Est-ce serieux? What you call re-li-ah-ble?

FORMAN: (Moves to her.)
Here — on this card —
(Quickly takes card from pocket and pushes it
into her hands.)
Go to that address! Don't let anyone see it!

TERESE: (Quickly looking at card while FORMAN
looks away— begins slowly to read.)
Meester — Sheer — lock —

FORMAN: (With a quick warning exclamation and sudden
turn, seizes her, covering her mouth with one
hand; they stand a moment, he looks slowly
round.)
Some one might hear you! Go to that address
in the morning.

The front door bell rings. FORMAN motions her off with quick, short
motion. She goes out. FORMAN goes out to open the house door —
quickly.

(CONT/)

Sound of house door opening — a solid, heavy sound — not sharp.
Enter SID PRINCE, walking in quickly. He is a short, stoutish, dapper
little fellow. He carries a small black satchel, wears overcoat and hat,
gloves, etc., and is well dressed and jaunty. He wears diamond scarf
pin, rings, etc., is quick in movements and always on the alert.
FORMAN follows him on, standing near archway.

PRINCE: (Going across towards piano.)
                 Don't waste toime, you fool; tell 'em I'm 'ere,
                 can't yer?

FORMAN: Did you wish to see Mr. Chetwood, sir, or was
                 it Miss Chetwood?

PRINCE: (Stopping and turning to FORMAN.)
                 Well, I'll be blowed! You act as if I'd never
                 been 'ere before! 'Ow do you know but I was
                 born in this 'ere 'ouse? Go on and tell 'em as
                 it's Mr. Sidney Prince, Esq.
                 (He puts satchel, which is apparently heavy, on
                 seat at foot of piano.)

FORMAN: Oh yes, sir — I beg your pardon! I'll announce
                 you immediate, sir.
                 (Goes out upstairs.)

PRINCE takes off hat, gloves, etc., laying them so as to cover the
satchel. Looks about room. Walks over to the heavy desk and glances
at it. Swings door of the desk open in easy business-like way.

PRINCE: Ah!
                 (As if he had found what he was looking for.
                 Not an exclamation of surprise. Drops on one
                 knee and gives the lock a turn. Rises and goes
                 over to his satchel—which he uncovers and
                 opens. Feels about for something.)

MADGE and LARRABEE come downstairs and enter. PRINCE sees
them, but does not stop what he is doing.

MADGE: (Going across to PRINCE.)
                 Oh, is that you, Sid? I'm so glad you've come.

LARRABEE:	Hallo, Sid! … Did you get my note?
PRINCE:	(Going right on with what he is doing.) Well, I'm 'ere, ain't I? (Business at satchel.) That's what it is, I take it? (Motion of head towards desk.)
MADGE:	Yes … We're awfully glad you turned up, Sid. We might have had to get in some stranger to do it. (Going across to below piano in front of PRINCE.)
PRINCE:	(Standing up and looking at LARRABEE and MADGE) That would be nice now, wouldn't it? If your game 'appens to be anything off colour —!!!
LARRABEE:	Oh — it isn't so specially dark.
PRINCE:	That different. (Goes across to desk with tools from satchel.) I say, Larrabee —

Quick "Sh!" from MADGE just behind him.

LARRABEE:	(At same time.) Shut up!

(They look round. PRINCE looks up surprised.)

LARRABEE:	For Heaven's sake, Sid, remember — my name is Chetwood here.
PRINCE:	Beg your pardon. My mistake. Old times when we was learnin' the trade together—eh!
LARRABEE:	Yes, yes!
PRINCE:	I 'ardly expected you'd be doin' the 'igh tone thing over 'ere, wen I first come up with you workin' the Sound Steamer out O' New York.

LARRABEE: Come! Don't let's go into that now.

PRINCE: Well, you needn't get so 'uffy about it! You
                  wouldn't a' been over 'ere at all, if it 'adn't
                  been for me … An' youd a' never met Madge
                  'ere neither — and a devil of a life of it you
                  might a' been leadin'.

LARRABEE: Yes, yes.

MADGE: We know all that, Sid — but can't you open
                  that box for us now? We've no time to lose.

PRINCE: Open it! I should say I could! It's one o' those
                  things it'll fall open if you let it alone long
                  enough! I'd really like to know where you
                  picked up such a relic as this 'ere box! It's an
                  old timer and no mistake!
                  (About to try some tools on lock, looks about.)
                  All clear, you say, no danger lurking?

LARRABEE: (Shaking head.)
                  Not the least!

MADGE moves away a little, glancing cautiously about. PRINCE tries
tools. LARRABEE remains near piano. Both watch him as he tries
tools in the lock.

PRINCE: (at lock)
                  You're not robbing yourselves, I trust?

LARRABEE: (near PRINCE)
                  It does look a little like it!

PRINCE: I knew you was on some rum lay — squatting
                  down in this place for over a year; but I never
                  could seem to —
                  (business)
                  get a line on you.
                  (He works a moment, then crosses to get a tool
                  out of satchel, and goes near light on piano and
                  begins to adjust it.)
                              (CONT/)

23

(This must bring him where he commands
stage. Stopping and looking sharply at
MADGE and LARRABEE.)
What do we get here? Oof, I trust?

LARRABEE: Sorry to disappoint you, but it isn't.

PRINCE: That's too bad!

MADGE: (Shakes head.)
Only a bundle of papers, Sid.

PRINCE works at tool an instant before speaking.

PRINCE: Pipers!

LARRABEE: Um!
(Grunt of assent.)

PRINCE: Realize, I trust?

MADGE: We can't tell — it may be something — it may
be nothing.

PRINCE: Well, if it's something, I'm in it, I hope.

MADGE: Why, of course, Sid — whatever you think is
due for opening the box.

PRINCE: Fair enough.
(As if it was all settled to go on.)
Now 'ere.
(Glances round quickly.)
Before we starts 'er goin' what's the general
surroundin's?

LARRABEE: What's the good of wasting time on —
(Going near PRINCE.)

PRINCE: (Up to him.)
If I'm in this, I'm in it, ain't I? An' I want to
know wot I'm in.

MADGE: Why don't you tell him, Jimmie?

PRINCE: If anything 'appened, 'ow'd I let the office
                know 'oo to look out for?

LARRABEE: Well — I'm willing to give him an idea of
                what it is but I won't give the name of the —
                (Hesitates.)

MADGE goes up to arch.

PRINCE: That's all I ask — wot it is. I don't want no
                names.

LARRABEE: (Nearer PRINCE and speaking lower.)
                You know we've been working the Continent.
                Pleasure places and all that.

PRINCE: So I've 'eard.

MADGE motions them to wait. Looking off quietly. Nods them to
proceed.

LARRABEE: It was over there — Homburg was the place.
                We ran across a young girl who'd been havin'
                trouble. Sister just died. Mother seemed wrong
                here.
                (Touches forehead.)

PRINCE: Well — you run across 'er.

LARRABEE: Madge took hold and found that this sister of
                hers had been having some kind of love affair
                with a — well — with a foreign gentleman of
                exceedingly high rank — or at least —
                expectations that way.

PRINCE: A foreign gentleman?

LARRABEE: That's what I said.

PRINCE: I don't so much care about that, yer know. My
                lay's 'ere at home.

Sir Arthur Conan Doyle

LARRABEE: Well, this is good enough for me.

PRINCE: 'Ow much was there to it?

LARRABEE: Promise of marriage.

PRINCE: Broke it, of course.

LARRABEE: Yes — and her heart with it. I don't know what
              more she expected — anyway, she did expect
              more. She and her child died together.

PRINCE: Oh—dead!

LARRABEE: Yes, but the case isn't; there are evidences —
              letters, photographs, jewellery with inscriptions
              that he gave her. The sister's been keeping
              them …
              (A glance about.)
              We've been keeping the sister … You see?

PRINCE: (Whistles.)
              Oh, it's the sister you've got 'ere? An' what's
              'er little game?

LARRABEE: To get even.

PRINCE: Ah! To get back on 'im for the way 'e treated
              'er sister?

LARRABEE: Precisely.

PRINCE: She don't want money?

LARRABEE: No.

PRINCE: An' your little game?

LARRABEE: (Shrug of shoulders.)
              Whatever there is in it.

PRINCE: These papers an' things ought to be worth a
              little Something!

LARRABEE:	I tell you it wouldn't be safe for him to marry until he gets them out of the way! He knows it very well. But what's more, the family knows it!
PRINCE:	Oh — family! … Rich, I take it.
LARRABEE:	Rich isn't quite the word. They're something else.
PRINCE:	You don't mean —

LARRABEE moves nearer PRINCE and whispers a name in his ear.

PRINCE:	My Gawd! Which of 'em?
LARRABEE:	(Shakes head.) I don't tell you that.
PRINCE:	Well, we are a-movin' among the swells now, ain't we? But this 'ere girl — the sister o' the one that died — 'ow did you manage to get 'er into it?
MADGE:	I picked her up, of course, and sympathized and consoled. I invited her to stay with me at my house in London. Jimmy came over and took this place — and when I brought her along a week later it was all ready — and a private desk safe for the letters and jewellery.
LARRABEE:	(Turning.) Yes — combination lock and all … Everything worked smooth until a couple of weeks ago, when we began to hear from a firm of London solicitors, some veiled proposals were made—which showed that the time was coming. They wanted the things out of the way. Suddenly all negotiations on their side stopped. The next thing for me to do was to threaten. I wanted the letters for this, but when I went to get them — (CONT/)

27

I found that in some way the girl had managed to change the lock on us. The numbers were wrong — and we couldn't frighten or starve her into opening the thing.

PRINCE: Oh — I see it now. You've got the stuff in there!
(Indicating safe.)

LARRABEE: That's what I'm telling you! It's in there, and we can't get it out! She's juggled the lock.

PRINCE: (Going at once to safe.)
Oh, well, it won't take long ta rectify that triflin' error.
(Stops.)
But wot gets me is the w'y they broke off with their offers that way — can you make head or tail of that?

LARRABEE: Yes.
(Goes nearer to PRINCE.)
It's simple enough.

PRINCE turns to him for explanation.

They've given it up themselves, and have got in Sherlock Holmes on the case.

PRINCE: (Suddenly starting.)
Wot's that!
(Pause.)
Is 'Olmes in this?

LARRABEE: That's what they told me!

MADGE: But what can he do, Sid? We haven't —

PRINCE: 'Ere, don't stand talking about that — I'll get the box open.
(Goes to piano in front of LARRABEE.)
You send a telegram, that's all I want!
(CONT/)

(Tears page out of his note-book and writes
hurriedly The other two watch him,
LARRABEE a little suspiciously. Silence for a
few moments while he writes.)
Where's your nearest telegraph office?

MADGE: Round the corner.
(Going to above piano.)

PRINCE: (Down to LARRABEE and giving him the
telegram he has written.)
Run for it! Mind what I say — run for it.

LARRABEE is looking at him hard.

PRINCE: That's to Alf Bassick. He's Professor
Moriarty's confidential man. Moriarty is king
of 'em all in London. He runs everything that's
shady — an' 'Olmes 'as been settin' lines all
round 'im for months — and he didn't know it
— an' now he's beginnin' to find out that
'Olmes is trackin' 'im down — and there's the
devil to pay. 'E wants any cases 'Olmes is on
— it's a dead fight between 'em! 'E'll take the
case just to get at 'Olmes! 'E'll kill 'im before
'e's finished with 'im, you can lay all you've
got on it.

LARRABEE: What are you telling him?

PRINCE: Nothing whatever, except I've got a job on as I
wants to see 'im about in the mornin' … Read
it yourself.

LARRABEE looks at what PRINCE has written.

PRINCE: But don't take all night over it! You cawn't tell
wot might 'appen.
(Crosses to safe.)

MADGE: Go on, Jim!

LARRABEE crosses, MADGE following him.

29

LARRABEE: (To MADGE near archway.)
                   Keep your eyes open.

MADGE: (To LARRABEE.)
                   Don't you worry!

LARRABEE goes out.

MADGE is looking after him. Quick sound of door closing. PRINCE
drops down to work — real work now — at desk. Short pause.
MADGE stands watching PRINCE a moment. She moves over to near
piano and picks up a book carelessly, which she glances at with perfect
nonchalance. After a time she speaks without taking eyes from book.

MADGE: I've heard of this Professor Moriarty.

PRINCE: If you 'aven't you must've been out in the
                   woods.

MADGE: You say he's king of them all.

PRINCE: (Working.)
                   Bloomin' Hemperor — that's wot I call 'im.

MADGE: He must be a good many different things.

PRINCE: You might see it that way if you looked around
                   an' didn't breathe too 'ard!

MADGE: What does he do?

PRINCE: I'll tell you one thing he does!
                   (Turns to her and rests a moment from work.)
                   He sits at 'ome — quiet and easy — an runs
                   nearly every big operation that's on. All the
                   clever boys are under him one way or another
                   — an' he 'olds them in 'is 'and without
                   moving a muscle! An' if there's a slip and the
                   police get wind of it there ain't never any 'old
                   on 'im. They can't touch him. And wot's more,
                   they wouldn't want to if they could.

MADGE: Why not?

PRINCE: Because they've tried it — that's w'y — an'
                       the men as did try it was found shortly after a-
                       floatin' in the river — that is, if they was found
                       at all! The moment a man's marked there ain't
                       a street that's safe for 'im! No — nor yet an
                       alley.
                       (Resumes drilling.)

MADGE: (After pause.)
                       What's the idea of telling him about this? He
                       might not want —

PRINCE: (Turning to her,)
                       I tell yer, 'e'll come into anything that gives
                       'im a chance at 'Olmes — he wants ter trap
                       'im — that's wot is an just what he'll do
                       (Resumes work.)

PRINCE works rapidly, drill going in suddenly as if he had one hole
sunk. He tries a few tools in it and quickly starts another hole with
drills. MADGE starts forward at business of drill.

MADGE: (Recovering to careless.)
                       Have you got it, Sid?

PRINCE: Not yet — but I'll be there soon.
                       (Works.)
                       I know where I am now.

Sound of door closing outside. Enter LARRABEE hurriedly. He is
breathless from running.

LARRABEE: Well, Sid. How goes it?

PRINCE: (Working.)
                       So-so.

LARRABEE: Now about this Professor Moriarty?
                       (Gets chair from near piano and sits behind
                       PRINCE.)

PRINCE: (Working.)
                       Ask 'er.

31

MADGE: It's all right, Jim. It was the proper thing to do.

Music. Melodramatic, very pp. Hardly audible.

MADGE and LARRABEE move near PRINCE, looking over him
eagerly. He quickly introduces small punch and hammers rapidly;
sound of bolts, etc., falling inside lock as if loosened. Eagerness of all
three increases with final sound of loose iron work inside lock, and
PRINCE at once pulls open the iron doors. All three give a quick look
within. MADGE and LARRABEE start back with subdued
exclamation. PRINCE looks in more carefully, then turns to them.
Pause. LARRABEE in moving back pushes chair along with him.
Pause. Music stops.

MADGE: (Turning to LARRABEE.)
                          Gone!

LARRABEE: (To MADGE,)
                          She's taken 'em out.

PRINCE: (Rising to his feet.)
                          What do you mean?

LARRABEE: The girl!

MADGE stops and goes quickly to safe in front of PRINCE and
dropping down feels carefully about inside. Others watch her closely.
PRINCE gives back a little for her.

(NOTE. — Their dialogue since opening of safe has dropped to low
excited tones, almost whispers, as they would if it were a robbery.
Force of habit in their intense excitement.)

MADGE: (Rises and turns to LARRABEE.)
                          She's got them!

PRINCE: 'Ow can you tell as she 'asn't done the trick
                          already?

LARRABEE: (Quick turn on PRINCE.)
                          What's that?

PRINCE: She wants to get even, you say.

MADGE: Yes! yes!

PRINCE: Well, then, if she's got the thing out of the box
                    there — ain't it quite likely she's sent 'em
                    along to the girl as 'e wants to marry.
                    (Brief pause.)

MADGE: No! She hasn't had the chance.

LARRABEE: She couldn't get them out of this room. We've
                    Watched her too close for that.

MADGE: Wait!
                    (Turns and looks rapidly about piano, etc.)

LARRABEE hurriedly looks about under cushions.

LARRABEE: Here!
                    (Strides towards archway.)
                    I'll get her down She'll tell us where they are
                    or strangle for it!
                    (Turns hurriedly.)
                    Wait here! When I get her in, don't give her
                    time to think!

LARRABEE goes out. PRINCE comes to the end of the piano looking
off after LARRABEE.

Music. Very pp.

Brief pause. MADGE glances nervously.

PRINCE: Wot's he goin' to do?

MADGE: There's only one thing, Sid. We've got to get it
                    out of her or two years' work is wasted.

Muffled cry of pain from ALICE in distance. Pause.

PRINCE: (Glances off anxiously.)
                    Look 'ere, I don't so much fancy this sort of
                    thing.
                    (Goes to safe and collects tools.)

MADGE: Don't you worry, we'll attend to it!

Sound of LARRABEE approaching outside and speaking angrily
Nearer and nearer. Footsteps heard just before entrance. LARRABEE
drags ALICE FAULKNER on, jerking her across him.

LARRABEE: (As he brings ALICE on.)
                         Now, we'll see whether you will or not!
                         (Pause for an instant.)

NOTE. — This scene should be played well up stage.

Music stops.

LARRABEE: (Coming down.)
                         Now tell her what we want.

ALICE: (Low voice — slight shake of head.)
                         You needn't tell me, I know well enough.

MADGE: (Drawing nearer to ALICE with quiet cat-like
                         glide. Smiling.)
                         Oh no dear you don't know. It isn't anything
                         about locks, or keys, or numbers this time.
                         (Points slowly to the open safe.)
                         We want to know what you've done with
                         them!

Pause. ALICE looks at MADGE calmly. No defiance or suffering in
her expression.

MADGE: (Comes closer and speaks with set teeth.)
                         Do you hear! We want to know what you've
                         done with them.

ALICE: (Low voice—but clear and distinct.)
                         You will not know from me.

LARRABEE: (Sudden violence, yet subdued, as if not
                         wishing servants to overhear.)
                         We will know from you — and we'll know
                         before —
                         (As if to cross MADGE to ALICE.)

MADGE: (Motioning him.)
                          Wait, Jim!
                          (Moves down with him a little.)

LARRABEE: (To MADGE, violently.)
                          I tell you, they're in this room — she couldn't
                          have got them out — and I'm going to make
                          her —
                          (As if to seize ALICE.)

MADGE: (Detaining him.)
                          No! Let me speak to her first!

LARRABEE after an instant's sullen pause, turns and walks up stage.
Watches from above sullenly. MADGE turns to ALICE again.

MADGE: Don't you think, dear, it's about time to
                          remember that you owe us a little
                          consideration? Wasn't it something, just a little
                          something, that we found you friendless and ill
                          in Homburg and befriended you?

ALICE: It was only to rob me.

MADGE: Wasn't it something that we brought you and
                          your mother across to England with us — that
                          we kept you here — in our own home — and
                          supported and cared for you —

ALICE: So that you could rob me.

MADGE: My dear child — you have nothing of value.
                          That package of letters wouldn't bring you
                          sixpence.

ALICE: Then why do you want it? Why do you
                          persecute me and starve me to get it?
                          (Pause — MADGE looking at her cruelly.)
                          All your friendship to me and my mother was a
                          pretence — a sham. It was only to get what
                          you wanted away from me when the time
                          came.

MADGE: Why, we have no idea of such a thing!

ALICE: (Turning slightly on MADGE.)
                    I don't believe you.

LARRABEE: (Who has controlled himself with difficulty.)
                    Well, believe me, then.

ALICE turns to him, frightened but calm. No forced expressions of
pain and despair anywhere in the scene.

LARRABEE: (Moves towards her.)
                    You're going to tell us what you've done with
                    that package before you leave this room to-
                    night!

MADGE backs away a step or two.

ALICE: Not if you kill me.

LARRABEE: (Seizing ALICE violently by the arms or wrists
                    at back of her.)
                    It isn't killing that's going to do it — it's
                    something else.

Music melodramatic and pathetic.

LARRABEE gets ALICE'S arms behind her, and holds her as if
wrenching or twisting them from behind. She gives slight cry of pain.
MADGE comes to her. PRINCE looks away during following —
appearing not to like the scene but not moving.

MADGE: (Sharp hard voice.)
                    Tell us where it is! Tell us and he'll stop.

LARRABEE: (A little behind — business of gripping as if
                    wrenching her arms.)
                    Out with it!

ALICE: (Suppressed cry or moan.)
                    Oh!

(NOTE. — ALICE has little expression of pain on her face. The idea
is to be game.)

MADGE: Where is it?

LARRABEE: Speak quick now! I'll give you a turn next time
that'll take it out of you.

MADGE: (Low voice.)
Be careful, Jimmie!

LARRABEE: (Angry.)
Is this any time to be careful? I tell you we've
got to get it out of her — and we'll do it too!
(Business.)
Will you tell?
(Business.)
Will you tell?
(Business.)
Will you —

Loud ringing of door bell in distant part of house.

NOTE. — This must on no account be close at hand.

After bell music stops.

PRINCE: (Quick turn on ring. Short sharp whisper as he
starts up.)
Lookout!

All stand listening an instant. ALICE, however, heard nothing, as the
pain has made her faint, though not unconscious. LARRABEE pushes
ALICE into chair facing fire-place. He then hides her. MADGE goes
quickly and cautiously draws picture from a small concealed window.
LARRABEE stands near ALICE close up to her. Steps heard outside.
LARRABEE turns quickly, hearing steps. Make these steps distinct—
slow—not loud.

LARRABEE: (Speaking off.)
Here!

Enter FORMAN. He stands waiting.

LARRABEE: Don't go to that door; see who it is.

FORMAN simply waits — no surprise on his face. MADGE turning and speaking in low but clear voice. LARRABEE stands so that FORMAN will not see ALICE.

MADGE: (Standing on ottoman.)
Tall, slim man in a long coat — soft hat — smooth face — carries … an ebony cane — (Short, quick exclamation from PRINCE.)

PRINCE: (Breaks in with quick exclamation under breath. MADGE stopped by PRINCE'S exclamation.)
Sherlock 'Olmes! He's 'ere!

Pause. PRINCE quickly conceals his satchel above safe — also closing door of safe. Music melodramatic, very pp.

LARRABEE: (Moving towards piano, turns out lamp.)
We won't answer the bell.

PRINCE: (Turning from tools, etc., and stopping him quickly.)
Now that won't do, ye know! Looks crooked at the start!

LARRABEE: You're right! We'll have him in — and come the easy innocent.
(He turns up the lamp again.)

MADGE: There's the girl!

PRINCE: (At piano.)
Get her away — quick!

ALICE is beginning to notice what goes on in a dreamy way.

LARRABEE: Take her up the back stairway!

MADGE takes ALICE quickly and forces her to door as they speak.

MADGE: (Stopping to speak to LARRABEE and speaking out very distinctly.) She's in poor health and can't see anyone — you understand.

LARRABEE: Yes! yes! Lock her in the room — and stay by the door.

MADGE and ALICE quickly go out. LARRABEE closes door at once and stands an instant, uncertain. Then he goes to and opens lid of box on wall seat, and gets a loaded club — an ugly looking weapon — and shoves it into PRINCE'S hand.

LARRABEE: You get out there! (Indicating.) Keep quiet there till he gets in the house — then come round to the front.

PRINCE: I come round to the front after 'e's in the 'ouse — that plain.

LARRABEE: Be ready for 'im when he comes out! If he's got the things in spite of us, I'll give you two sharp whistles! If you don't hear it, let him pass.

PRINCE: But if I do 'ear the two whistles—?

LARRABEE: Then let 'im have it.

PRINCE gets off at window, which he closes at once. LARRABEE moves rapidly, kicking door of desk shut as he passes. Stands at piano, leaning on it carelessly. Turns to FORMAN.

LARRABEE: Go on, answer the bell.

FORMAN bows slightly and goes. LARRABEE strolls about trying to get into an assumption of coolness. Picks up book off piano. Sound of heavy door closing outside. Brief pause. Enter SHERLOCK HOLMES, hat and stick in hand — wearing a long coat or ulster, and gloves. He lingers in the archway, apparently seem nothing in particular, and slowly drawing off gloves. Then moves to the wall seat close at hand and sits.

Music stops.

After quite a time LARRABEE turns, throws book on piano, and saunters towards HOLMES in rather an ostentatious manner.

LARRABEE: Mr. Holmes, I believe.

HOLMES: (Rises and turning to LARRABEE as if mildly surprised.)
                   Yes, sir.

LARRABEE: Who did you wish to see, Mr. Holmes?

HOLMES: (Looking steadily at LARRABEE an instant. Speaks very quietly.)
                   Thank you so much — I sent my card — by the butler.

LARRABEE: (Stands motionless an instant — after an instant pause.)
                   Oh—very well.

Long pause. Enter FORMAN down stairs. LARRABEE moves up near piano and turns to hear what FORMAN says.

FORMAN: (To HOLMES.)
                   Miss Faulkner begs Mr. Holmes to excuse her. She is not well enough to see anyone this evening.

HOLMES takes out note-book and pencil and writes a word or two on a card or leaf of the book. Tears it out of book. Pulls out watch and glances at it. Hands the card to FORMAN, taking off coat first.

HOLMES: Hand Miss Faulkner this — and say that I have—

LARRABEE: I beg your pardon, Mr. Holmes, but it's quite useless — really.

HOLMES: Oh — I'm so sorry to hear it.

HOLMES turns quietly to LARRABEE and looks at him.
LARRABEE is a trifle affected by HOLMES' quiet scrutiny.

LARRABEE: Yes — Miss Faulkner is — I regret to say —
quite an invalid. She is unable to see anyone —
her health is so poor.

HOLMES: Did it ever occur to you that she might be
confined to the house too much?

An instant's pause.

LARRABEE: (Suddenly in low threatening tone, but not too
violent.)
How does that concern you?

HOLMES: (Easily.)
It doesn't … I simply made the suggestion.

The two look at one another an instant. HOLMES turns quietly to
FORMAN.

Holmes: That's all.
(Motions him slightly.)
Go on. Take it up.

FORMAN goes out up stairway. After a moment LARRABEE turns,
breaking into hearty laughter.

LARRABEE: Ha! ha! This is really too good.
(Strolling about laughing.)
Why, of course he can take up your card — or
your note — or whatever it is, if you wish it so
much; I was only trying to save You the
trouble.

HOLMES: (Who has been watching him through
foregoing speech.)
Thanks — hardly any trouble at all to send a
card.
(Seats himself in an easy languid way — picks
up Punch.)

LARRABEE: (Endeavours to be easy, careless and patronizing.)
Do you know, Mr. Holmes, you interest me very much.

HOLMES: (Easily.)
Ah!

LARRABEE: Upon my word, yes! We've all heard of your wonderful methods.
(Coming towards HOLMES.)
Your marvellous insight — your ingenuity in picking up and following clues — and the astonishing manner in which you gain information from the most trifling details …
Now, I dare say — in this brief moment or two you've discovered any number of things about me.

HOLMES: Nothing of consequence, Mr. Chetwood — I have scarcely more than asked myself why you rushed off and sent that telegram in such a frightened hurry — what possible excuse you could have had for gulping down that tumbler of raw brandy at the "Lion's Head" on the way back — why your friend with the auburn hair left so suddenly by the terrace window — and what there can possibly be about the safe in the lower part of that desk to cause you such painful anxiety.

Pause. LARRABEE standing motionless looking at HOLMES.
HOLMES picks up paper and reads.

LARRABEE: Ha! ha! very good! Very good indeed! If those things were only true now, I'd be wonderfully impressed. It would absolutely —

He breaks off as FORMAN enters — coming down stairs. He quietly crosses to LARRABEE, who is watching him, and extends salver with a note upon it. HOLMES is looking over paper languidly.
LARRABEE takes note. FORMAN retires.

LARRABEE: You'll excuse me, I trust.

HOLMES remains silent, glancing over paper and looking quietly at
FORMAN. LARRABEE reads the note hastily.

LARRABEE: (First a second's thought after reading, as he
sees that HOLMES is not observing him —
then speaking.)
Ah — it's from — er — Faulkner! Well really!
She begs to be allowed to see — Mr. Holmes.
She absolutely implores it!
(HOLMES looks slowly up as though scarcely
interested.)
Well, I suppose I shall have to give way.
(Turns to FORMAN.)
Judson!

FORMAN: Sir.

LARRABEE: (Emphasizing words in italics.)
Ask Miss Faulkner to come down to the
drawing-room. Say that Mr. Holmes is waiting
to see her.

FORMAN: Yes, sir.
(Bows and goes out upstairs.)

LARRABEE: (Trying to get on the free and easy style again.)
It's quite remarkable, upon my soul! May I
ask—
(Turns toward HOLMES.)
— if it's not an impertinent question, what
message you sent up that could have so
aroused Miss Faulkner's desire to come down?

HOLMES: (Looking up at LARRABEE innocently.)
Merely that if she wasn't down here in five
minutes I'd go up.

LARRABEE: (Slightly knocked.)
Oh, that was it!

HOLMES: Quite so.
                    (Rises and takes his watch out.)
                    And unless I am greatly mistaken I hear the
                    young lady on the stairs. In which case she has
                    a minute and a half to spare.
                    (Moving by piano — taking opportunity to
                    look at keys, music, etc.)

Enter MADGE LARRABEE downstairs as if not quite strong. She has
made her face pale, and steadies herself a little by columns, side of
arch, furniture, etc., as she comes on, but not overdoing this. She gives
the impression of a person a little weak, but endeavouring not to let it
be seen.

LARRABEE: (Advancing to MADGE.)
                    Alice — or — that is, Miss Faulkner, let me
                    introduce Mr. Sherlock Holmes.

HOLMES is near piano. MADGE goes a step to him with extended
hand. HOLMES meets MADGE and takes her hand in the utmost
confidence.

MADGE: Mr. Holmes!
                    (Coming toward him with extended hand.)

HOLMES: (Meeting MADGE.)
                    Miss Faulkner!

MADGE: I'm really most charmed to meet you —
                    although it does look as if you had made me
                    come down in spite of myself, doesn't it? But it
                    isn't so at all, Mr. Holmes. I was more than
                    anxious to come, only the doctor has forbidden
                    me seeing anyone — but when Cousin Freddie
                    said I might come, of course that fixed the
                    responsibility on him, so I have a perfectly
                    clear conscience.

HOLMES: I thank you very much for consenting to see
                    me, Miss Faulkner, but regret that you were put
                    to the trouble of making such a very rapid
                    change of dress.

MADGE slightest possible start, and recover at once.

MADGE:　　　　　　Ye — yes! I did hurry a trifle, I confess.
　　　　　　　　　(Crosses toward LARRABEE.)
　　　　　　　　　Mr. Holmes is quite living up to his reputation,
　　　　　　　　　isn't he, Freddie?

LARRABEE:　　　　Yes … But he didn't quite live up to it a
　　　　　　　　　moment ago.

MADGE:　　　　　　Oh, didn't he! I'm so sorry.
　　　　　　　　　(Sits on seat at foot of piano.)

LARRABEE:　　　　No. He's been telling me the most astonishing
　　　　　　　　　things.

MADGE:　　　　　　And they weren't true?

LARRABEE:　　　　Well hardly!
　　　　　　　　　(HOLMES sits in arm-chair.)
　　　　　　　　　He wanted to know what there was about the
　　　　　　　　　safe in the lower part that desk that caused me
　　　　　　　　　such horrible anxiety! Ha! ha! ha!

MADGE:　　　　　　(Above LARRABEE'S laugh — to
　　　　　　　　　HOLMES.)
　　　　　　　　　Why, this isn't anything.
　　　　　　　　　(To LARRABEE.)
　　　　　　　　　Is there?

LARRABEE:　　　　That's just it! Ha! ha! ha!
　　　　　　　　　(With a quick motion swings back the doors.)
　　　　　　　　　There's a safe there, but nothing in it.

MADGE joins him in laughter.

MADGE:　　　　　　(As she laughs.)
　　　　　　　　　Really Mr. Holmes, that's too grotesque, ha!
　　　　　　　　　ha!

HOLMES, seated in arm-chair among the cushions, regards MADGE
and LARRABEE with a peculiar whimsical look.

LARRABEE: (Laughing.)
                Perhaps you'll do better next time!
                (Closes safe door.)

MADGE: Yes, next time —
                (HOLMES is looking at them.)
                You might try on me, Mr. Holmes.
                (Looking playfully at HOLMES, greatly
                enjoying the lark.)

LARRABEE: Yes, what do you think of her?

HOLMES: It is very easy to discern one thing about Miss
                Faulkner— and that is, that she is particularly
                fond of the piano that her touch is exquisite,
                her expression wonderful, and her technique
                extraordinary. While she likes light music very
                well, she is extremely fond of some of the great
                masters, among whom are Chopin, Liszt. She
                plays a great deal indeed; I see it is her chief
                diversion — which makes it all the more
                remarkable that she has not touched the piano
                for three days.

Pause.

MADGE: (Turning to LARRABEE —a trifle
                disconcerted by HOLMES'S last words, but
                nearly hiding it with success.)
                Why that's quite surprising, isn't it?

LARRABEE: Certainly better than he did for me.

HOLMES: (Rising..)
                I am glad to somewhat repair my shattered
                reputation, and as a reward, will Miss Faulkner
                be so good as to play me something of which I
                am particularly fond?

MADGE: I shall be delighted — if I can.
                (Looks questioningly at HOLMES.)

HOLMES:	If you can! Something tells me that Chopin's Prelude Number Fifteen is at your finger ends.
MADGE:	Oh yes! (Rising and forgetting her illness, and going to keyboard — crossing in front of piano.) I can give you that.
HOLMES:	It will please me so much.
MADGE:	(Stopping suddenly as she is about to sit at piano.) But tell me, Mr. Holmes, how did you know so much about my playing — my expression — technique?
HOLMES:	Your hands.
MADGE:	And my preference for the composers you mentioned?
HOLMES:	Your music-rack.
MADGE:	How simple! But you said I hadn't played for three days. How did—
HOLMES:	The keys.
MADGE:	The keys?
HOLMES:	A light layer of dust.
MADGE:	Dust! Oh dear! (Quick business with handkerchief on keyboard.) I never knew Terèse to forget before. (To HOLMES.) You must think us very untidy, I'm sure.
HOLMES:	Quite the reverse. I see from many things that you are not untidy in the least, and therefore I am compelled to conclude that the failure of Térêse is due to something else.

47

MADGE: (A little under breath — and hesitatingly —yet compelled by HOLMES' pointed statement to ask.)
Wh—what?

HOLMES: To some unusual excitement or disturbance that has recently taken place in this house.

MADGE: (After an instant's pause.)
You're doing very well, Mr. Holmes, and you deserve your Chopin.
(Sits, makes preparation to play rather hurriedly in order to change the subject.)

HOLMES: Thanks.

LARRABEE looks toward safe, far from easy in his mind, and leans on piano, giving HOLMES a glance as he turns to MADGE. MADGE strikes a few preliminary chords during above business and soon begins to play the composition spoken of. Shortly after the music begins, and while LARRABEE is looking to front or elsewhere, HOLMES reaches quietly back and pulls the bell crank. No sound of bell heard, the music supposed to make it inaudible. He then sinks into seat just at bell. After a short time FORMAN enters and stands waiting just in the archway. LARRABEE does not see FORMAN at first, but happening to turn discovers him standing there and speaks a warning word to MADGE under his breath. MADGE, hearing LARRABEE speak, looks up and sees FORMAN. She stops playing in the midst of a bar — a hesitating stop. Looks at FORMAN a moment.

MADGE: What are you doing here, Judson?

Brief pause because FORMAN seems surprised.

FORMAN: I came to see what was wanted, ma'am.

Brief pause.

MADGE: What was wanted?

Brief pause.

LARRABEE: Nobody asked you to come here.

FORMAN: I beg pardon, sir. I answered the bell.

LARRABEE: (Becoming savage.)
                  What bell?

FORMAN: The drawing-room bell, sir.

LARRABEE: (Threateningly.)
                  What do you mean, you blockhead!

FORMAN: I'm quite sure it rang, sir.

LARRABEE: (Loud voice.)
                  Well, I tell you it did not ring!

Pause. The LARRABEES look angrily at FORMAN.

HOLMES: (Quietly — after slight pause — clear incisive
                  voice.)
                  Your butler is right Mr. Chetwood — the bell
                  did ring.

Brief pause. LARRABEE and MADGE looking at HOLMES.

LARRABEE: How do you know?

HOLMES: I rang it.

MADGE rises.

LARRABEE: (Roughly.)
                  What do you want?

HOLMES rises, takes card from case or pocket.

HOLMES: I want to send my card to Miss Faulkner.
                  (Gives card to FORMAN.)

FORMAN stands apparently paralysed.

LARRABEE:	(Angrily — approaching HOLMES.) What right have you to ring for servants and give orders in my house?
HOLMES:	(Turning on LARRABEE.) What right have you to prevent my cards from reaching their destination — and how does it happen that you and this woman are resorting to trickery and deceit to prevent me from seeing Alice Faulkner? (The situation is held an instant and then he turns quietly to FORMAN.) Through some trifling oversight, Judson, neither of the cards I handed you have been delivered. See that this error — does not occur again.

FORMAN stands, apparently uncertain what to do.

FORMAN:	My orders, sir —
HOLMES:	(Quick — sharp.) Ah! you have orders! (A sudden sharp glance at LARRABEE and back in an instant.)
FORMAN:	I can't say, sir, as I —
HOLMES:	(Quickly breaking in.) You were told not to deliver my card!
LARRABEE:	(Step or two up.) What business is this of yours, I'd like to know?
HOLMES:	I shall satisfy your curiosity on that point in a very short time.
LARRABEE:	Yes — and you'll find out in a very short time that it isn't safe to meddle with me! It wouldn't be any trouble at all for me to throw you out into the street.

HOLMES: (Sauntering easily towards him—shaking
                   finger ominously.)
                   Possibly not — but trouble would swiftly
                   follow such an experiment on your part.

LARRABEE: It's a cursed lucky thing for you I'm not
                   armed.

HOLMES: Yes — well, when Miss Faulkner comes down
                   you can go and arm yourself.

LARRABEE: Arm myself! I'll call the police! And what's
                   more, I'll do it now.

HOLMES steps down and faces LARRABEE

HOLMES: You will not do it now. You will remain where
                   you are until the lady I came here to see has
                   entered this room.

LARRABEE: What makes you so sure of that?

HOLMES: (In his face.)
                   Because you will infinitely prefer to avoid an
                   investigation of your very suspicious conduct
                   Mr. James Larrabee —

A sharp start from both LARRABEE and MADGE on hearing
HOLMES address the former by his proper name.

HOLMES: — an investigation that shall certainly take
                   place if you or your wife presume further to
                   interfere with my business
                   (Turns to FORMAN.)
                   As for you, my man—it gives me great
                   pleasure recall the features of an old
                   acquaintance. Your recent connection with the
                   signing of another man's name to a small piece
                   of paper has made your presence at Bow Street
                   much desired. You either deliver that card to
                   Miss Faulkner at once — or you sleep in the
                   police station to night.
                                    (CONT/)

51

Sir Arthur Conan Doyle

It is a matter of small consequence to me
which you do.
(Turns and strolls near fire, picking book from
mantelpiece—and sits.)

FORMAN stands motionless but torn with conflicting fears.

FORMAN: (Finally in a low painful voice—whispers
               hoarse.)
               Shall I go sir?

MADGE moves to near LARRABEE, at piano.

LARRABEE: Go on. Take up the card — it makes no
               difference to me.

MADGE: (Quick sharp aside to LARRABEE.)
               If she comes down can't he get them away
               from her?

LARRABEE: (To MADGE.)
               If he does Sid Prince is waiting for him
               outside.

FORMAN appearing to be greatly relieved, turns and goes out up
stairs with HOLMES' card.

Pathetic music, very pp.

A pause—no one moves.

Enter ALICE FAULKNER. She comes down a little — very weak —
looking at LARRABEE, then seeing HOLMES for first time.

Stop music.

HOLMES: (On seeing ALICE, rises and puts book on
               mantel. After a brief pause, turns and comes
               down to LARRABEE.)
               A short time since you displayed an acute
               anxiety to leave the room. Pray do not let me
               detain you or your wife — any longer.

The LARRABEES do not move. After a brief pause, HOLMES shrugs shoulders slightly and goes over to ALICE. HOLMES and ALICE regard each other a moment.

ALICE: This is Mr. Holmes?

HOLMES: Yes.

ALICE: You wished to see me?

HOLMES: Very much indeed, Miss Faulkner, but I am
                    sorry to see —
                    (placing chair near her)
                    — you are far from well.

ALICE: (A step. LARRABEE gives a quick glance
                    across at her, threateningly, and a gesture of
                    warning, but keeping it down.)
                    Oh no —
                    (Stops as she catches LARRABEE'S angry
                    glance.)

HOLMES: (Pausing as he is about to place chair, and
                    looking at her.)
                    No?
                    (Lets go of his chair.)
                    I beg your pardon — but —
                    (Goes to her and takes her hand delicately —
                    looks at red marks on her wrist. Looking up at
                    her.)
                    What does this mean?

ALICE: (Shrinking a little. Sees LARRABEE'S cruel
                    glance.)
                    Oh— nothing.

HOLMES looks steadily at her an instant.

HOLMES: Nothing?

ALICE: (Shaking head.)
                    No!

HOLMES: And the —
           (Pointing lightly.)
           — mark here on your neck. Plainly showing
           the clutch of a man's fingers?
           (Indicating a place on her neck where more
           marks appear.)
           Does that mean nothing also?

Pause. ALICE turns slightly away without answering.

HOLMES: (Looking straight before him to front.)
           It occurs to me that I would like to have an
           explanation of this … Possibly —
           (Turns slowly towards LARRABEE.)
           — you can furnish one, Mr. Larrabee?

Pause.

LARRABEE: (Doggedly.)
           How should I know?

HOLMES: It seems to have occurred in your house.

LARRABEE: (Advancing a little, becoming violently angry.)
           What if it did? You'd better understand that it
           isn't healthy for you or anyone else to interfere
           with my business.

HOLMES: (Quickly—incisively.)
           Ah! Then it is your business. We have that
           much at least.

LARRABEE stops suddenly and holds himself in.

HOLMES: (Turning to ALICE.)
           Pray be seated, Miss Faulkner.
           (Placing chair as if not near enough.)

ALICE hesitates an instant — then decides to remain standing for the
present. LARRABEE stands watching and listening to interview
between HOLMES and ALICE.

ALICE:	I don't know who you are, Mr. Holmes, or why you are here.
HOLMES:	I shall be very glad to explain. So far as the question of my identity is concerned, you have my name and address as well as the announcement of my profession upon the card, which I observe you still hold clasped tightly in the fingers of your left hand.

ALICE at once looks at the card in her hand.

ALICE:	(A look at him.) A — detective! (Sits on ottoman, looking at HOLMES.)
HOLMES:	(Draws near her and sits.) Quite so. And my business is this. I have been consulted as to the possibility of obtaining from you certain letters and other things which are supposed to be in your possession, and which — I need not tell you — are the source of the greatest anxiety.
ALICE	(Her manner changing and no longer timid and shrinking.) It is quite true I have such letters, Mr. Holmes, but it will be impossible to get them from me; others — have tried — and failed.
HOLMES:	What others have or have not done, while possibly instructive in certain directions, can in no way affect my conduct, Miss Faulkner. I have come to you frankly and directly, to beg you to pity and forgive.
ALICE:	There are some things, Mr. Holmes, beyond pity — beyond forgiveness.
HOLMES:	But there are other things that are not. (ALICE looks at him.) (CONT/)

	I am able to assure you of the sincere penitence — the deep regret — of the one who inflicted the injury, and of his earnest desire to make — any reparation in his power.

ALICE: How can reparation be made to the dead?

HOLMES: How indeed! And for that very reason, whatever injury you yourself may be able to inflict by means of these things can be no reparation — no satisfaction — no indemnity to the one no longer here. You will be acting for the living — not the dead. For your own satisfaction, Miss Faulkner, your own gratification, your own revenge!

ALICE starts slightly at the idea suggested and rises. Pause. HOLMES rises, moves his chair back a little, standing with his hand on it.

ALICE: (Stands a moment, very quiet low voice.) I know — from this and from other things that have happened — that a — a marriage is — contemplated.

HOLMES: It is quite true.

ALICE: I cannot give up what I intend to do, Mr. Holmes. There are other things beside revenge — there is punishment. If I am not able to communicate with the family — to which this man proposes to ally himself — in time to prevent such a thing — the punishment will come later — but you may be perfectly sure it will come.
          (HOLMES is about to speak. She motions him not to speak.)
          There is nothing more to say!

HOLMES gives a signal.

ALICE: (She looks at HOLMES an instant.)
          Good night, Mr. Holmes.
          (She turns and starts to go.)

HOLMES: But my dear Miss Faulkner, before you —

A confused noise of shouting and terrified screams from below followed by sounds of people running up a stairway and through the halls.

HOLMES: What's that?

All stop and listen. Noise louder. Enter FORMAN, breathless and white. At same time smoke pours in through archway.

FORMAN: (Gasping.)
                       Mr. Chetwood! Mr. Chetwood!

MADGE and LARRABEE:
                       What is it?

HOLMES keeps his eyes sharply on ALICE. ALICEstands back alarmed.

FORMAN: The lamp — in the kitchen, sir! It fell off the
                       table — an' everything down there is blazin',
                       sir.

MADGE: The house — is on fire!
                       (She gives a glance towards safe, forgetting
                       that the package is gone— but instantly
                       recovers.)

LARRABEE hurriedly goes out, MADGE after him.FORMAN disappears. Noise of people running downstairs, etc. ALICE, on cue "Blazin', sir," gives a scream and looks quickly at chair, at the same time making an involuntary start toward it. She stops upon seeing HOLMES and stands. Noises grow less and die away outside and below.

HOLMES: Don't alarm yourself, Miss Faulkner —
                       (Slight shake of head.)
                       —there is no fire.

ALICE: (Shows by tone that she fears something.)
                       No fire!
                       (Stands, dreading what may come.)

HOLMES: The smoke was all arranged for by me.
                      (Slight pause.)

ALICE: Arranged for?
                      (Looks at HOLMES.)

HOLMES quickly moves to large upholstered chair which ALICE
glanced at and made start towards a moment since.

ALICE: What does it mean, Mr. Holmes?

HOLMES feels rapidly over chair. Rips away upholstery. ALICE
attempts to stop him — but is too late, and backs to piano almost in a
fainting condition. HOLMES stands erect with a package in
hand.

HOLMES: That I wanted this package of letters, Miss
                      Faulkner.

ALICE stands looking at HOLMES speechless — motionless —meets
HOLMES' gaze for a moment, and then covers her face with her
hands, and very slight motion of convulsive sob or two. HOLMES
with a quick motion steps quickly in a business-like way to the seat
where his coat, hat and cane are, and picks up coat, throwing it over
his arm as if to go at once. As he is about to take his hat, he catches
sight of ALICE'S face and stops dead where he is.

Music. Very pp. Scarcely audible.

HOLMES stands looking at her, motionless. She soon looks up at him
again, brushing hand across face as if to clear away any sign of crying.
The tableau of the two looking at one another is held a moment or two.
HOLMES' eyes leave her face and he looks down an instant. After a
moment he lays his coat, hat and cane back on seat. Pauses an instant.
Turns toward her.

HOLMES: (Low voice. Brief pause.)
                      I won't take them, Miss Faulkner.
                      (He looks down an instant. Her eyes are upon
                      his face steadily.)
                      As you—
                      (Still looking down.)
                                   (CONT/)

> — as you —very likely conjecture, the alarm
> of fire was only to make you betray their
> hiding-place — which you did … and I —
> availed myself of that betrayal — as you see.
> But now that I witness your great distress — I
> find that I cannot keep them — unless —
> (Looking up at her.)
> — you can possibly — change your mind and
> let me have them — of your own free will …
> (He looks at her a moment. She shakes her
> head very slightly.)
> I hardly supposed you could.
> (Looks down a moment. Looks up.)
> I will therefore — return it to you.
> (Very slight pause, and he is about to start
> toward her as if to hand her the Package.)

Sound of quick footsteps outside. Enter LARRABEE, with a revolver in his hand, followed by MADGE.

Stop music.

LARRABEE: So! You've got them, have you? And now, I
               suppose we're going to see you walk out of the
               house with them.
               (Handles revolver with meaning.)

HOLMES looks quietly at LARRABEE an instant.

HOLMES: On the contrary, you're going to see me return
               them to their rightful owner.

LARRABEE: (With revolver.)
               Yes — I think that'll be the safest thing for Mr.
               Sherlock Holmes to do.

HOLMES stops dead and looks at LARRABEE and walks quietly down facing him.

HOLMES: You flatter yourself Mr. Larrabee.
                            (CONT/)

The reason I did not leave the house with this
package of papers is not because of you, or
what you may do — or say — or think — or
feel! It is on account of this young lady! I care
that for your cheap bravado
(Looks at revolver and smiles.)
Really?
(He looks quietly in LARRABEE'S eyes an
instant, then turns and goes to ALICE.)
Miss Faulkner permit me to place this in your
hands
(Gives her the package.)

ALICE takes the package with sudden eagerness—then turns and
keeps her eyes steadily on HOLMES.

HOLMES: Should you ever change your mind and be so
                       generous, forgiving as to wish to return these
                       letters to the one who wrote them, you have my
                       address. In any event, rest assured there will be
                       no more cruelty, no more persecution in this
                       house. You are perfectly safe with your
                       property now — for I shall so arrange that your
                       faintest cry of distress will be heard! And if
                       that cry is heard — it will be a very unfortunate
                       thing for those who are responsible. Good
                       night Miss Faulkner.
                       (Pause—turns to LARRABEE and MADGE.
                       Coming to them.)
                       As for you sir and you, madam, I beg you to
                       understand that you continue your persecution
                       of that young lady at your peril.

ALICE looks at HOLMES an instant, uncertain what to do. He makes
a slight motion indicating her to go. ALICE, after slight pause crosses
in front of HOLMES and goes out. LARRABEE makes slight move
towards ALICE, but is checked by a look from HOLMES. HOLMES
waits motionless eyes on ALICE until exit. Then he looks after her for
a moment, turns and takes his coat and hat. Looks at them an instant.

HOLMES: Good evening—
                       (Walks out and the sound of heavy door
                       closing is heard outside.)

Pause LARRABEE and MADGE stand whereHOLMES left them.
Sound of window opening SIDPRINCE hurries in at window.

PRINCE: (sharp but subdued)
                        Well! 'E didn't get it, did 'e?

LARRABEE shakes head. PRINCE looks at him, puzzled, and then
turns towards MADGE.

PRINCE: Well — wot is it? Wot's the pay if 'e didn't?

MADGE: He gave it to her.

PRINCE: What! — 'e found it?

MADGE indicates "Yes" by slight movement.

PRINCE: An' gave it to the girl?

MADGE repeats slight affirmative motion.

PRINCE: Well 'ere — I say! Wot are you waiting for?
                        Now's the chance — before she 'ides it again!
                        (Starting as if to go.)

MADGE: (stopping PRINCE)
                        No! Wait!
                        (Glances round nervously.)

PRINCE: Wot's the matter!
                        (Going to LARRABEE.)
                        Do you want to lose it?

LARRABEE: No! you're right! It's all a cursed bluff!
                        (Starting as if to go.)

MADGE: (meeting them, as if to stop them)
                        No, no, Jim!

LARRABEE: I tell you we will! Now's our chance to get a
                        hold of it!
                        (Pushing her aside.)

PRINCE: Well, I should say so!

Three knocks are heard just as PRINCE and LARRABEE reach
archway. A distant sound of three heavy blows, as if struck from
underneath up against the floor, reverberates through the house. All
stop motionless.

Pause.

Music, melodramatic agitato, very pp. till Curtain.

LARRABEE: (in a low voice)
                          What's that?

MADGE: Someone at the door.

LARRABEE: (low voice)
                          No — it was on that side!

PRINCE glances round alarmed. MADGE rings bell. Enter FORMAN
All stand easily as if nothing out of the usual.

MADGE: I think someone knocked, Judson.

FORMAN at once goes out quietly but quickly. Sound of door outside
closing again. FORMAN re-enters.

FORMAN: I beg pardon, ma'am, there's no one at the
                          door.

MADGE: That's all.

FORMAN goes.

PRINCE: (speaks almost in a whisper from above the
                          piano)
                          'E's got us watched! Wot we want to do is to
                          leave it alone an the Hemperor 'ave it!

MADGE: (low voice — taking a step or two toward
                          PRINCE)
                          Do you mean — Professor Moriarty?

PRINCE: That's 'oo I mean. Once let 'im get at it and
'e'll settle it with 'Olmes pretty quick
(Turns to LARRABEE).
Meet me at Leary's — nine sharp — in the
morning. Don't you worry a minute. I tell you
the Professor'll get at 'im before to-morrow
night! 'E don't wait long either! An' w'en he
strikes — it means death.
(He goes out at window.)

Brief pause. After PRINCE goes MADGE looks after him.
LARRABEE, with a despairing look on his face, leans on chair —
looks round puzzled. His eyes meet MADGE'S as lights fade away.

CURTAIN.

ACT II
In two scenes with a Dark Change

Scene 1
PROFESSOR MORIARTY'S Underground Office. Morning

SCENE 1.—This scene is built inside the Second. PROFESSOR MORIARTY'S underground office. A large vault-like room, with rough masonry walls and vaulted ceiling. The general idea of this place is that it has been converted from a cellar room of a warehouse into a fairly comfortable office or head-quarters. There are no windows.

The colour or tone of this set must not be similar to the third Act set, which is a gloomy and dark bluish-brown. The effect in this set should be of masonry that has long ago been whitewashed and is now old, stained and grimy. Maps on wall of England, France, Germany, Russia, etc. Also a marked map of London — heavy spots upon certain localities. Many charts of buildings, plans of floors—possible tunnelings, etc. Many books about — on impoverished shelves, etc.

PROFESSOR ROBERT MORIARTY is seated at a large circular desk facing the front. He is looking over letters, telegrams, papers, etc., as if morning mail. He is a middle-aged man, with massive head and grey hair, and a face full of character, overhanging brow, heavy jaw. A man of great intellectual force, extremely tall and thin. His forehead domes out in a white curve, and his two eyes are deeply sunken in his head. Clean-shaven, pale, ascetic-looking. Shoulders rounded, and face protruding forward, and for ever oscillating from side to side in a curiously reptilian fashion. Deep hollow voice.

The room is dark, with light showing on his face, as if from lamp. Pause. MORIARTY rings a gong at desk, which has a Peculiar sound. In a second, buzzer outside door replies twice. He Picks up a speaking tube and puts it to his mouth.

MORIARTY: (Speaking into tube in a low voice.)
                   Number.
                   (He Places tube to his ear and listens, then
                   speaks into it again.)
                   Correct.
                              (CONT/)

64

> (Drops tube. He moves a lever up against wall
> and the bolt of the door slides back with a solid
> heavy sound.)

Enter JOHN noiselessly. No sound of steps. He stands just within the door in the half darkness.

MORIARTY: Has any report come in from Chibley?

JOHN: Nothing yet, sir.

MORIARTY: All the others are heard from?

JOHN: Yes, sir.

MORIARTY: I was afraid we'd have trouble there. If
                 anything happened we lose Hickson — one of
                 our best men. Send Bassick.

JOHN goes out. Bolt slides back. Buzzer outside door rings twice.
MORIARTY picks up tube and speaks into it.

MORIARTY: (Speaking into tube.)
                 Number.
                 (Listens. Speaks into tube again.)
                 Correct.
                 (He slides back bolt of door.)

Enter BASSICK noiselessly Bolt of door slides back. BASSICK goes
to MORIARTY'S desk at once and stands. MORIARTY motions to
sit. He does so.

MORIARTY: Before we go into anything else, I want to refer
                 to Davidson.

BASSICK: I've made a note of him myself, sir; he's
                 holding back money.

MORIARTY: Something like six hundred short on that last
                 haul, isn't it?

BASSICK: Certainly as much as that.

MORIARTY:	Have him attended to. Craigin is the one to do it. (BASSICK writes a memo quickly.) And see that his disappearance is noticed. Have it spoken of. That finishes Davidson … Now as to this Blaisdell matter — did you learn anything more?
BASSICK:	The whole thing was a trap.
MORIARTY:	What do you mean?
BASSICK:	Set and baited by an expert.
MORIARTY:	But those letters and papers of instructions— you brought them back, or destroyed them, I trust?
BASSICK:	I could not do it, sir — Manning has disappeared and the papers are gone!

Music melodramatic. Cue, as MORIARTY looks at BASSICK.

MORIARTY:	Gone! Sherlock Holmes again. That's bad for the Underwood trial.
BASSICK:	I thought Shackleford was going to get a postponement.
MORIARTY:	He tried to — and found he was blocked.
BASSICK:	Who could have done it?

MORIARTY turns and looks at BASSICK almost hypnotically — his head vibrating from side to side as if making him speak the name.

BASSICK:	Sherlock Holmes?
MORIARTY:	Sherlock Holmes again. (His eyes still on BASSICK.)

BASSICK: (As if fascinated by MORIARTY. Slight
                   affirmative motion.)
                   He's got hold of between twenty and thirty
                   papers and instructions in as many different
                   jobs, and some as to putting a man or two out
                   of the way — and he's gradually completing
                   chains of evidence which, if we let him go on,
                   will reach to me as sure as the sun will rise.
                   Reach to me! —Ha! (Sneer.) He's playing
                   rather a dangerous game! Inspector Wilson
                   tried it seven years ago. Wilson is dead. Two
                   years later Henderson took it up. We haven't
                   heard anything of Henderson lately, eh?

BASSICK: (Shaking head.)
                   Not a thing, sir.

MORIARTY: Ha!
                   (Sneer.)
                   This Holmes is rather a talented man. He hopes
                   to drag me in at the Underwood trial, but he
                   doesn't realize what can happen between now
                   and Monday. He doesn't know that there isn't
                   a street in London that'll be safe for him if I
                   whisper his name to Craigin — I might even
                   make him a little call myself — just for the
                   satisfaction of it —
                   (Business of head swaying, etc.)
                   — just for the satisfaction of it.
                   (BASSICK watches MORIARTY with some
                   anxiety.)
                   Baker Street, isn't it? His place — Baker Street
                   — eh?

BASSICK: Baker Street, sir.

MORIARTY: We could make it safe. We could make it
                   absolutely secure for three streets each way.

BASSICK: Yes, sir, but—

MORIARTY: We could.
                                   (CONT/)

67

We've done it over and over again elsewhere
— Police decoyed. Men in every doorway.
(Sudden turn to him.)
Do this to-night — in Baker Street! At nine
o'clock call his attendants out on one pretext
and another, and keep them out — you
understand! I'll see this Sherlock Holmes
myself — I'll give him a chance for his life. If
he declines to treat with me —

He takes a savage-looking bulldog revolver from under desk and
examines it carefully, slowly placing it in breast pocket. Ring of
telephone bell is heard, but not until the revolver business is finished.

The music stops.

MORIARTY gives a nod to BASSICK, indicating him to attend to
phone. BASSICK rises and goes to and picks up telephone.
MORIARTY resumes business of examining papers on his desk.

BASSICK: (Speaks into receiver and listens as indicated.)
                    Yes — yes—Bassick—What name did you
                    say? Oh, Prince, yes. He'll have to wait — Yes
                    —I got his telegram last night — Well, tell him
                    to come and speak to me at the phone.
                    (Longer wait.)
                    Yes— I got your telegram, Prince, but I have
                    an important matter on. You'll have to wait—
                    Who?
                    (Suddenly becomes very interested.)
                    What sort of a game is it? — Where is he now?
                    —- Wait a moment.
                    (To MORIARTY.)
                    Here's something, sir. Sid Prince has come
                    here over some job, and he says he's got
                    Holmes fighting against him.

MORIARTY: (Quickly turning to BASSICK.)
                    Eh? Ask him what it is. Ask him what it is.
                    (BASSICK is about to speak through the
                    telephone. Quickly.)
                    Wait!
                              (CONT/)

(BASSICK stops.)
Let him come here.
(BASSICK turns in surprise.)

BASSICK: No one sees you — no one knows you. That
                           has meant safety for years.

MORIARTY: No one sees me now. You talk with him — I'll
                           listen from the next room.
                           (BASSICK looks at him hesitatingly an
                           instant.)
                           This is your office — you understand — your
                           office — I'll be there.

BASSICK turns to telephone.

BASSICK: (Speaking into telephone.)
                           Is that you, Prince? — Yes, I find I can't come
                           out — but I'll see you here — What interest
                           have they got? What's the name?
                           (Listening a moment. Looks round to
                           MORIARTY.)
                           He says there's two with him — a man and a
                           woman named Larrabee. They won't consent
                           to any interview unless they're present.

MORIARTY: Send them in.

BASSICK: (Speaking into telephone.)
                           Eh, Prince — ask Beads to come to the
                           telephone — Beads —eh — ?
                           (Lower voice.)
                           Those people with Prince, do they seem to be
                           all right? Look close yes? — Well — take
                           them out through the warehouse and down by
                           the circular stairway and then bring them up
                           here by the long tunnel — Yes, here — Look
                           them over as you go along to see they're not
                           carrying anything — and watch that no one
                           sees you come down — Yes —
                           (Hangs up ear-piece, turns and looks at
                           MORIARTY.)
                           I don't like this, sir!

MORIARTY: (Rises.)
        You don't like this! You don't like this! I tell
        you it's certain death unless we can settle with
        this man Holmes.

(The buzzer rings three times.)

MORIARTY: (Moves towards opening.)
        Your office, you understand — your office.

BASSICK looks at MORIARTY. MORIARTY goes out. BASSICK,
after MORIARTY is well off, goes and takes MORIARTY'S place at
the back of the desk. Rings gong at desk. Buzzer replies twice from
outside.

BASSICK: (Speaking into tube.)
        Send John here.

BASSICK pushes back bolt. Enter JOHN noiselessly. He stands just
within door. Bolt of door slides back when door shuts.

BASSICK: There are some people coming in here, you
        stand over there, and keep your eye on them
        from behind. If you see anything suspicious,
        drop your handkerchief. If it's the woman pick
        it up — if it's the man leave it on the floor.

Three knocks are distinctly heard on door from outside. On last knock
JOHN goes near wall.

BASSICK: (Picks up tube and speaks into it.)
        Number.
        (Listens—speaking into tube.)
        Are the three waiting with you?
        (Listens—drops tube and pushes lever back,
        and the bolt slides back from the door. The
        door slowly swings open.)

Enter SID PRINCE, followed by MADGE and LARRABEE. The door
Closes and the bolts slide back with a clang. At the sound of the bolts
LARRABEE looks round at door very sharply, realizing that they are
all locked in. BASSICK motions MADGE to chair.

         (CONT/)

MADGE sits. LARRABEE is suspicious, and does not like the look of the place. PRINCE remains standing. BASSICK sits behind desk. JOHN is in the dark, watching LARRABEE and MADGE, with a handkerchief in hand.

BASSICK: I understand you to say — through our private telephone — that you've got something with Sherlock Holmes against you.

PRINCE: Yes, sir — we 'ave.

BASSICK: Kindly let me have the particulars.

LARRABEE gives "H'm," indicating that he wants to hear.

PRINCE: Jim and Madge Larrabee here, which you used to know in early days, they have picked up a girl at 'Omburg, where her sister had been havin' a strong affair of the 'eart with a very 'igh young foreign nob who promised to marry 'er — but the family stepped in and threw the whole thing down. 'E be'aved very bad to 'er an had let 'imself out an written her letters an given her rings and tokens, yer see — and there was photographs too. Now as these various things showed how 'e'd deceived and betrayed 'er, they wouldn't look nice at all considerin' who the young man was, an' wot 'igh titles he was comin' into. So when this girl up an' dies of it all, these letters and things all fall into the 'ands of the sister — which is the one my friends 'ere has been nursin' all along — together with 'er mother.

BASSICK: (To LARRABEE.)
Where have you had the people?

LARRABEE: We took a house up the Norrington Road.

BASSICK: How long have you been there?

LARRABEE: Two years, the fourteenth of next month.

BASSICK: And those letters and — other evidences of the
                    young man's misconduct — when will they
                    reach their full value?

LARRABEE is about to answer, but PRINCE jumps in quickly.

PRINCE: It's now, don't you see. It's now — There's a
                    marriage comin' on, an' there's been offers,
                    an' the problem is to get the papers in our
                    'ands.

BASSICK: Where are they?

PRINCE: Why, the girl's got 'old of 'em, sir!

BASSICK turns for explanation of this to LARRABEE.

LARRABEE: We had a safe for her to keep them in,
                    supposing that when the time came we could
                    open it, but the lock was out of order and we
                    got Prince in to help us. He opened it last night,
                    and the package containing the things was
                    gone — she had taken them out herself.

BASSICK: What did you do when you discovered this?

PRINCE: Do — I 'adn't any more than got the box open,
                    sir, an' given one look at it, when Sherlock
                    Holmes rings the front door bell.

BASSICK: (Intent.)
                    There — at your house?

LARRABEE: At my house.

BASSICK: He didn't get those letters?

LARRABEE: Well, he did get them, but he passed them back
                    to the Faulkner girl.

BASSICK: (Rises—in surprise.)
                    Passed them back, eh? What did that mean?
                    (Goes down a little, thinking.)

LARRABEE: (Slight shrug of shoulders.)
There's another thing that puzzles me. There was an accident below in the kitchen — a lamp fell off the table and scattered burning oil about, the butler came running up, yelling fire. We ran down there, and a few buckets of water put it out.

MORIARTY suddenly appears at his desk. Lights on his face.

MORIARTY: I have a suggestion to make.
(All turn in surprise and look at MORIARTY.)
The first thing we must do is to get rid of your butler — not discharge him — get rid of him.
(To BASSICK.)
Craigin for that! To-day! As soon as it's dark. Give him two others to help —Mr. Larrabee will send the man into the cellar for something —they'll be ready for him there. Doulton's van will get the body to the river.
(MADGE shudders slightly.)
It need not inconvenience you at all, Madam, we do these things quietly.

BASSICK is writing orders.

MORIARTY: (To BASSICK.)
What's the Seraph doing?

BASSICK: He's on the Reading job to-morrow night.

MORIARTY: Put him with Craigin to-day to help with that butler. But there's something else we want. Have you seen those letters, the photographs, and whatever else there may be? Have you seen them? Do you know what they're like?

MADGE: I have, sir. I've looked them through carefully several times.

(CONT/)

MORIARTY:	Could you make me a counterfeit set of these things and tie them up so that they will look exactly like the package Sherlock Holmes held in his hand last night?
MADGE:	I could manage the letters—but —
MORIARTY:	If you manage the letters, I'll send some one who can manage the rest — from your description. Bassick — that old German artist —eh —?
BASSICK:	Leuftner.
MORIARTY:	Precisely! Send Leuftner to Mrs. Larrabee at eleven. (Looks at watch.) Quarter past ten — that gives you three quarters of an hour to reach home. I shall want that counterfeit packet an eleven to-night — twelve hours to make it.

MADGE: It will be ready, sir.

MORIARTY: Good! Bassick — notify the Lascar that I may require the Gas Chamber at Stepney to-night.

BASSICK: The Gas Chamber?

MORIARTY:	Yes. The one backing over the river — and have Craigin there a quarter before twelve with two others. Mr. Larrabee — (Turning slightly to him.) — I shall want you to write a letter to Mr. Sherlock Holmes which I shall dictate — and tonight I may require a little assistance from you both. (Taking in PRINCE with his glance.) Meet me here at eleven.
LARRABEE:	This is all very well, sir, but you have said nothing about — the business arrangements. I'm not sure that! —

MORIARTY: (Turning front.)
                 You have no choice.

LARRABEE: No choice.
                 (Looks fiercely to MORIARTY.)

MADGE rises to quiet him. JOHN drops handkerchief. Pause.

MORIARTY: (Looking at him.)
                 No choice.
                 (PRINCE aghast.)
                 I do what I please. It pleases me to take hold of
                 this case.

LARRABEE: (Angry—crossing to desk.)
                 Well, what about pleasing me?

BASSICK looks across at LARRABEE.

MORIARTY: (Perfectly quiet—looks at LARRABEE an
                 instant.)
                 I am not so sure but I shall be able to do that as
                 well. I will obtain the original letters from Miss
                 Faulkner and negotiate the for much more than
                 you could possibly obtain. In addition — you
                 will have an opportunity to sell the counterfeit
                 package to Holmes tonight, for a good round
                 sum. And the money obtained from both these
                 sources shall be divided as follows: you will
                 take one hundred per cent, and I — nothing.

Brief pause of astonishment.

LARRABEE: Nothing!

MORIARTY: Nothing!

LARRABEE moves to PRINCE.

BASSICK: But we cannot negotiate those letters until we
                 know who they incriminate. Mr. Larrabee has
                 not yet informed us.

MORIARTY: Mr. Larrabee —
                   (LARRABEE looks round to MORIARTY.)
                   — is wise in exercising caution. He values the
                   keystone to his arch. But he will consent to let
                   me know.

LARRABEE goes to MADGE.

MADGE: (Going across to MORIARTY.)
                   Professor Moriarty, that information we would
                   like to give — only to you.
                   (Looking toward BASSICK.)

MORIARTY motions BASSICK away. BASSICK moves a little.
MORIARTY hands a card and pencil to MADGE from desk. MADGE
writes a name and hands it to MORIARTY. He glances at name on
card, then looks more closely. Looks up at MADGE astonished.

MORIARTY: This is an absolute certainty.

LARRABEE: Absolute.

MORIARTY: It means that you have a fortune.

PRINCE drinks in every word and look.

MORIARTY: Had I known this, you should hardly have had
                   such terms.

LARRABEE: Oh well — we don't object to a —

MORIARTY: (Interrupting.)
                   The arrangement is made, Mr. Larrabee — I
                   bid you good morning.
                   (Bowing with dignity and Pulling lever back.)

LARRABEE, PRINCE and MADGE move toward door. Bolts, etc.,
slide back on door. BASSICK motions JOHN, who stands ready to
conduct the party. BASSICK crosses to door. All bow a little and go
out, followed by JOHN — business of door closing, bolts, etc.
BASSICK turns at door and looks at MORIARTY.

MORAIRTY: Bassick, place your men at nine to-night for
                   Sherlock Holmes' house in Baker Street.

BASSICK: You will go there yourself sir!

MORIARTY: I will go there myself — myself
                   (Revolver out.)
                   I am the one to attend to this.

BASSICK: But this meeting to-night at twelve, to trap
                   Holmes in the Gas Chamber in Swandem Lane.

MORIARTY: If I fail to kill him in Baker Street, we'll trap
                   him to-night in Swandem Lane. Either way I
                   have him, Bassick. I have him. I have him.

Lights off gradually but not too slow on this act, and leave light on
MORIARTY'S face last.

Music. Swell out forte for change.

DARK CHANGE

Scene 2
SHERLOCK HOLMES'S Apartments in Baker Street. Evening

SCENE II. — In SHERLOCK HOLMES' rooms in Baker Street —the
large drawing-room of his apartments. An open, cheerful room, but not
too much decorated. Rather plain. The walls are a plain tint, the ceiling
ditto. The furniture is comfortable and goody but not elegant. Books,
music, violins, tobacco pouches, pipes, tobacco, etc., are scattered in
places about the room with some disorder. Various odd things are
hung about. Some very choice pictures and etchings hang on the walls
here and there, but the pictures do not have heavy gilt frames. All
rather simple. The room gives more an impression of an artist's studio.
A wide door up right side to hall (and thus by stairway to street door).
Door communicating with bedroom or dining-room. A fireplace with
cheerful grate fire burning, throwing a red glow into room. Through a
large arch can be seen a laboratory and a table with chemicals and
various knick-knacks.

(CONT/)

77

The lighting should be arranged so that after the dark change the first thing that becomes visible — even before the rest of the room — is the glow of the fire, the blue flame of the spirit lamp — and SHERLOCK HOLMES seated among cushions on the floor before the fire. Light gradually on, but still leaving the effect of only firelight.

Music stops, just as lights up.

SHERLOCK HOLMES is discovered on the floor before the fire. He is in a dressing-gown and slippers and has his pipe. HOLMES leans against the chesterfield. A violin is upon the chesterfield, and the bow near it, as if recently laid down. Other things Scattered about him. He sits smoking awhile in deep thought. Enter BILLY, the boy page, or buttons. He comes down to back of table.

BILLY: Mrs. 'Udson's compliments, sir, an' she wants to know if she can see you?

HOLMES: (Without moving, looking into fire thoughtfully.)
Where is Mrs. Hudson?

BILLY: Downstairs in the back kitchen, sir.

HOLMES: My compliments and I don't think she can — from where she is.

BILLY: She'll be very sorry, sir.

HOLMES: Our regret will be mutual.

BILLY hesitates.

BILLY: She says it was terribly important, sir, as she wants to know what you'll have for your breakfast in the mornin'.

HOLMES: Same.

Slight pause.

BILLY: Same as when, sir?

HOLMES: This morning.

BILLY: You didn't 'ave nothing, sir — you wasn't
                 'ere.

HOLMES: Quite so — I won't be here tomorrow.

BILLY: Yes, sir. Was that all, sir?

HOLMES: Quite so.

BILLY: Thank you, sir.

BILLY goes out. After long pause bell rings off. Enter BILLY.

BILLY: It's Doctor Watson, sir. You told me as I could
                 always show 'im up.

HOLMES: Well! I should think so.
                 (Rises and meets WATSON.)

BILLY: Yes, sir, thank you, sir. Dr. Watson, sir!

Enter DR. WATSON. BILLY, grinning with pleasure as he passes in,
goes out at once.

HOLMES: (Extending left hand to WATSON.)
                 Ah, Watson, dear fellow.

WATSON: (Going to HOLMES and taking his hand.)
                 How are you, Holmes?

HOLMES: I'm delighted to see you, my dear fellow,
                 perfectly delighted, upon my word — but —
                 I'm sorry to observe that your wife has left you
                 in this way.

WATSON   (Laughing.)
                 She has gone on a little visit.
                 (Puts hat on chair between bookcases.)
                 But how did you know?

HOLMES: (Goes to laboratory table and puts spirit lamp
           out, then turns up lamp on table. All lights up.)
           How do I know? Now, Watson, how absurd
           for you to ask me such a question as that. How
           do I know anything?
           (Comes down a little way. Gives a very little
           sniff an instant, smelling something.)
           How do I know that you've opened a
           consulting room and resumed the practice of
           medicine without letting me hear a word about
           it? How do I know that you've been getting
           yourself very wet lately? That you have an
           extremely careless servant girl — and that
           you've moved your dressing-table to the other
           side of your room?

WATSON: (Turning and looking at HOLMES in
           astonishment.)
           Holmes, if you'd lived a few centuries ago,
           they'd have burned you alive.
           (Sits.)

HOLMES: Such a conflagration would have saved no
           considerable trouble and expense.
           (Strolls over to near fire.)

WATSON: Tell me, how did you know all that?

HOLMES: (Pointing.)
           Too simple to talk about.
           (Pointing at WATSON'S shoe.)
           Scratches and clumsy cuts — on the side of
           shoe there just where the fire strikes it,
           somebody scraped away crusted mud — and
           did it badly — badly. There's your wet feet
           and careless servant all on one foot. Face badly
           shaved on one side — used to be on left —
           light must have come from other side —
           couldn't well move your window — must have
           moved your dressing-table.
           (Goes to mantel and gets cocaine, etc.)

WATSON: Yes, by Jove! But my medical practice — I
               don't see how you —

HOLMES: (Glancing up grieved.)
               Now, Watson! How perfectly absurd of you to
               come marching in here, fairly reeking with the
               odour of iodoform, and with the black mark of
               nitrate of silver on the inner side of your right
               forefinger and ask me how I know —

WATSON: (Interrupting with a laugh.)
               Ha! ha! of course. But how the deuce did you
               know my wife was away and —

HOLMES: (Breaking in.)
               Where the deuce is your second Waistcoat
               button, and what the deuce is yesterday's
               boutonniere doing in to-day's lapel — and why
               the deuce do you wear the expression of a —

WATSON: (Toying with a cigarette and laughing.)
               Ha, ha, ha!

HOLMES: Ho!
               (Sneer.)
               Elementary! The child's play of deduction!

HOLMES has a neat morocco case and a phial in hand, which he
brings to the table and lays carefully upon it. As WATSON sees
HOLMES with the open case he looks restless and apparently
annoyed at what HOLMES is about to do, throwing cigarette on table.
HOLMES opens the case and takes therefrom a hypodermic syringe,
carefully adjusting the needle. Fills from phial. Then back left cuff of
shirt a little. Pauses, looks at arm or wrist a moment. Inserts needle.
Presses piston home.

Music. A weird bar or two — keeping on a strange pulsation on one
note for cocaine business. Begin as HOLMES fills syringe.

WATSON has watched him with an expression of deep anxiety but
with effort to restrain himself from speaking.

WATSON: (As HOLMES puts needle in case again.
Finally speaks.)
Which is it to-day? Cocaine or morphine or —

HOLMES: Cocaine, my dear fellow. I'm back to my old
love. A seven per cent. solution.
(Offering syringe and phial.)
Would you like to try some?

WATSON: (Emphatically — rise.)
Certainly not.

HOLMES: (As if surprised.)
Oh! I'm sorry!

WATSON: I have no wish to break my system down
before time.

Pause.

HOLMES: Quite right, my dear Watson — quite right —
but, see, my time has come.
(Goes to mantel and replaces case thereon.
Throws himself languidly into chesterfield and
leans back in luxurious enjoyment of the drug.)

WATSON: (Goes to table, resting hand on upper corner,
looking at HOLMES seriously.)
Holmes, for months I have seen you use these
deadly drugs — in ever-increasing doses.
When they lay hold of you there is no end. It
must go on, and on — until the finish.

HOLMES: (Lying back dreamily.)
So must you go on and on eating your
breakfast — until the finish.

WATSON: (Approaches HOLMES.)
Breakfast is food. These are poisons — slow
but certain. They involve tissue changes of a
most serious nature.

HOLMES: Just what I want. I'm bored to death with my present tissues, and I'm trying to get a brand-new lot.

WATSON: (Going near HOLMES — putting hand on HOLMES' shoulder.)
Ah Holmes — I am trying to save you.

HOLMES   (Earnest at once — places right hand on WATSON'S arm.)
You can't do it, old fellow — so don't waste your time.

Music stops.

They look at one another an instant. WATSON sees cigarette on table—picks it up and sits.

HOLMES: Watson, to change the subject a little. In the enthusiasm which has prompted you to chronicle and — if you will excuse my saying so, to somewhat embellish — a few of my little — adventures, you have occasionally committed the error — or indiscretion — of giving them a certain tinge of romance which struck me as being a trifle out of place. Something like working an elopement into the fifth proposition of Euclid. I merely refer to this in case you should see fit at some future time — to chronicle the most important and far-reaching case in my career — one upon which I have laboured for nearly fourteen months, and which is now rapidly approaching a singularly diverting climax — the case of Professor Robert Moriarty.

WATSON: Moriarty! I don't remember ever having heard of the fellow.

HOLMES: The Napoleon of crime. The Napoleon!

(CONT/)

83

Sitting motionless like an ugly venomous spider in the centre of his web — but that web having a thousand radiations and the spider knowing every quiver of every one of them.

WATSON: Really! This is very interesting.
(Turns chair facing HOLMES.)

HOLMES: Ah — but the real interest will come when the Professor begins to realize his position — which he cannot fail to do shortly. By ten o'clock to-morrow night the time will be ripe for the arrests. Then the greatest criminal trial of the century … the clearing up of over forty mysteries … and the rope for every one.

WATSON: Good! What will he do when he sees that you have him?

HOLMES: Do? He will do me the honour, my dear Watson, of turning every resource of his wonderful organization of criminals to the one purpose of my destruction.

WATSON: Why, Holmes, this is a dangerous thing.
(Rises.)

HOLMES: Dear Watson, it's perfectly delightful! It saves me any number of doses of those deadly drugs upon which you occasionally favour me with your medical views! My whole life is spent in a series of frantic endeavours to escape from the dreary common places of existence! For a brief period I escape! You should congratulate me!

WATSON: But you could escape them without such serious risks! Your other cases have not been so dangerous, and they were even more interesting. Now, the one you spoke of — the last time I saw you — the recovery of those damaging letters and gifts from a young girl who —

HOLMES suddenly rises — stands motionless. WATSON looks at him surprised. Brief pause. Then WATSON sits in arm-chair.

WATSON: A most peculiar affair as I remember it. You were going to try an experiment of making her betray their hiding-place by an alarm of fire in her own house — and after that —

HOLMES: Precisely — after that.

Pause.

WATSON: Didn't the plan succeed?

HOLMES: Yes — as far as I've gone.

WATSON: You got Forman into the house as butler?

HOLMES: (nods)
Forman was in as butler.

WATSON: And upon your signal he overturned a lamp in the kitchen—
(HOLMES moves up and down)
—scattered the smoke balls and gave an alarm of fire?

HOLMES nods and mutters "Yes" under his breath.

WATSON: And the young lady — did she —

HOLMES: (Turning and interrupting.)
Yes, she did, Watson.
(Going down near him as if he had recovered himself.)
The young lady did. It all transpired precisely as planned. I took the packet of papers from its hiding-place — and as I told you I would handed it back to Miss Faulkner.

WATSON: But you never told me why you proposed to hand it back.

HOLMES: For a very simple reason my dear Watson That
                           would have been theft for me to take it. The
                           contents of the packet were the absolute
                           property of the young lady.

WATSON: What did you gain by this?

HOLMES: Her confidence, and so far as I was able to
                           secure it, her regard. As it was impossible for
                           me to take possession of the letters,
                           photographs and jewellery in that packet
                           without her consent, my only alternative is to
                           obtain that consent — to induce her to give it
                           to me of her own free will. Its return to her
                           after I had laid hands on it was the first move
                           in this direction. The second will depend
                           entirely upon what transpires to-day. I expect
                           Forman here to report in half an hour.

Light hurried footsteps outside. Short quick knock at door and enter
TÉRÉSE in great haste and excitement. WATSON rises and turns and
faces her near table. HOLMES turns towards fire-place.

TÉRÉSE: I beg you to pardon me, sir, ze boy he say to
                           come right up as soon as I come.

HOLMES: Quite right! quite right!

TÉRÉSE: Ah! I fear me zere is trouble — Messieurs —
                           ze butlair— you assesstant — ze one who sent
                           me to you —

HOLMES: Forman?
                           (Turning to her.)

TÉRÉSE: Heem! Forman. Zere ees somesing done to
                           heem! I fear to go down to see.

HOLMES: Down where?

WATSON watches.

TÉRÉSE: Ze down.
                 (Gesture.)
                 Ze cellaire of zat house. Eet ees a dreadful
                 place. He deed not come back. He went down
                 — he deed not return.
                 (Business of anguish.)

HOLMES goes to table — rings bell and takes revolver from drawer
and slides it into his hip pocket, at same time unfastening dressing-
gown.

HOLMES: (During business.)
                 Who sent him down?

TÉRÉSE: M'sieur of ze house, M'sieur Chetwood.

HOLMES: Larrabee?

TÉRÉSE: Yes.

HOLMES: (During business.)
                 Has he been down there long?

TÉRÉSE: No — for I soon suspect — ze dreadful noise
                 was heard. Oh —
                 (Covers face.)
                 — ze noise! Ze noise!

HOLMES: What noise?
                 (Goes to her and seizes her arm.)

TÉRÉSE: Ze noise!

HOLMES: Try to be calm and answer me. What did it
                 sound like?

TÉRÉSE: Ze dreadful cry of a man who eez struck down
                 by a deadly seeng.

Enter BILLY

HOLMES: Billy! Coat — boots, and order a cab — quick!
                               (CONT/)

87

(Back again to table, takes a second revolver out.)

BILLY: (Darting off at door.)
Yes, sir.

HOLMES: (To TÉRÉSE.)
Did anyone follow him down?

BILLY is back in a second.

TÉRÉSE: I did not see.

HOLMES: Don't wait. The cab.

BILLY shoots off having placed coat over chesterfield and boots on floor.

HOLMES: Take this Watson and come with me.
(Handing WATSON a revolver. WATSON advances a step to meet HOLMES and takes revolver.)

TÉRÉSE: I had not better go also?

HOLMES: No … Wait here!
(Ready to go. About to take off dressing gown)

Hurried footsteps heard outside.

Pause.

HOLMES: Ha! I hear Forman coming now.

Enter FORMAN.

TÉRÉSE: (Seeing FORMAN — under her breath.)
Ah!
(Backing a little.)

FORMAN coming rapidly on is covered with black coal stains, and his clothing otherwise stained. He has a bad bruise on forehead.
(CONT/)

But he must not be made to look grotesque. There must be no suspicion of comedy about his entrance. Also he must not be torn, as BILLY is later in the scene. HOLMES just above table stops taking off his dressing gown, slips it back on shoulders again.

FORMAN: (To HOLMES in an entirely matter of fact
                                   tone.)
                                   Nothing more last night, sir. After you left,
                                   Prince came in, they made a start for her room
                                   to get the package away, but I gave the three
                                   knocks with an axe on the floor beams as you
                                   directed, and they didn't go any farther. This
                                   morning, a little after nine—

HOLMES: One moment.

FORMAN: Yes, sir?

HOLMES: (Quietly turns to TÉRÉSE.)
                                   Mademoiselle — step into that room and rest
                                   yourself.
                                   (Indicating bedroom door.)

TÉRÉSE: (Who has been deeply interested in
                                   FORMAN'S report.)
                                   Ah!
                                   (Shaking head.)
                                   I am not tired, Monsieur.

HOLMES: Step in and walk about, then. I'll let you know
                                   when you are required.

TÉRÉSE   (After an instant's pause sees it.)
                                   Oui, Monsieur.
                                   (Goes out.)

HOLMES goes over and quickly closes the door after her — he then turns to WATSON, but remains at the door with right ear alert to catch any sound from within.

HOLMES: Take a look at his head, Watson.
                                   (Listens at door.)

89

WATSON at once goes to FORMAN.

FORMAN: It's nothing at all.

HOLMES: Take a look at his head, Watson.

WATSON: An ugly bruise, but not dangerous.
                         (Examining head.)

WATSON goes quickly and stands near end of chesterfield facing
around to FORMAN.

HOLMES: Very well … At a little after nine, you say —
                         (HOLMES has attention on door, where
                         TÉRÉSE went off while listening to FORMAN
                         —but not in such a marked way as to take the
                         attention off from what he says, and after a few
                         seconds sits on chesterfield.)

FORMAN: Yes, sir!
                         (Coming down a little.)
                         This morning a little after nine, Larrabee and
                         his wife drove away and she returned about
                         eleven without him. A little later, old Leuftner
                         came and the two went to work in the library. I
                         got a look at them from the outside and found
                         they were making up a counterfeit of the
                         Package we're working for! You'll have to
                         watch for some sharp trick, sir.

HOLMES: They'll have to watch for the trick, my dear
                         Forman. And Larrabee what of him?

FORMAN: He came back a little after three

HOLMES: How did he seem?

FORMAN: Under great excitement, sir.

HOLMES: Any marked resentment towards you?

FORMAN: I think there was, sir — though he tried not to
                         show it.

HOLMES: He has consulted some one outside. Was the
               Larrabee woman's behaviour different also?

FORMAN: Now I come to think of it, she gave me an ugly
               look as she came in.

HOLMES: Ah, an ugly look. She was present at the
               consultation. They were advised to get you out
               of the way. He sent you into the cellar on some
               pretext. You were attacked in the dark by two
               men — possibly three — and received a bad
               blow from a sand club. You managed to strike
               down one of your assailants with a stone or
               piece of timber and escaped from the others in
               the dark crawling out through a coal grating.

FORMAN: That's what took place sir.

HOLMES: They've taken in a partner, and a dangerous
               one at that. He not only directed this
               conspiracy against you, but he advised the
               making of the counterfeit package as well.
               Within a very short time I shall receive an offer
               from Larrabee to sell the package of letters. He
               will indicate that Miss Faulkner changed her
               mind, and has concluded to get what she can
               for them. He will desire to meet me on the
               subject — and will then endeavour to sell me
               his bogus package for a large sum of money.
               After that —

Enter BILLY with a letter.

BILLY: Letter, sir! Most important letter, sir!
               (After giving HOLMES letter, he stands
               waiting.)

HOLMES: Unless I am greatly mistaken — the said
               communication is at hand.
               (Lightly waves letter across before face once
               getting the scent.)
                              (CONT/)

It is. Read it, Watson, there's a good fellow,
my eyes —
(With a motion across eyes. Half smile.)
You know, cocaine — and all those things you
like so much.

BILLY goes with letter to WATSON. WATSON takes letter and up to
lamp.

WATSON: (Opens letter and reads.)
                 "Dear Sir."

After WATSON is at lamp, FORMAN waits.

HOLMES: Who — thus — addresses me?
                 (Slides further on to chesterfield, supporting
                 head on pillows.)

WATSON: (Glances at signature.)
                 "James Larrabee."

HOLMES: (Whimsically.)
                 What a surprise! And what has James to say
                 this evening?

WATSON: "Dear Sir."

HOLMES: I hope he won't say that again.

WATSON: "I have the honour to inform you that Miss
                 Faulkner has changed her mind regarding the
                 letters, etc., which you wish to obtain, and has
                 decided to dispose of them for a monetary
                 consideration. She has placed them in my
                 hands for this purpose, and if you are in a
                 position to offer a good round sum, and to pay
                 it down at once in cash, the entire lot is yours.
                 If you wish to negotiate, however, it must be
                 to-night, at the house of a friend of mine, in the
                 city. At eleven o'clock you will be at the
                 Guards' Monument at the foot of Waterloo
                 Place.
                                 (CONT/)

> You will see a cab with wooden shutters to the
> windows. Enter it and the driver will bring you
> to my friend's house. If you have the cab
> followed, or try any other underhand trick, you
> won't get what you want. Let me know your
> decision. Yours truly, James Larrabee."

HOLMES during the reading of the letter begins to write something in
a perfectly leisurely way. The light of the fire is upon him, shining
across the room — on his left — as he writes.

HOLMES: Now see if I have the points. To-night, eleven
                   o'clock — Guards' Monument — cab with
                   wooden shutters. No one to come with me. No
                   one to follow cab — or I don't get what I want.

WATSON: Quite right.

HOLMES: Ah!

WATSON: But this cab with the wooden shutters.
                   (Coming down and placing letter on table.)

HOLMES: A little device to keep me from seeing where I
                   am driven. Billy!

BILLY: (Going to HOLMES at once.)
                   Yes, sir.

HOLMES: (Reaching out letter to BILLY back of him
                   without looking.)
                   Who brought it?

BILLY: It was a woman, sir.

HOLMES: (Slight dead stop as he is handing letter.)
                   Ah — old, young?
                   (He does not look round for these questions,
                   but faces the was front or nearly so.)

BILLY: Very old sir.

HOLMES: In a cab?

93

BILLY:	Yes, sir.
HOLMES:	Seen the driver before?
BILLY:	Yes sir — but I can't think where.
HOLMES:	(Rising.) Hand this over to the old lady — apologize for the delay and look at the driver again.
BILLY:	(Takes letter.) Yes sir. (Goes out.)
WATSON:	My dear Holmes — you did not say you would go?
HOLMES:	Certainly I did.
WATSON:	But it is the counterfeit.
HOLMES:	(Moves towards bedroom door.) The counterfeit is what I want.
WATSON:	Why so?
HOLMES:	(Turning to WATSON an instant.) Because with it I shall obtain the original (Turns and speaks off at door.) Mademoiselle! (Turns back.)
WATSON:	But this fellow means mischief.

Enter TÉRESE She comes into and stands a little way inside the room.

HOLMES:	(Facing WATSON — touching himself lightly.) This fellow means the same.

As HOLMES turns away to TÉRÉSE, WATSON crosses and stands with back to fire.

HOLMES: (to TÉRÉSE)
Be so good Mademoiselle as to listen to every word. To-night at twelve o'clock I meet Mr. Larrabee and purchase from him the false bundle of letters to which you just now heard us refer, as you were listening at the keyhole of the door.

TÉRÉSE: (Slightly confused but staring blankly.)
Oui, Monsieur.

HOLMES: I wish Miss Faulkner to know at once that I propose to buy this package to night.

TÉRÉSE: I will tell her, Monsieur.

HOLMES: That is my wish. But do not tell her that I know this packet and its contents to be counterfeit. She is to suppose that I think I am buying the genuine.

TÉRÉSE: Oui, Monsieur, je comprends. When you purchase you think you have the real.

HOLMES: Precisely.
(Motions her up to door and moving towards door with her.)
One thing more. Tomorrow evening I shall want you to accompany her to this place, here. Sir Edward Leighton and Count von Stalburg will be here to receive the package from me. However, you will receive further instructions as to this in the morning.

TÉRÉSE: Oui, Monsieur.
(Turns and goes out at once.)

HOLMES: Forman.

FORMAN: Yes, sir.

HOLMES: Change to your beggar disguise No. 14 and go
                    through every place in the Riverside District.
                    Don't stop till you get a clue to this new
                    partner of the Larrabees. I must have that.
                    (Turns away towards WATSON.)
                    I must have that.

FORMAN: Very well, sir.
                    (Just about to go.)

Enter BILLY.

BILLY: If you please, sir, there's a man a-waitin' at the
                    street door — and 'e says 'e must speak to Mr.
                    Forman, sir, as quick as 'e can.

HOLMES — who was moving — stops suddenly and stands
motionless — eyes front. Pause.

Music. Danger. Melodramatic. Very low. Agitato. B String.

HOLMES: (After a pause.)
                    We'd better have a look at that man, Billy,
                    show him up.

BILLY: 'E can't come up, sir — 'e's a-watchin' a man
                    in the Street. 'E says 'e's from Scotland Yard.

FORMAN: (Going toward door.)
                    I'd better see what it is, sir.

HOLMES: No!

FORMAN stops. Pause. Music heard throughout this pause, but
without swelling forte in the least. HOLMES stands motionless a
moment.

HOLMES: Well —
                    (A motion indicating FORMAN to go.)
                    — take a look at first. Be ready for anything.

FORMAN: Trust me for that, sir.
                    (Goes out.)

HOLMES: Billy, see what he does.

BILLY: Yes, sir.

HOLMES stands an instant thinking.

WATSON: This is becoming interesting.

HOLMES does not reply He goes up to near door and listens then moves to window and glances down to street then turns goes down to table.

WATSON: Look here Holmes you've been so kind as to give me a half look into this case —

HOLMES: (Looking up at him.)
                     What case?

WATSON: This strange case of — Miss —

HOLMES: Quite so. One moment my dear fellow
                     (Rings bell.)

After slight wait enter BILLY.

HOLMES: Mr. Forman—is he there still?

BILLY: No, sir — 'e's gone.
                     (Second's pause.)

HOLMES: That's all.

BILLY: Yes sir. Thank you sir.
                     (Goes out.)

Music stops.

HOLMES: As you were saying, Watson.
                     (Eyes front.)
                     …strange case — of —
                     (Stops but does not change position. As if listening or thinking.)

WATSON: Of Miss Faulkner.

HOLMES   (Abandoning further anxiety and giving
                 attention to WATSON.)
                 Precisely. This strange case of Miss Faulkner.
                 (Eyes down an instant as he recalls it.)

WATSON: You've given me some idea of it. Now don't
                 you it would be only fair to let me have the
                 rest?

HOLMES looks at him.

HOLMES: What shall I tell you?

WATSON: Tell me what you propose to do with that
                 counterfeit package — which you are going to
                 risk your life to obtain.

HOLMES looks at WATSON an instant before speaking.

HOLMES: I intend, with the aid of the counterfeit, to
                 make her willingly hand me the genuine. I
                 shall accomplish this by a piece of trickery and
                 deceit of which I am heartily ashamed — and
                 which I would never have undertaken if I — if
                 I had known her — as I do now (Looks to the
                 front absently.) It's too bad. She's — she's
                 rather a nice girl, Watson.
                 (Goes over to mantel and gets a pipe.)

WATSON: (Following HOLMES with his eyes.)
                 Nice girl, is she?

HOLMES nods "Yes" to WATSON. Brief pause. He turns with pipe
in hands and glances towards WATSON, then down.

WATSON: Then you think that possibly —

Enter BILLY quickly.

BILLY: I beg pardon, sir.
                              (CONT/)

98

> Mr. Forman's just sent over from the chemist's on the corner to say 'is 'ead is a-painin' 'im a bit, an' would Dr. Watson —

WATSON, on hearing his name, turns and looks in direction of BILLY.

BILLY: —kindly step over and get 'im something to put on it.

WATSON: (Moving at once towards door.)
Yes — certainly — I'll go at once.
(Picking up hat off chair.)
That's singular.
(Stands puzzled.)
It didn't look like anything serious.
(At door.)
I'll be back in a minute, Holmes.
(Goes out.)

HOLMES says nothing.

HOLMES: Billy.

BILLY: Yes, sir.

HOLMES: Who brought that message from Forman?

BILLY: Boy from the chemist's, sir.

HOLMES: Yes, of course, but which boy?

BILLY: Must-a-bin a new one, sir — I ain't never seen 'im before.

Music. Danger. Melodramatic. Very low. Agitato.

HOLMES: Quick, Billy, run down and look after the doctor. If the boy's gone and there's a man with him it means mischief. Let me know, quick. Don't stop to come up, ring the door bell. I'll hear it. Ring it loud. Quick now.

BILLY: Yes, sir.
                          (Goes out quickly.)

HOLMES waits motionless a moment, listening.

Music heard very faintly.

HOLMES moves quickly towards door. When half-way to the door he
stops suddenly, listening; then begins to glide backward toward table,
stops and listens — eyes to the front; turns towards door listening.
Pipe in left hand — waits — sees pipe in hand — picks up match —
lights pipe, listening, and suddenly shouts of warning from BILLY —
turns — at the same time picking up revolver from off table and puts
in pocket of dressing-gown, with his hand clasping it. HOLMES at
once assumes easy attitude, but keeps eyes on door. Enter
MORIARTY. He walks in at door very quietly and deliberately. Stops
just within doorway, and looks fixedly at HOLMES, then moves
forward a little way. His right hand behind his back. As MORIARTY
moves forward, HOLMES makes slight motion for the purpose of
keeping him covered with revolver in his pocket. MORIARTY, seeing
what HOLMES is doing, stops.

MORIARTY: (Very quiet low voice.)
                          It is a dangerous habit to finger loaded firearms
                          in the pocket of one's dressing-gown.

HOLMES: You'll be taken from here to the hospital if you
                          keep that hand behind you.

After slight pause MORIARTY slowly takes his hand from behind his
back and holds it with the other in front of him.

HOLMES: In that case, the table will do quite as well.
                          (Places his revolver on the table.)

MORIARTY: You evidently don't know me.

HOLMES: (Takes pipe out of mouth, holding it. With very
                          slight motion toward revolver.)
                          I think it quite evident that I do. Please take a
                          chair, Professor.
                          (Indicating arm-chair.)
                                              (CONT/)

> I can spare five minutes — if you have
> anything to say.

Very slight pause—then MORIARTY moves his right hand as if to take something from inside his coat. Stops instantly on HOLMES covering him with revolver, keeping hand exactly where it was stopping.

HOLMES: What were you about to do?

MORIARTY: Look at my watch.

HOLMES: I'll tell you when the five minutes is up.

Slight pause. MORIARTY comes slowly forward. He advances to back of arm-chair. Stands motionless there an instant, his eyes on HOLMES. He then takes off his hat, and stoops slowly, putting it on floor, eyeing HOLMES the while. He then moves down a little to right of chair, by its side. HOLMES now places revolver on table, but before he has quite let go of it, MORIARTY raises his right hand, whereupon HOLMES quietly takes the revolver back and holds it at his side. MORIARTY has stopped with right hand near his throat, seeing HOLMES' business with revolver. He now slowly pulls away a woolen muffler from his throat and stands again with hands down before him. HOLMES' forefinger motionless on table. MORIARTY moves a little in front of chair. This movement is only a step or two. As he makes it HOLMES moves simultaneously on the other side of the table so that he keeps the revolver between them on the table. That is the object of this business.

MORIARTY: All that I have to say has already crossed your
                 mind.

HOLMES: My answer thereto has already crossed yours.

MORIARTY: It is your intention to pursue this case against
                 me?

HOLMES: That is my intention to the very end.

MORIARTY: I regret this — not so much on my own
                 account — but on yours.

HOLMES: I share your regrets, Professor, but solely
                     because of the rather uncomfortable position it
                     will cause you to occupy.

MORIARTY: May I inquire to what position you are pleased
                     to allude, Mr. Holmes?

HOLMES motions a man being hanged with his left hand — slight
Pause. A tremor of passion. MORIARTY slowly advances towards
HOLMES. He stops instantly as HOLMES' hand goes to his revolver,
having only approached him a step or two.

MORIARTY: And have you the faintest idea that you would
                     be permitted to live to see the day?

HOLMES: As to that, I do not particularly care, so that I
                     might bring you to see it.

MORIARTY makes a sudden impulsive start towards HOLMES, but
stops on being covered with the revolver. He has now come close to
the table on the other side of HOLMES. This tableau is held briefly.

MORIARTY: (Passionately but in a low tone.)
                     You will never bring me to see it. You will
                     find —
                     (He stops, recollecting himself as HOLMES
                     looks at him — changes to quieter tone.)
                     Ah! you are a bold man Mr. Holmes to
                     insinuate such a thing to my face —
                     (Turning towards front.)
                     — but it is the boldness born of ignorance.
                     (Turning still further away from HOLMES in
                     order to get his back to him and after doing so
                     suddenly raising his right hand to breast he is
                     again stopped with hand close to pocket by
                     hearing the noise of HOLMES'S revolver
                     behind him. He holds that position for a
                     moment then passes the matter off by feeling
                     muffler as if adjusting it. He mutters to
                     himself.)
                     You'll never bring me to see it, you'll never
                     bring me to see it.
                                    (CONT/)

(Then begins to move in front of table still
keeping his back towards HOLMES. Business
as he moves forward of stopping suddenly on
hearing the noise of revolver sliding along
table then when in front of table slowly turns
so that he brings his hands into view of
HOLMES then a slight salute with hand and
bow and back slowly with dignity into chair.)

Business of HOLMES seating himself on stool opposite MORIARTY,
revolver business and coming motionless.

MORIARTY: (After HOLMES'S business.)
                    I tell you it is the boldness born of ignorance.
                    Do you think that I would be here if I had not
                    made the streets quite safe in every respect?

HOLMES: (Shaking head.)
                    Oh no! I could never so grossly overestimate
                    your courage as that.

MORIARTY: Do you imagine that your friend the doctor,
                    and your man Forman will soon return?

HOLMES: Possibly not.

MORIARTY: So it leaves us quite alone — doesn't it, Mr.
                    Holmes — quite alone — so that we can talk
                    the matter over quietly and not be disturbed. In
                    the first place I wish to call your attention to a
                    few memoranda which I have jotted down —
                    (suddenly put both hands to breast pocket) —
                    which you will find —

HOLMES: Look out! Take your hands away.

Music: Danger pp

MORIARTY again stopped with his hands at breast pocket.

HOLMES: · Get your hands down.

MORIARTY does not lower his hands at first request.

HOLMES: A little further away from the memorandum
           book you are talking about.

MORIARTY: (Lowers hands to his lap. Slight pause, raising
           hands again slowly as he speaks.)
           Why, I was merely about to —

HOLMES: Well, merely don't do it.

MORIARTY: (Remonstratingly—his hands still up near
           breast.)
           But I would like to show you a —

HOLMES: I don't want to see it.

MORIARTY: But if you will allow me —

HOLMES: I don't care for it at all. I don't require any
           notebooks. If you want it so badly we'll have
           someone get it for you.

MORIARTY slowly lowers hands again.

HOLMES: (Rings bell on table with left hand.)
           I always like to save my guests unnecessary
           trouble.

MORIARTY: (After quite a pause.)
           I observe that your boy does not answer the
           bell.

HOLMES: No. But I have an idea that he will before long.

MORIARTY: (Leaning towards HOLMES and speaking with
           subdued rage and significance.)
           It may possibly be longer than you think, Mr.
           Holmes.

HOLMES: (Intensely.)
           What! That boy!

MORIARTY: (Hissing at HOLMES.)
           Yes, your boy.

Hold the tableau for a moment, the two men scowling at each other. HOLMES slowly reaching left hand out to ring bell again. MORIARTY begins to raise right hand slowly towards breast pocket, keeping it concealed beneath his muffler as far as possible. On slight motion of HOLMES' left hand, he lowers it again, giving up the attempt this time.

HOLMES: At least we will try the bell once more,
                 Professor.
                 (Rings bell.)

Short wait.

MORIARTY: (After pause.)
                 Doesn't it occur to you that he may Possibly
                 have been detained, Mr. Holmes?

HOLMES: It does. But I also observe that you are in very
                 much the same predicament.
                 (Pause.)

HOLMES rings bell for the third time. Noise on stairway outside. Enter BILLY with part of his coat, and with sleeves of shirt and waistcoat badly torn.

Music stops.

BILLY: (Up near door.)
                 I beg pardon, sir—someone tried to 'old me
                 sir!
                 (Panting for breath.)

HOLMES: It is quite evident however that he failed to do
                 so.

BILLY: Yes sir — 'e's got my coat sir but 'e 'asn't got
                 me!

HOLMES: Billy!

BILLY: (Cheerfully.)
                 Yes sir.
                 (Still out of breath.)

HOLMES: The gentleman I am pointing out to you with this six-shooter desires to have us get something out of his left hand coat pocket.

MORIARTY gives a very slight start or movement of right hand to breast pocket, getting it almost to his pocket, then recollecting himself, seeing that HOLMES has got him covered.

HOLMES: Ah, I thought so. Left-hand coat pocket. As he is not feeling quite himself to-day, and the exertion might prove injurious, suppose you attend to it.

BILLY: Yes sir.
        (He goes quickly to MORIARTY puts hand in his pocket and draws out a bull dog revolver.) Is this it sir?

HOLMES: It has the general outline of being it. Quite so. Put it on the table.

MORIARTY makes a grab for it.

HOLMES: Not there Billy. Look out. Push it a little further this way.

BILLY does so placing it so that it is within easy reach of HOLMES.

HOLMES: That's more like it.

BILLY: Shall I see if he's got another sir?

HOLMES: Why, Billy, you surprise me, after the gentleman has taken the trouble to inform you that he hasn't.

BILLY: When sir?

HOLMES: When he made a snatch for this one. Now that we have your little memorandum book, Professor, do you think of anything else you'd like before Billy goes?

MORIARTY does not reply.

HOLMES:	Any little thing that you've got, that you want? No! Ah, I am sorry that's all, Billy.

Pause. MORIARTY motionless, eyes on HOLMES. HOLMES puts his own revolver in his pocket quietly. MORIARTY remains motionless, his eyes on HOLMES, waiting for a chance.

BILLY:	Thank you, sir. (Goes out.)

HOLMES carelessly picks up MORIARTY'S weapon, turns it over in his hands a little below table for a moment, then tosses it back on table again—during which business MORIARTY looks front savagely.

HOLMES:	(tapping revolver with pipe): Rather a rash project of yours Moriarty— even though you have made the street quite safe in every respect — to make use of that thing — so early in the evening and in this part of the town.
MORIARTY:	Listen to me. On the 4th of January you crossed my path — on the 23rd you incommoded me. And now, at the close of April, I find myself placed in such a position through your continual interference that I am in positive danger of losing my liberty.
HOLMES:	Have you any suggestion to make?
MORIARTY:	(head swaying from side to side) No! (Pause and look fiercely at HOLMES.) I have no suggestion to make. I have a fact to state. If you do not drop it at once your life is not worth that. (Snap of finger.)
HOLMES:	I shall be pleased to drop it — at ten o'clock to-morrow night.

MORIARTY: Why then?

HOLMES: Because at that hour, Moriarty … your life will
not be worth that.
(A snap of finger.)
You will be under arrest.

MORIARTY: At that hour, Sherlock Holmes, your eyes will
be closed in death.

Both look at one another motionless an instant.

HOLMES: (Rising as if rather bored.
I am afraid, Professor, that in the pleasure of
this conversation I am neglecting more
important business.
(Turns away to mantel and business of looking
for match, etc.)

MORIARTY rises slowly, picks up hat, keeping his eyes on
HOLMES. Suddenly catches sight of revolver on table — pause —
and putting hat on table.

MORIARTY: (Nearing HOLMES and looking towards door.)
I came here this evening to see if peace could
not be arranged between us.

HOLMES: Ah yes.
(Smiling pleasantly and pressing tobacco in
pipe.)
I saw that. That's rather good.

MORIARTY;   (Passionately.)
You have seen fit not only to reject my
proposals, but to make insulting references
coupled with threats of arrest.

HOLMES: Quite so! Quite so!
(Lights match and holds it to pipe)

MORIARTY: (Moving a little so as to be nearer table.)
Well—
       (CONT/)

> (Slyly picking up revolver.)
> —you have been warned of your danger —
> you do not heed that warning—perhaps you
> will heed this!

Making a sudden plunge and aiming at HOLMES' head rapidly snaps
the revolver in quick attempt to fire.

HOLMES turns quietly toward him still holding match to pipe so that
the last snap of hammer is directly in his face. Very slight pause on
MORIARTY being unable to fire — and back up at same time boiling
with rage.

HOLMES: Oh! ha! — here!
                   (As if recollecting something. Tosses away
                   match and feeling quickly in left pocket of
                   dressing gown brings out some cartridges and
                   tosses them carelessly on table towards
                   MORIARTY.)
                   I didn't suppose you'd want to use that thing
                   again, so I took all your cartridges out and put
                   them in my pocket. You'll find them all there,
                   Professor.
                   (Reaches over and rings bell on table with right
                   hand.)

Enter BILLY.

HOLMES: Billy!

BILLY: Yes, sir!

HOLMES: Show this gentleman nicely to the door.

BILLY: Yes sir! This way sir!
                   (Standing within door.)

PROFESSOR MORIARTY looks at HOLMES a moment, then flings
revolver down and across the table, clenches fist in HOLMES' face,
turns boiling with rage, picks hat up, and exits quickly at door,
muttering aloud as he goes.

HOLMES:	(After exit of MORIARTY.) Billy! Come here!
BILLY:	Yes, sir! (BILLY comes quickly down.)
HOLMES:	Billy! You're a good boy!
BILLY:	Yes, sir! Thank you, sir! (Stands grinning up at HOLMES.)

The lights go out suddenly.

No music at end of this Act.

CURTAIN

ACT III

The Stepney Gas Chamber. Midnight.

SCENE. — The Gas Chamber at Stepney. A large, dark, grimy room on an upper floor of an old building backing on wharves etc. Plaster cracking off, masonry piers or chimney showing. As uncanny and gruesome appearance as possible. Heavy beams and timbers showing. Door leads to the landing and then to the entrance. Another door leads to a small cupboard. The walls of the cupboard can be seen when the door is opened. Large window, closed. Grimy and dirty glass so nothing can be seen through it. The window is nailed with spike nails securely shut. Black backing — no light behind. Strong bars outside back of windows, to show when window is broken. These bars must not be seen through the glass. Trash all over the room. The only light in the room on the rise of the curtain is from a dim lantern — carried on by McTAGUE.

Characteristic Music for Curtain.

CRAIGIN and LEARY are discovered. CRAIGIN is sitting on a box. He sits glum and motionless, waiting. LEARY is sitting on table his feet on the chair in front of it.

McTAGUE enters with safety lamp. He stops just within a moment, glancing around in the dimness. Soon moves up near a masonry pier, a little above the door, and leans against it, waiting. CRAIGIN, LEARY and McTAGUE are dressed in dark clothes and wear felt -soled shoes.

LEARY: What's McTague doing 'ere?

McTAGUE: I was sent 'ere.

All dialogue in this part of Act in low tones, but distinct, to give a weird effect, echoing through the large grimy room among the deep shadows.

LEARY: I thought the Seraph was with us in this job.

CRAIGIN: 'E ain't.

LEARY: Who was the last you put the gas on?

Pause.

111

CRAIGIN: I didn't 'ear 'is name.
                  (Pause.)
                  'E'd been 'oldin' back money on a 'aul out
                  some railway place.

Pause.

McTAGUE: What's this 'ere job he wants done?
                  (Sits on box, placing lamp on floor by his
                  side.)

Pause.

CRAIGIN: I ain't been told.

Pause.

LEARY: As long as it's 'ere we know what it's likely to
                  be.

Door opens slowly and hesitatingly. Enter SID PRINCE. He stands
just within door, and looks about a little suspiciously as if uncertain
what to do. Pause. He notices that the door is slowly closing behind
him and quietly holds it back. But he must not burlesque this
movement with funny business. McTAGUE holds lantern up to see
who it is, at the same time rising and coming down near PRINCE.

PRINCE: Does any one of you blokes know if this is the
                  place where I meet Alf Bassick?

Pause. Neither of the other men take notice of PRINCE. McTAGUE
goes back to where he was sitting before PRINCE'S entrance.

PRINCE: (After waiting a moment.)
                  From wot you say, I take it you don't.

CRAIGIN: We ain't knowin' no such man. 'E may be 'ere
                  and 'e may not.

PRINCE: Oh!
                  (Comes a little farther into room and lets the
                  door close.)
                                  (CONT/)

112

It's quite right then, thank you.
(Pause. No one speaks.)
Nice old place to find, this 'ere is.
(No one answers him.)
And when you do find it —
(Looks about)
— I can't say it's any too cheerful.
(He thereupon pulls out a cigarette-case, puts a cigarette in his mouth, and feels in pocket for matches. Finds one. About to light it. Has moved a few steps during this.)

CRAIGIN: Here! ...

PRINCE stops.

CRAIGIN: Don't light that! ... It ain't safe!

PRINCE stops motionless, where above speech caught him, for an instant. Pause. PRINCE begins to turn his head slowly and only a little way, glances carefully about, as if expecting to see tins of nitro-glycerine. He sees nothing on either side, and finally turns towards CRAIGIN.

PRINCE: If it ain't askin' too much wot's the matter with the place? It looks all roight to me.

CRAIGIN: Well don't light no matches, and it'll stay lookin' the same.

Pause. Door opens, and BASSICK enters hurriedly. He looks quickly about.

BASSICK: Oh, Prince, you're here. I was looking for you outside.

PRINCE: You told me to be 'ere, sir. That was 'ow the last arrangement stood.

BASSICK: Very well!
                  (Going across PRINCE and glancing about to see that the other men are present.)
                  You've got the rope Craigin?

113

Voices are still kept low.

CRAIGIN: (Pointing to bunch of loose rope on floor near him.)
It's 'ere.

BASSICK: That you, Leary?

LEARY: 'Ere, sir!

BASSICK: And McTague?

McTAGUE: 'Ere, sir!

BASSICK: You want to be very careful with it to-night —
you've got a tough one.

CRAIGIN: You ain't said who, as I've 'eard.

BASSICK: (Low voice.)
Sherlock Holmes.

Brief pause.

CRAIGIN: (After the pause.)
You mean that, sir?

BASSICK: Indeed, I do!

CRAIGIN: We're goin' to count 'im out.

BASSICK: Well, if you don't and he gets away — I'm
sorry for you, that's all.

CRAIGIN: I'll be cursed glad to put the gas on 'im — I
tell you that.

LEARY: I say the same myself.

Sound of MORIARTY and LARRABEE coming.

BASSICK: Sh! Professor Moriarty's coming.

McTAGUE places lamp on box.

LEARY: Not the guv'nor?

BASSICK: Yes. He wanted to see this.

The three men retire a little up stage, waiting. BASSICK moves to meet MORIARTY. PRINCE moves up out of way. Door opens. Enter MORIARTY, followed by LARRABEE. Door slowly closes behind them. LARRABEE waits a moment near door and then retires up near PRINCE. They watch the following scene. All speeches low — quiet — in undertone.

MORIARTY: Where's Craigin?

CRAIGIN steps forward.

MORIARTY: Have you got your men?

CRAIGIN: All 'ere, sir.

MORIARTY: No mistakes to-night.

CRAIGIN: I'll be careful o' that.

MORIARTY: (Quick glance about.)
                   That door, Bassick.
                   (Points up, back to audience.)

BASSICK: A small cupboard, sir.
                   (Goes quickly up and opens the door wide to
                   show it.)

LEARY catches up lantern and swings it near the cupboard door.

MORIARTY: No outlet?

BASSICK: None whatever, sir.

LEARY swings lantern almost inside cupboard to let MORIARTY See. All this dialogue in very low tones, but distinct and Impressive. BASSICK closes door after lantern business.

115

MORIARTY: (Turns and points.)
                   That window?

BASSICK: (Moving over a little.)
                   Nailed down, sir!

LEARY turns and swings the lantern near window so that
MORIARTY can see.

MORIARTY: A man might break the glass.

BASSICK: If he did that he'd come against heavy iron
                   bars outside.

CRAIGIN: We'll 'ave 'im tied down afore 'e could break
                   any glass sir.

MORIARTY: (Who has turned to CRAIGIN.)
                   Ah! You've used it before. Of course you
                   know if it's airtight?

BASSICK: Every crevice is caulked sir.

MORIARTY: (Turns and points as if at something directly
                   over footlights.)
                   And that door?

LEARY comes down and gives lantern a quick swing as if lighting
place indicated.

BASSICK: (From same position.)
                   The opening is planked up solid sir as you can
                   see and double thickness.

MORIARTY: Ah!
                   (Satisfaction. Glances at door through which
                   he entered.)
                   When the men turn the gas on him they leave
                   by that door?

BASSICK: Yes sir.

MORIARTY: It can be made quite secure?

BASSICK: Heavy bolts on the outside sir and solid bars
                    over all.

MORIARTY: Let me see how quick you can operate them.

BASSICK: They tie the man down, sir — there's no need
                    to hurry.

MORIARTY: (Same voice.)
                    Let me see how quick you can operate them.

BASSICK: (Quick order.)
                    Leary!
                    (Motions him to door.)

LEARY: (Handing lamp to CRAIGIN.)
                    Yes sir!
                    (He jumps to and goes out closing it at once
                    and immediately the sound of sliding bolts and
                    the dropping of bars are heard from outside.)

This is a very important effect as it is repeated at the end of the Act.
CRAIGIN places lamp on box.

MORIARTY: That s all.

Sounds of bolts withdrawn and LEARY enters and waits.

MORIARTY: (Goes to CRAIGIN.)
                    Craigin — you'll take your men outside that
                    door and wait till Mr. Larrabee has had a little
                    business interview with the gentleman. Take
                    them up the passage to the left so Holmes does
                    not see them as he comes in.
                    (To BASSICK.)
                    Who's driving the cab to night?

BASSICK: I sent O'Hagan. His orders are to drive him
                    about for an hour so he doesn't know the
                    distance or the direction he's going, and then
                    stop at the small door at upper Swandem Lane.
                    He's going to get him out there and show him
                    to this door.

MORIARTY: The cab windows were covered, of course?

BASSICK: Wooden shutters, sir, bolted and secure. There isn't a place he can see through the size of a pin.

MORIARTY: (Satisfied.)
                   Ah! …
                   (Looks about.)
                   We must have a lamp here.

BASSICK: Better not, sir — there might be some gas left.

MORIARTY: You've got a light there.
                   (Pointing to miner's safety lamp on box.)

BASSICK: It's a safety lamp, sir.

MORIARTY: A safety lamp! You mustn't have that here! The moment he sees that he'll know what you're doing and make trouble.
                   (Sniffs.)
                   There's hardly any gas. Go and tell Lascar we must have a good lamp.

BASSICK goes out.

MORIARTY: (Looks about.)
                   Bring that table over here.

CRAIGIN and McTAGUE bring table.

MORIARTY: Now, Craigin — and the rest of you — One thing remember. No shooting to-night! Not a single shot. It can be heard in the alley below. The first thing is to get his revolver away before he has a chance to use it. Two of you attract his attention in front — the other come up on him from behind and snatch it out of his pocket. Then you have him. Arrange that, Craigin.

CRAIGIN: I'll attend to it, sir.

The three men retire. Enter BASSICK with large lamp. Glass shade to lamp of whitish colour. BASSICK crosses to table and Places lamp on it.

BASSICK: (To McTAGUE.)
                    Put out that lamp.

McTAGUE is about to pick up lamp.

CRAIGIN: Stop!

McTAGUE waits.

CRAIGIN: We'll want it when the other's taken away.

BASSICK: He mustn't see it, understand.

MORIARTY: Don't put it out — cover it with something.

CRAIGIN: Here!
                    (He goes up, takes lantern, and pulling out a
                    large box from several others places lantern
                    within and pushes the open side against the
                    wall so that no light from lantern can be seen
                    from front.)

MORIARTY: That will do.

BASSICK: (Approaching MORIARTY.)
                    You mustn't stay longer, sir. O'Hagan might
                    be a little early.

MORIARTY: Mr. Larrabee —
                    (Moving a step forward.)
                    You understand! — they wait for you.

LARRABEE: (Low — quiet.)
                    I understand, sir.

MORIARTY: I give you this opportunity to get what you can
                    for your trouble. But anything that is found on
                    him after you have finished — is subject —
                                (CONT/)

119

(Glances at CRAIGIN and others.)
— to the usual division.

LARRABEE: That's all I want.

MORIARTY: When you have quite finished and got your
money suppose you blow that little whistle
which I observe hanging from your watch
chain — and these gentlemen will take their
turn.

BASSICK holds door open for MORIARTY. LARRABEE moves up
out of way as MORIARTY crosses.

MORIARTY: (Crosses to door. At door, turning to
CRAIGIN.)
And, Craigin —

CRAIGIN crosses to MORIARTY.

MORIARTY: At the proper moment present my compliments
to Mr. Sherlock Holmes, and say that I wish
him a pleasant journey to the other side.
(Goes out, followed by BASSICK.)

LARRABEE glances about critically. As MORIARTY goes, PRINCE
throws cigarette on floor in disgust, which LEARY picks up as he goes
later, putting it in his pocket.

LARRABEE: You'd better put that rope out of sight.

CRAIGIN picks up rope, which he carries with him until he goes out
later. LEARY and McTAGUE move across noiselessly at back.
CRAIGIN stops an instant up stage to examine the window, looking at
the caulking, etc., and shaking the frames to see that they are securely
spiked. Others wait near door. He finishes at window. LARRABEE is
examining package near lamp, which he has taken from his pocket. As
LEARY crosses he picks up rope which was lying up centre and hides
it in barrel. McTAGUE in crossing bumps up against PRINCE, and
both look momentarily at each other very much annoyed.

CRAIGIN: (Joins LEARY and McTAGUE at door. Speaks to LARRABEE from door.)
You understand, sir, we're on this floor just around the far turn of the passage — so 'e won't see us as 'e's commin' up.

LARRABEE: I understand.
(Turning to CRAIGIN.)

CRAIGIN: An' it's w'en we 'ears that whistle, eh?

LARRABEE: When you hear this whistle.

CRAIGIN, LEARY and McTAGUE go out noiselessly. Pause. Door remains open. PRINCE, who has been very quiet during foregoing scene, begins to move a little nervously and looks about. He looks at his watch and then glances about again. LARRABEE is still near lamp, looking at package of papers which he took from his pocket.

PRINCE: (Coming down in a grumpy manner, head down, not looking at LARRABEE.)
Look 'ere, Jim, this sort of thing ain't so much in my line.

LARRABEE: (At table.)
I suppose not.

PRINCE: (Still eyes about without looking at LARRABEE.)
When it comes to a shy at a safe or drillin' into bank vaults, I feels perfectly at 'ome, but I don't care so much to see a man —
(Stops — hesitates.)
Well, it ain't my line!

LARRABEE: (Turning.)
Here!
(Going to him and urging him toward door and putting package away.)
All I want of you is to go down on the corner below and let me know when he comes.

PRINCE: (Stops and turns to LARRABEE.)
                    'Ow will I let you know?

LARRABEE: Have you got a whistle?

PRINCE: (Pulls one out of pocket.)
                    Cert'nly.

LARRABEE: Well when you see O'Hagan driving with him
                    Come down the alley there and blow it twice.
                    (Urging PRINCE a little nearer door.)

PRINCE: Yes—but ain't it quite loikely to call a cab at
                    the same time?

LARRABEE: What more do you want — take the cab and go
                    home.

PRINCE: Oh, then you won't need me 'ere again.

LARRABEE: No.

PRINCE turns to go.

PRINCE: (Going to door — very much relieved.)
                    Oh, very well — then I'll tear myself away.
                    (Goes out.)

Music. Pathetic, melodramatic, agitato, pp.

LARRABEE crosses to table and looks at lamp, gets two chairs and
places them on either side of table; As he places second chair he stops
dead as if having heard a noise outside, listens, and is satisfied all is
well. Then thinking of the best way to conduct negotiations with
Holmes, takes out cigar, and holds it a moment unlighted as he thinks.
Then takes out match and is about to light it when ALICE
FAULKNER enters. He starts up and looks at her. She stands looking
at him, frightened and excited.

Music stops.

LARRABEE: What do you want?

ALICE: It's true, then?

LARRABEE: How did you get to this place?

ALICE: I followed you — in a cab.

LARRABEE: What have you been doing since I came up
                here? Informing the police, perhaps.

ALICE: No — I was afraid he'd come — so I waited.

LARRABEE: Oh — to warn him very likely?

ALICE: Yes.
                (Pause.)
                To warn him.
                (Looks about room.)

LARRABEE: Then it's just as well you came up.

ALICE: I came to make sure —
                (Glances about.)

LARRABEE: Of what?

ALICE: That something else — is not going to be done
                besides — what they told me.

LARRABEE: Ah — somebody told you that something else
                was going to be done?

ALICE: Yes.

LARRABEE: So! We've got another spy in the house.

ALICE: You're going to swindle and deceive him — I
                know that. Is there anything more?
                (Advancing to him a little.)

LARRABEE: What could you do if there was?

ALICE: I could buy you off. Such men as you are
                always open to sale.

LARABEE: How much would you give?

ALICE: The genuine package — the real ones. All the proofs — everything

LARRABEE: (Advancing above table, quietly but with quick interest.)
Have you got it with you?

ALICE: No, but I can get it.

LARRABEE: Oh —
(Going to table. Slightly disappointed.)
So you'll do all that for this man? You think he's your friend, I suppose?

ALICE: I haven't thought of it.

LARRABEE: Look what he's doing now. Coming here to buy those things off me.

ALICE: They're false. They're counterfeit.

LARRABEE: He thinks they're genuine, doesn't he? He'd hardly come here to buy them if he didn't.

ALICE: He may ask my permission still.

LARRABEE: Ha!
(Sneer—turning away.)
He won't get the chance.

ALICE: (Suspicious again.)
Won't get the chance. Then there is something else.

LARRABEE: Something else!
(Turning to her.)
Why, you see me here myself, don't you? I'm going to talk to him on a little business. How could I do him any harm?

ALICE:	(Advancing.) Where are those men who came up here?
LARRABEE:	What men?
ALICE:	Three villainous looking men — I saw them go in at the street door —
LARRABEE:	Oh — those men. They went up the other stairway. (Pointing over shoulder.) You can see them in the next building — if you look out of this window. (Indicating window.)

ALICE at once goes rapidly toward the window and making a hesitating pause near table as she sees LARRABEE crossing above her but moving on again quickly LARRABEE at same time crosses well up stage, keeping his eye on ALICE as she moves towards the window and tries to look out, but finding she cannot she turns at once to LARRABEE. He is standing near door.

Music. Melodramatic. Danger. Keep down. pp Agitato

Hold this an instant where they stand looking at one another, ALICE beginning to see she has been trapped.

ALICE:	(Starting toward door.) I'll look in the passage-way, if you please.
LARRABEE:	(Taking one step down before door, quietly.) Yes — but I don't please.
ALICE:	(Stops before him.) You wouldn't dare to keep me here.
LARRABEE:	I might dare — but I won't. You'd be in the way.
ALICE:	Where are those men?
LARRABEE:	Stay where you are and you'll see them very soon.

LARRABEE goes to door and blows whistle as quietly as possible. Short pause. No footsteps heard, as the men move noiselessly. Enter CRAIGIN, McTAGUE and LEARY, appearing suddenly noiselessly. They stand looking in some astonishment at ALICE.

Music stops.

ALICE:
I knew it.
(Moving back a step, seeing from this that they are going to attack Holmes.)
Ah!
(Under breath. After pause she turns and hurries to window, trying to look out or give an alarm. Then runs to cupboard door. LARRABEE watching her movements. Desperately.)
You're going to do him some harm.

LARRABEE:
Oh no, it's only a little joke — at his expense.

ALICE:
(Moving toward him a little.)
You wanted the letters, the package I had in the safe! I'll get it for you. Let me go and I'll bring it here — or whatever you tell me —
(LARRABEE sneers meaningly.)
I'll give you my word not to say anything to anyone — not to him — not to the policemen—not anyone!

LARRABEE:
(Without moving.)
You needn't take the trouble to get it — but you can tell me where it is — and you'll have to be quick about it too—

ALICE:
Yes — if you'll promise not to go on with this.

LARRABEE:
Of course! That's understood.

ALICE:
(Excitedly.)
You promise!

LARRABEE:
Certainly I promise. Now where is it?

ALICE: Just outside my bedroom window — just
                          outside on the left, fastened between the shutter
                          and the wall — you can easily find it.

LARRABEE: Yes — I can easily find it.

ALICE: Now tell them — tell them to go.

LARRABEE: (Going down to men.)
                          Tie her up so she can't make a noise. Keep her
                          out there until we have Holmes in here, and
                          then let O'Hagan keep her in his cab. She
                          mustn't get back to the house —not till I've
                          been there.

ALICE listens dazed, astonished.

CRAIGIN: (Speaks low.)
                          Go an' get a hold, Leary. Hand me a piece of
                          that rope.

McTAGUE brings rope from under his coat. Business of getting
rapidly ready to gag and tie ALICE. Much time must not be spent on
this; quick, business-like. McTAGUE takes handkerchief from pocket
to use as gag.

LARRABEE: (Taking a step or two down before ALICE so
                          as to attract her attention front.)
                          Now then, my pretty bird—
                          (ALICE begins to move back in alarm and
                          looking at LARRABEE.)

ALICE: You said — you said if I told you —

LARRABEE: Well — we haven't done him any harm yet,
                          have we?

LEARY is moving quietly round behind her.

ALICE: Then send them away.

LARRABEE: Certainly. Go away now, boys, there's no more
                          work for you to-night.

ALICE: (Looking at them terrified.)
                        They don't obey you. They are —

LEARY seizes her. She screams and resists, but CRAIGIN and
McTAGUE come at once, so that she is quickly subdued and gagged
with handkerchief, etc., and her hands tied. As the Struggle takes
place, men work up to near cupboard with ALICE. LARRABEE also
eagerly watching them tie ALICE up. This is not prolonged more than
is absolutely necessary. Just as they finish, a shrill whistle is heard in
distance outside at back, as if from street far below. All stop —
listening —picture.

CRAIGIN: Now out of the door with her —
                        (Starting to door.)

(The prolonged shrill whistle is heard again.)

LARRABEE: By God, he's here.

CRAIGIN: What!

LARRABEE: That's Sid Prince, I put him on the watch.

CRAIGIN: We won't have time to get her out.

LARRABEE: Shut her in there.
                        (Pointing to cupboard.)

LEARY: Yes — that'll do.

CRAIGIN: In with her.

LEARY and CRAIGIN, almost on the word, take her to cupboard.
McTAGUE goes and keeps watch at door.

CRAIGIN: (As he holds ALICE.)
                        Open that door! Open that door!

LEARY goes and opens cupboard door. As LEARY leaves she breaks
away from CRAIGIN and gets almost to right when CRAIGIN catches
her again. As he takes hold of her she faints, and he throws her into
cupboard in a helpless condition. LEARY closes cupboard door and
they stand before it.

LEARY: (Still at cupboard door. Others have turned so
                    as to avoid suspicion if Holmes comes in on
                    them.)
                    There ain't no lock on this 'ere door.

LARRABEE: No lock!

LEARY: No.

LARRABEE: Drive something in.

CRAIGIN: Here, this knife.
                    (Hands LEARY a large clasp-knife, opened
                    ready.)

LARRABEE: A knife won't hold it.

CRAIGIN: Yes, it will. Drive it in strong.

LEARY drives blade in door frame with all his force.

LEARY: 'E'll have to find us 'ere.

CRAIGIN: 'Es — and he won't either — we'll go on and
                    do 'im up.
                    (Going to door.)

LARRABEE: No, you won't.

Men stop. Pause.

LARRABEE: I'll see him first, if you please.

CRAIGIN and LARRABEE facing each other savagely an instant well
down stage.

McTAGUE: Them was orders, Craigin.

LEARY: So it was.

McTAGUE: There might be time to get back in the passage.

(CONT/)

129

Sir Arthur Conan Doyle

(He listens at door and cautiously looks off —
turns back into room.)
They ain't got up one flight yet.

LEARY: Quick then.
                   (Moving toward door.)

McTAGUE, LEARY and CRAIGIN go out. Door does not close.
LARRABEE glances at door anxiously. Makes a quick dash up to it,
and forces knife in with all his strength. Quickly pulls off coat and hat,
throwing them on boxes, and sits quietly chewing an end of cigar.
Enter SHERLOCK HOLMES at door, walking easily as though on
some ordinary business.

Stop music.

HOLMES: (Seeing the apartment with a glance as he
                   enters and Pausing, disappointed. His little
                   laugh, with no smile.)
                   How the devil is it that you crooks always
                   manage to hit on the same places for your
                   scoundrelly business?
                   (Chuckles of amusement.)
                   Well! I certainly thought, after all this driving
                   about in a closed cab you'd show me
                   something new.

LARRABEE: (Looking up nonchalantly.)
                   Seen it before, have you?

HOLMES: (Standing still.)
                   Well, I should think so!
                   (Moves easily about recalling dear old times.)
                   I nabbed a friend of yours in this place while
                   he was trying to drop himself out of that
                   window. Ned Colvin, the cracksman.

LARRABEE: Colvin. I never heard of him before.

HOLMES: No? Ha! ha! Well, you certainly never heard of
                   him after. A brace of counterfeiters used these
                   regal chambers in the spring of '90.
                                 (CONT/)

130

One of them hid in the cupboard. We pulled him out by the heels.

LARRABEE: (Trying to get in on the nonchalance.)
Ah! Did you? And the other?

HOLMES: The other? He was more fortunate.

LARRABEE: Ah — he got away, I suppose.

HOLMES: Yes, he got away. We took his remains out through that door to the street.
(Indicating door.)

LARRABEE: Quite interesting.
(Drawled a little — looks at end of his cigar.)

HOLMES is looking about.

LARRABEE: Times have changed since then.

HOLMES darts a lightning glance at LARRABEE. Instantly easy again and glancing about as before.

HOLMES: (Dropping down near LARRABEE.)
So they have, Mr. Larrabee — so they have.
(A little confidentially.)
Then it was only cracksmen, counterfeiters, and petty swindlers of various kinds — Now—
(Pause, looking at LARRABEE.)

LARRABEE turns and looks at HOLMES.

LARRABEE: Well? What now?

HOLMES: Well —
(Mysteriously.)
Between you and me, Larrabee — we've heard some not altogether agreeable rumors; rumours of some pretty shady work not far from here — a murder or two of a very peculiar kind — and I've always had a suspicion —
(CONT/)

(Stops. Sniffs very delicately. Motionless pause. Nods ominously to LARRABEE, who is looking about, and gets over towards window. When within reach he runs his hand lightly along the frame.)
My surmise was correct — it is.

LARRABEE: (Turning to HOLMES.)
It is what?

HOLMES: Caulked.

LARRABEE: What does that signify to us?

HOLMES: Nothing to us, Mr. Larrabee, nothing to us, but it might signify a good deal to some poor devil who's been caught in this trap.

LARRABEE: Well if it's nothing to us suppose we leave it and get to business. My time is limited.

HOLMES: Quite so, of course. I should have realized that reflections could not possibly appeal to you. But it so happens I take a deep interest in anything that pertains to what are known as the criminal classes and this same interest makes me rather curious to know —(looking straight at LARRABEE, who looks up at him) — how you happened to select such a singularly gruesome place for an ordinary business transaction.

LARRABEE: (Looking at HOLMES across the table.)
I selected this places Mr. Holmes, because I thought you might not be disposed to take such liberties here as you practised in my own house last night.

HOLMES: Quite so, quite so.
(Looks innocently at LARRABEE.)
But why not?

They look at one another an instant.

LARRABEE: (Significantly.)
You might not feel quite so much at home.

HOLMES: Oh — ha!
(A little laugh.)
You've made a singular miscalculation.
I feel perfectly at home, Mr. Larrabee!
Perfectly!
(He seats himself at table in languid and leisurely manner, takes cigar from pocket and lights it.)

LARRABEE: (Looks at him an instant.)
Well, I'm very glad to hear it.

LARRABEE now takes out the counterfeit package of papers, etc., and tosses it on the table before them. HOLMES looks on floor slightly by light of match, unobserved by LARRABEE.

Here is the little packet which is the object of this meeting. (He glances at HOLMES to see effect of its production.)

HOLMES looks at it calmly as he smokes.

LARRABEE: I haven't opened it yet, but Miss Faulkner tells me everything is there.

HOLMES: Then there is no need of opening it, Mr. Larrabee.

LARRABEE: Oh, well — I want to see you satisfied.

HOLMES: That is precisely the condition in which you now behold me. Miss Faulkner is a truthful young lady. Her word is sufficient.

LARRABEE: Very well. Now what shall we say, Mr. Holmes?
(Pause.)
Of course, we want a pretty large price for this. Miss Faulkner is giving up everything. She would not be satisfied unless the result justified it.

HOLMES: (Pointedly.)
                   Suppose, Mr. Larrabee, that as Miss Faulkner
                   knows nothing whatever about this affair, we
                   omit her name from the discussion.

Slight pause of two seconds.

LARRABEE: Who told you she doesn't know?

HOLMES: You did. Every look, tone, gesture —
                   everything you have said and done since I have
                   been in this room has informed me that she has
                   never consented to this transaction. It is a little
                   speculation of your own.
                   (Tapping his fingers on end of table.)

LARRABEE: Ha!
                   (Sneer.)
                   I suppose you think you can read me like a
                   book.

HOLMES: No — like a primer.

LARRABEE: Well, let that pass. How much'll you give?

HOLMES: A thousand pounds.

LARRABEE: I couldn't take it.

HOLMES: What do you ask?

LARRABEE: Five thousand.

HOLMES: (Shakes head.)
                   I couldn't give it.

LARRABEE: Very well —
                   (Rises.)
                   We've had all this trouble for nothing.
                   (As if about to put up the packet.)

HOLMES: (Leaning back in chair and remonstrating.)
                                (CONT/)

Oh — don't say that, Mr. Larrabee! To me the occasion has been doubly interesting. I have not only had the pleasure of meeting you again but I have also availed myself of the opportunity of making observations regarding this place which may not come amiss.

LARRABEE looks at HOLMES contemptuously. He places chair under table.

LARRABEE: Why, I've been offered four thousand for this little—

HOLMES: Why didn't you take it?

LARRABEE: Because I intend to get more.

HOLMES: That's too bad.

LARRABEE: If they offered four thousand they'll give five.

HOLMES: They won't give anything.

LARRABEE: Why not?

HOLMES: They've turned the case over to me.

LARRABEE: Will you give three thousand?

HOLMES: (Rising.)
Mr. Larrabee, strange as it may appear, my time is limited as well as yours. I have brought with me the sum of One thousand pounds, which is all that I wish to pay. If it is your desire to sell at this figure kindly appraise me of the fact at once. If not, permit me to wish you a very good evening.

Pause. LARRABEE looks at him.

LARRABEE: (After the pause glances nervously round once, fearing he heard something)
(CONT/)

135

Go on!
(Tosses packet on table.)
You can have them. It's too small a matter to
haggle over.

HOLMES reseats himself at once, back of table, and takes wallet from
his pocket, from which he produces a bunch of bank notes.
LARRABEE stands watching him with glittering eye. HOLMES
counts out ten one hundred pound notes and lays the remainder of the
notes on the table with elbow on them, while he counts the first over
again.

LARRABEE:	(Sneeringly.) Oh—I thought you said you had brought just a thousand.
HOLMES:	(Not looking up; counting the notes.) I did. This is it.
LARRABEE:	You brought a trifle more, I see.
HOLMES:	(Counting notes.) Quite so. I didn't say I hadn't brought any more.
LARRABEE:	Ha! (Sneers.) You can do your little tricks when it comes to it, can't you?
HOLMES:	It depends on who I'm dealing with. (Hands LARRABEE one thousand pounds in notes.)

LARRABEE takes money and keeps a close watch at same time on the
remaining pile of notes lying at HOLMES' left. HOLMES, after
handing the notes to LARRABEE, lays cigar he was smoking on the
table, picks up packet which he puts in his pocket with his right hand,
and is almost at the same time reaching with his left hand for the notes
he placed upon the table when LARRABEE makes a Sudden lunge
and snatches the pile of bank notes, jumping back On the instant.
HOLMES springs to his feet at the same time.

HOLMES: Now I've got you where I want you, Jim
                   Larrabee! You've been so cunning and so
                   cautious and so wise, we couldn't find a thing
                   to hold you for — but this little slip will get
                   you in for robbery —

LARRABEE: Oh! You'll have me in, will you?
                   (Short sneering laugh.)
                   What are your views about being able to get
                   away from here yourself?

HOLMES: I do not anticipate any particular difficulty.

LARRABEE: (Significantly.)
                   Perhaps you'll change your mind about that.

HOLMES: Whether I change my mind or not, I certainly
                   shall leave this place, and your arrest will
                   shortly follow.

LARRABEE: My arrest? Ha, ha! Robbery, eh — Why, even
                   if you got away from here you haven't got a
                   witness. Not a witness to your name.

HOLMES: (Slowly backing, keeping his eyes sharply on
                   LARRABEE as he does so.)
                   I'm not so sure of that, Mr. Larrabee! — Do
                   you usually fasten that door with a knife?
                   (Pointing toward door with left arm and hand,
                   but eyes on LARRABEE.)

LARRABEE turns front as if bewildered. Tableau an instant. Very
faint moan from within cupboard. HOLMES listens motionless an
instant, then makes quick dash to door and seizing knife wrenches it
out and flings it on the floor. LARRABEE seeing HOLMES start
toward door of cupboard springs up to head him off.

LARRABEE: Come away from that door.

But HOLMES has the door torn open and ALICE FAULKNER out
before LARRABEE gets near.

Sir Arthur Conan Doyle

HOLMES:	Stand back! (Turning to LARRABEE, supporting ALICE at same time.) You contemptible scoundrel! What does this mean!
LARRABEE:	I'll show you what it means cursed quick. (Taking a step or two, blows the little silver whistle attached to his watch chain.)
HOLMES:	(Untying ALICE quickly.) I'm afraid you're badly hurt Miss Faulkner.

Enter CRAIGIN. He stands there a moment near door, watching HOLMES. He makes a signal with hand to others outside door and then moves noiselessly. McTAGUE enters noiselessly, and remains a little behind CRAIGIN below door. ALICE shakes her head quickly, thinking of what she sees, and tries to call HOLMES attention to CRAIGIN and McTAGUE.

ALICE:	No! — Mr. Holmes. (Pointing to CRAIGIN and McTAGUE.)
HOLMES:	(Glances round.) Ah, Craigin — delighted to see you.

CRAIGIN gives slight start.

HOLMES:	And you too McTague. I infer from your presence here at this particular juncture that I am not dealing with Mr. Larrabee alone.
LARRABEE:	Your inference is quite correct, Mr. Holmes.
HOLMES:	It is not difficult to imagine who is at the bottom of such a conspiracy as this.

CRAIGIN begins to steal across noiselessly. McTAGUE remains before door, HOLMES turns to ALICE again.

HOLMES:	I hope you're beginning to feel a little more yourself, Miss Faulkner—because we shall leave here very soon.

ALICE: (Who has been shrinking from the sight of
                      CRAIGIN and McTAGUE.)
                      Oh yes — do let us go, Mr. Holmes.

CRAIGIN: (Low, deep voice, intense.)
                      You'll 'ave to wait a bit, Mr. 'Olmes. We 'ave
                      a little matter of business we'd like to talk
                      over.

HOLMES turning to CRAIGIN.

Enter LEARY and glides up side in the shadow and begins to move
towards HOLMES. In approaching from corner he glides behind door
of cupboard as it stands open and from there down on HOLMES at
cue. As HOLMES turns to CRAIGIN, ALICE leans against wall of
cupboard .

HOLMES: All right, Craigin, I'll see you to-morrow
                     morning in your cell at Bow Street.

CRAIGIN: (Threateningly.)
                     Very sorry sir but I cawn't wait till morning Its
                     got to be settled to night.

HOLMES: (Looks at CRAIGIN an instant.)
                     All right, Craigin, we'll settle it to-night.

CRAIGIN: It's so very himportant, Mr. 'Olmes — so very
                     important indeed that you'll 'ave to 'tend to it
                     now.

At this instant ALICE sees LEARY approaching rapidly from behind
and screams. HOLMES turns, but LEARY is upon him at the same
time. There is a very short struggle and HOLMES throws LEARY
violently off, but LEARY has got HOLMES' revolver. As they
struggle ALICE steps back to side of room up stage. A short deadly
pause. HOLMES motionless, regarding the men. ALICE'S back
against wall. After the pause LEARY begins to revive.

CRAIGIN: (Low voice to LEARY.)
                     'Ave you got his revolver?

LEARY: (Showing revolver.)
'Ere it is.
(Getting slowly to his feet.)

HOLMES: (Recognizing LEARY in the dim light.)
Ah, Leary! It is a pleasure indeed. It needed
only your blithe personality to make the party
complete.
(Sits and writes rapidly on pocket pad, pushing
lamp away a little and picking up cigar which
he had left on the table, and which he keeps in
his mouth as he writes.)
There is only one other I could wish to
welcome here, and that is the talented author of
this midnight carnival. We shall have him
however, by to-morrow night.

CRAIGIN: Though 'e ain't 'ere, Mr. 'Olmes, 'e gave me a
message for yer. 'E presented his koindest
compliments wished yer a pleasant trip across.

HOLMES: (Writing — cigar in mouth.)
That's very kind of him, I'm sure.
(Writes.)

LARRABEE: (Sneeringly.)
You're writing your will, I suppose?

HOLMES: (Writing — with quick glances at the rest.)
No.
(Shakes head.)
Only a brief description of one or two of you
gentlemen for the police. We know the rest.

LEARY: And when will you give it 'em, Mr. 'Olmes?

HOLMES: (Writes.)
In nine or nine and a half minutes, Leary.

LARRABEE: Oh, you expect to leave here in nine minutes,
eh?

HOLMES: No.
                   (Writing.)
                   In one. It will take me eight minutes to find a
                   policeman. This is a dangerous neighbourhood.

LARRABEE: Well, when you're ready to start, let us know.

HOLMES: (Rising and putting pad in pocket.)
                   I'm ready.
                   (Buttoning up coat.)

CRAIGIN. McTAGUE and LEARY suddenly brace themselves for
action, and stand ready to make a run for HOLMES. LARRABEE also
is ready to join in the struggle if necessary. HOLMES moves
backward from table a little to ALICE — she drops down a step
towards HOLMES.

CRAIGIN: Wait a bit. You'd better listen to me, Mr.
                   'Olmes. We're going to tie yer down nice and
                   tight to the top o' that table.

HOLMES: Well, by Jove! I don't think you will, That's
                   my idea, you know.

CRAIGIN: An' you'll save yourself a deal of trouble if ye
                   submit quiet and easy like — because if ye
                   don't ye moight get knocked about a bit —

ALICE: (Under her breath.)
                   Oh — Mr. Holmes!
                   (Coming closer to HOLMES.)

LARRABEE: (To ALICE.)
                   Come away from him! Come over here if you
                   don't want to get hurt.

Love music.

HOLMES: (To ALICE, without looking round, but
                   reaching her with left hand.)
                   My child, if you don't want to get hurt, don't
                   leave me for a second.

141

ALICE moves closer to HOLMES.

LARRABEE: Aren't you coming?

ALICE: (Breathlessly.)
                 No!

CRAIGIN: You'd better look out, Miss — he might get
                 killed.

ALICE: Then you can kill me too.

HOLMES makes a quick turn to her, with sudden exclamation under
breath. For an instant only he looks in her face — then a quick turn
back to CRAIGIN and men.

HOLMES: (Low voice — not taking eyes from men
                 before him.)
                 I'm afraid you don't mean that, Miss Faulkner.

ALICE: Yes, I do.

HOLMES: (Eyes on men — though they shift about
                 rapidly, but never toward ALICE.)
                 No.
                 (Shakes head a trifle.)
                 You would not say it — at another time or
                 place.

ALICE: I would say it anywhere — always.

Music stops.

CRAIGIN: So you'll 'ave it out with us, eh?

HOLMES: Do you imagine for one moment, Craigin, that
                 I won't have it out with you?

CRAIGIN: Well then — I'll 'ave to give you one — same
                 as I did yer right-'and man this afternoon.
                 (Approaching HOLMES.)

HOLMES   (To ALICE without turning — intense, rapid.)
                          Ah!

CRAIGIN stops dead.

HOLMES: You heard him say that. Same as he did my
                          right-hand man this afternoon.

ALICE: (Under breath.)
                          Yes! yes!

HOLMES: Don't forget that face.
                          (Pointing to CRAIGIN.)
                          In three days I shall ask you to identify it in the
                          prisoner's dock.

CRAIGIN: (Enraged.)
                          Ha!
                          (Turning away as if to hide his face.)

HOLMES: (Very sharp — rapid.)
                          Yes — and the rest of you with him. You
                          surprise me, gentlemen — thinking you're sure
                          of anybody in this room, and never once taking
                          the trouble to look at that window. If you
                          wanted to make it perfectly safe, you should
                          have had those missing bars put in.

HOLMES whispers something to ALICE, indicating her to make for
door.

Music till end of Act.

CRAIGIN, LEARY, McTAGUE and LARRABEE make very slight
move and say "Eh?" but instantly at tension again, and all motionless,
ready to spring on HOLMES. HOLMES and ALICE motionless,
facing them. This is held an instant.

LARRABEE: Bars or no bars, you're not going to get out of
                          here as easy as you expect.

HOLMES moves easily down near table.

143

HOLMES: There are so many ways, Mr. Larrabee, I
                  hardly know which to choose.

CRAIGIN: (Louder — advancing.)
                  Well, you'd better choose quick — I can tell
                  you that.

HOLMES: (Sudden — strong — sharp.)
                  I'll choose at once, Mr. Craigin — and my
                  choice —
                  (Quickly seizing chair.)
                  — falls on this.
                  (On the word he brings the chair down upon
                  the lamp frightful crash, extinguishing light
                  instantly.)

Every light out. Only the glow of HOLMES' cigar remains where he
stands at the table. He at once begins to move toward window keeping
cigar so that it will show to men and to front.

CRAIGIN: (Loud sharp voice to others.)
                  Trace 'im by the cigar.
                  (Moving at once toward window.)
                  Follow the cigar.

LARRABEE: Look out. He's going for the window.

LEARY goes quickly to window. McTAGUE goes and is ready by
safety lamp. HOLMES quickly fixes cigar in a crack or joint at side of
window so that it is still seen — smash of the window glass is heard.
Instantly glides across, well up stage, and down side to the door where
he finds ALICE. On crash of window CRAIGIN and LEARY give
quick shout of exclamation — they spring up stage toward the light of
cigar — sound of quick scuffle and blows in darkness.

LARRABEE: Get that light.

CRAIGIN: (Clear and distinct.)
                  The safety lamp. Where is it?

Make this shout for lantern very strong and audible to front.
McTAGUE kicks over box which concealed the safety lamp — lights
up. HOLMES and ALICE at door. ALICE just going out.

HOLMES: (Turning at door and pointing to window.)
                   You'll find that cigar in a crevice by the
                   window.

All start towards HOLMES with exclamations, oaths, etc. He makes
quick exit with ALICE and slams door after him. Sounds of heavy
bolts outside sliding quickly into place, and heavy bars dropping into
position. CRAIGIN, McTAGUE and LEARY rush against door and
make violent efforts to open it. After the first excited effort they turn
quickly back. As McTAGUE crosses he throws safely lamp on table.
LARRABEE, who has stopped near when he saw door closed, turns
front with a look of hatred on his face and mad with rage.

CURTAIN

ACT IV
Doctor Watson's Consulting Room, Kensington.
The following evening.

The place is London.

SCENE. — DR. WATSON'S house in Kensington. The consulting room. Oak paneling. Solid furniture. Wide double-doors opening to the hall and street door. Door communicating with doctor's inner medicine room. Another door, center, opens to private hallway of house. The windows are supposed to open at side of house upon an area which faces the street. These windows have shades or blinds on rollers which can quickly be drawn down. At the opening of the Act they are down, so that no one could see into the room from the street.

There is a large operating chair with high back, cushions, etc. Music for curtain, which stops an instant before rise.

DR. WATSON is seated behind his desk and MRS. SMEEDLEY, a seedy-looking middle-aged woman, is seated in the chair next to the desk with a medicine bottle in her hand.

WATSON: Be careful to make no mistake about the
                     medicine. If she's no better to-morrow I'll call.
                     You will let me know, of course.

MRS. SMEEDLEY: Oh yes, indeed I will. Good evening, sir.

WATSON: Good night, Mrs. Smeedley.

MRS. SMEEDLEY goes out. Sound of door closing heard after she is off. Pause. The doctor turns to his desk, and ringing bell, busies himself with papers.

Enter PARSONS—a servant.

WATSON: Parsons!

PARSONS comes a little towards WATSON.

WATSON: (Lower voice.)
                     That woman who just left — do you know her?

PARSONS:	(Trying to recollect.) I can't say as I recollect 'avin' seen 'er before. Was there anything—?
WATSON:	Oh no! Acted a little strange, that's all. I thought I saw her looking about the hall before she went out.
PARSONS:	Yes sir, she did give a look. I saw that myself, sir.
WATSON:	(After an instant's thought.) Oh well — I dare say it was nothing. Is there anyone waiting, Parsons?
PARSONS:	There's one person in the waiting-room, sir — a gentleman.
WATSON:	(Looks at watch.) I'll see him, but I've only a short time left. If any more come you must send them over to Doctor Anstruther. I spoke to him this afternoon about taking my cases. I have an important appointment at nine.
PARSONS:	Very well, sir. Then you'll see this gentleman, sir?
WATSON:	Yes.

PARSONS goes out. Short pause. WATSON busy at desk. PARSONS opens door and shows in SID PRINCE. He comes in a little way and pauses. PARSONS all through this Act closes the door after his exit, or after showing anyone in. WATSON looks up.

PRINCE:	(Speaking in the most dreadful husky whisper.) Good evenin', sir!
WATSON:	Good evening. (Indicating chair.) Pray be seated.

PRINCE: (Same voice all through.)
Thanks, I don't mind if I do.
(Coughs, then sits in chair near desk.)

WATSON: (Looking at him with professional interest.)
What seems to be the trouble?

PRINCE: Throat, sir.
(Indicating his throat to assist in making
himself understood.)
Most dreadful sore throat.

WATSON: Sore throat, eh?
(Glancing about for an instrument.)

PRINCE: Well, I should think it is. It's the most
'arrowing thing I ever 'ad! It pains me that
much to swallow that I —

WATSON: Hurts you to swallow, does it?
(Finding and picking up an instrument on the
desk.)

PRINCE: Indeed it does. Why, I can 'ardly get a bit of
food down.

WATSON rises and goes to cabinet, pushes gas burner out into
position and lights it.

WATSON: Just step this way a moment, please.
(PRINCE rises and goes up to WATSON, who
adjusts reflector over eye, etc. He has an
instrument in his hand which he wipes with a
napkin.)
Now, mouth open — wide as possible.
(PRINCE opens mouth and WATSON places
tongue holder on his tongue.)
That's it.
(Picks up dentist's mirror and warms it over
gas burner.)

148

PRINCE: (WATSON is about to examine throat when
                           PRINCE sees instrument and is trifle alarmed.)
                           Eh!

Business of WATSON putting in tongue holder and looking down
PRINCES throat — looking carefully this way and that.

WATSON: Say "Ah!"

PRINCE: (Husky voice.)
                           Ah!
                           (Steps away and places handkerchief to mouth
                           as if the attempt to say Ah! hurt him.)

WATSON discontinues, and takes instrument out of PRINCE'S
mouth.

WATSON: (A slight incredulity in his manner.)
                           Where do you feel this pain?

PRINCE: (Indicating with his finger.)
                           Just about there, doctor. Inside about there.

WATSON: That's singular. I don't find anything wrong.
                           (Gas burner back to usual position — and
                           placing instrument on cabinet.)

PRINCE: You may not foind anything wrong, but I feel it
                           wrong. If you would only give me something
                           to take away this awful agony.

WATSON: That's nothing. It'll pass away in a few hours.
                           (Reflectively.)
                           Singular thing it would have affected your
                           voice in this way. Well, I'll give you a gargle
                           — it may help you a little.

PRINCE: Yes — if you only would, doctor.

WATSON goes into surgery PRINCE watching him like a cat. Music.
Dramatic agitato, very pp. WATSON does not close the door of the
room, but pushes it part way so that it is open about a foot.

(CONT/)

149

PRINCE moves toward door, watching WATSON through it. Stops near door. Seems to watch for his chance, for he suddenly turns and goes quickly down and runs up blinds of both windows and moves back quickly, watching WATSON through the door again. Seeing that he still has time to spare, he goes to centre door and opens it, looking and listening off. Distant sound of a when door is open which stops when it is closed. PRINCE quickly turns back and goes off a little way at centre door, leaving it open so that he is seen peering up above and listening. Turns to come back, but just at the door he sees WATSON coming on and stops. WATSON suddenly enters and sees PRINCE in centre door and stops, with a bottle in his hand, and looks at PRINCE.

Music stops.

WATSON: What are you doing there?

PRINCE: Why, nothing at all, doctor. I felt such a
                 draught on the back o' my neck, don't yer
                 know, that I opened the door to see where it
                 came from!

WATSON goes down and rings bell on his desk, placing bottle on papers. Pause. Enter PARSONS.

WATSON: Parsons, show this man the shortest way to the
                 street door and close the door after him.

PRINCE: But, doctor, ye don't understand.

WATSON: I understand quite enough. Good evening.

PRINCE: Yer know, the draught plays hell with my
                 throat, sir — and seems to affect my —

WATSON: Good evening.
                 (He sits and pays no further attention to
                 PRINCE.)

PARSONS: This way, sir, if you please.

PRINCE: I consider that you've treated me damned
                 outrageous, that's wot I do, and ye won't hear
                 the last of this very soon.

PARSONS: (Approaching him.)
                    Come, none o' that now.
                    (Takes PRINCE by the arm.)

PRINCE: (As he walks toward door with PARSONS,
                    turns head back and speaks over his shoulder,
                    shouting out in his natural voice.)
                    Yer call yerself a doctor an' treats sick people
                    as comes to see yer this 'ere way.
                    (Goes out with PARSONS and continues
                    talking until slam of door outside.)
                    Yer call yerself a doctor! A bloomin' foine
                    doctor you are! (Etc.)

PARSONS has forced PRINCE out by the arm during foregoing
speech. Door closes after PRINCE. Sound of outside door closing
follows shortly. WATSON, after short pause, looks round room, not
observing that window shades are up. He rings bell. Enter PARSONS.

WATSON   (Rises and gathers up a few things as if to go.)
                    I shall be at Mr. Holmes's in Baker Street. If
                    there's anything special, you'll know where to
                    send for me. The appointment was for nine.
                    (Looks at watch.)
                    It's fifteen minutes past eight now —I'm going
                    to walk over.

PARSONS: Very well, sir.

Bell of outside door rings. PARSONS looks at WATSON, who shakes
his head.

WATSON: No. I won't see any more to-night. They must
                    go to Doctor Anstruther.

PARSONS: Yes, sir.
                    (He starts towards door to answer bell.)

WATSON looks and sees blinds up.

WATSON: Parsons!
                    (PARSONS turns.)
                    Why aren't those blinds down?

PARSONS: They was down a few minutes ago, sir!

WATSON: That's strange! Well, you'd better pull them
                down now.

PARSONS: Yes, sir.

Bell rings twice as PARSONS pulls second blind down. He goes out to
answer bell. Pause. Then enter PARSONS in a peculiar manner.

PARSONS: If you please, sir, it isn't a patient at all, sir.

WATSON: Well, what is it?

PARSONS: A lady sir —
                (WATSON looks up.)
                — and she wants to see you most particular,
                sir!

WATSON: What does she want to see me about?

PARSONS: She didn't say sir. Only she said it was of the
                hutmost himportance to 'er, if you could see
                'er, sir.

WATSON: Is she there in the hall?

PARSONS: Yes sir.

WATSON: Very well — I was going to walk for the
                exercise — I can take a cab.

PARSONS: Then you'll see the lady, sir.

WATSON: Yes.
                (PARSONS turns to go. WATSON continues
                his preparations.)
                And call a cab for me at the same time — have
                it wait.

PARSONS: Yes, sir.

PARSONS goes out. Pause. PARSONS appears, ushering in a lady —
and goes when she has entered. Enter MADGE LARRABEE. Her
manner is entirely different from that of the former scenes. She is an
impetuous gushing society lady with trouble on her mind.

MADGE:　　　　　　(As she comes in.)
　　　　　　　　　Ah! Doctor — it's awfully good of you to see
　　　　　　　　　me. I know what a busy man you must be but
　　　　　　　　　I'm in such trouble — oh, it's really too
　　　　　　　　　dreadful — You'll excuse my troubling you in
　　　　　　　　　this way, won't you?

WATSON:　　　　　Don't speak of it, madam.

MADGE:　　　　　　Oh, thank you so much! For it did look
　　　　　　　　　frightful my coming in like this — but I'm not
　　　　　　　　　alone — oh no! — I left my maid in the cab —
　　　　　　　　　I'm Mrs. H. de Witte Seaton —
　　　　　　　　　(Trying to find card-case.)
　　　　　　　　　Dear me — I didn't bring my card-case — or if
　　　　　　　　　I did I lost it.

WATSON:　　　　　Don't trouble about a card, Mrs. Seaton.
　　　　　　　　　(With gesture to indicate chair.)

MADGE:　　　　　　Oh, thank you.
　　　　　　　　　(Sitting as she continues to talk.)
　　　　　　　　　You don't know what I've been through this
　　　　　　　　　evening — trying to find some one who could
　　　　　　　　　tell me what to do.
　　　　　　　　　(WATSON sits in chair at desk.)
　　　　　　　　　It's something that's happened, doctor — it has
　　　　　　　　　just simply happened — I know that it wasn't
　　　　　　　　　his fault! I know it!

WATSON:　　　　　Whose fault?

MADGE:　　　　　　My brother's — my poor, dear, youngest
　　　　　　　　　brother — he couldn't have done such a thing,
　　　　　　　　　he simply couldn't and —

WATSON:　　　　　Such a thing as what, Mrs. Seaton?

153

MADGE: As to take the plans of our defences at Gibraltar from the Admiralty Offices. They think he stole them, doctor — and they've arrested him for it — you see, he works there. He was the only one who knew about them in the whole office — because they trusted him so. He was to make copies and — Oh, doctor, it's really too dreadful!
(Overcome, she takes out her handkerchief and wipes her eyes. This must all be perfectly natural, and not in the least particular overdone.)

WATSON: I'm very sorry, Mrs. Seaton —

MADGE: (mixed up with sobs):
Oh, thank you so much! They said you were Mr. Holmes's friend — several people told me that, several — they advised me to ask you where I could find him — and everything depends on it, doctor — everything.

WATSON: Holmes, of course. He's just the one you want.

MADGE: That's it! He's just the one — and there's hardly any time left! They'll take my poor brother away to prison to-morrow!
(Shows signs of breaking down again.)

WATSON: There, there, Mrs. Seaton — pray control yourself.

MADGE: (Choking down sobs.)
Now what would you advise me to do?

WATSON: I'd go to Mr. Holmes at once.

MADGE: But I've been. I've been and he wasn't there!

WATSON: You went to his house?

MADGE: Yes — in Baker Street. That's why I came to you! They said he might be here!

WATSON: No — he isn't here!
                   (Turns away slightly.)

MADGE looks deeply discouraged.

MADGE: But don't you expect him some time this
                   evening?

WATSON: No
                   (Shaking head.)
                   There's no possibility of his coming — so far
                   as I know.

MADGE: But couldn't you get him to come?
                   (Pause.)
                   It would be such a great favour to me — I'm
                   almost worn out with going about — and with
                   this dreadful anxiety! If you could get word to
                   him —
                   (Sees that WATSON is looking at her
                   strangely and sharply.)
                   — to come.

Brief pause.

WATSON: (Rising — rather hard voice.)
                   I could not get him to come madam. And I beg
                   you to excuse me I am going out myself —
                   (looks at watch) — on urgent business.
                   (Rings bell.)

MADGE: (Rising.)
                   Oh certainly! Don t let me detain you! And you
                   think I had better call at his house again?

WATSON: (Coldly.)
                   That will be the wisest thing to do.

MADGE: Oh, thank you so much.
                   (Extends her hand.)
                   You don t know how you've encouraged me!

WATSON withdraws his hand as he still looks at her. Enter
PARSONS He stands at door.

MADGE: Well — good night doctor.

WATSON simply bows coldly. MADGE turns to go. The crash of a
capsizing vehicle followed by excited shouts of men is heard. This
effect must be as if outside the house with doors closed and not close
at hand. MADGE stops suddenly on hearing the crash and all shouts.
WATSON looks at PARSONS.

WATSON: What's that Parsons?

PARSONS: I really can't say sir but it sounded to me like a
                          haccident.

MADGE: (Turning to WATSON.)
                          Oh dear! I do hope it isn't anything serious! It
                          affects me terribly to know that anyone is hurt.

WATSON: Probably nothing more than a broken-down
                          cab. See what it is, Parsons.

Bell and knock. MADGE turns and looks toward door again,
anxiously PARSONS turns to go. Sudden vigorous ringing of door
bell, followed by the sound of a knocker violently used.

PARSONS: There's the bell, sir! There's somebody 'urt,
                          sir, an' they're a-wantin' you!

WATSON: Well, don't allow anybody to come in!
                          (Looks at watch.)
                          I have no more time.
                          (Hurriedly gathers papers up.)

PARSONS: Very well, sir.
                          (Goes leaving door open.)

MADGE turns from looking off at door, and looks at WATSON
anxiously. Looks toward door again.

MADGE: But they're coming in, doctor.
                          (Retreats backward.)

WATSON: (Moving toward door.)
                     Parsons! Parsons!

Sound of voices. Following speeches outside are not in rotation, but jumbled together, so that it is all over very quickly.

VOICE: (Outside.)
                     We 'ad to bring 'im in, man.

VOICE: (Outside.)
                     There's nowhere else to go!

PARSONS: (outside)
                     The doctor can't see anybody.

VOICE: (Outside.)
                     Well let the old gent lay 'ere awhile can't yer.
                     It's common decency. Wot 'ave yer got a red
                     lamp 'angin' outside yer bloomin' door for?

VOICE: (Outside.)
                     Yes! yes! let him stay.

Enter PARSONS at door. Door closes and noise stops.

PARSONS: They would bring 'im in, sir. It's an old
                     gentleman as was 'urt a bit w'en the cab upset!

MADGE: Oh!

Sound of groans, etc. outside, and the old gentleman whining out complaints and threats.

WATSON: Let them put him here.
                     (Indicating operating chair.)
                     And send at once for Doctor Anstruther.

PARSONS: Yes, sir!

WATSON: Help him in Parsons.

PARSONS goes out.

MADGE: Oh doctor isn't it frightful.

WATSON: (Turning to centre door.)
                    Mrs Seaton if you will be so good as to step
                    this way, you can reach the hall, by taking the
                    first door to your left.

MADGE: (Hesitating.)
                    But I — I may be of some use doctor.

WATSON: (With a trifle of impatience.)
                    None whatever.
                    (Holds door open.)

MADGE: But doctor — I must see the poor fellow — I
                    haven't the power to go!

WATSON: (Facing MADGE.)
                    Madam, I believe you have some ulterior
                    motive in coming here! You will kindly —

Enter at door a white-haired old gentleman in black clerical clothes,
white tie, etc., assisted by PARSONS and the DRIVER. He limps as
though his leg were hurt. His coat is soiled. His hat is soiled as if it had
rolled in the street. MADGE has retired above desk and watches old
gent closely from there without moving. WATSON turns toward the
party as they come in.

HOLMES: (As he comes in.)
                    Oh, oh!
                    (He limps so that he hardly touches his right
                    foot to floor.)

PARSONS: (As he helps HOLMES in.)
                    This way, sir! Be careful of the sill, sir! That's
                    it. (Etc.)

DRIVER: (As he comes in, and also beginning outside
                    before entrance.)
                    Now we'll go in 'ere. You'll see the doctor an'
                    it'll be all right.

HOLMES: No, it won't be all right.

DRIVER:	It was a haccident. You cawn't 'elp a haccident.
HOLMES:	Yes, you can.
DRIVER:	He was on the wrong side of the street. I turned hup — (Etc.)
PARSONS:	Now over to this chair. (Indicating operating chair.)
HOLMES:	(Pushing back and trying to stop at the desk chair.) No, I'll sit here.
PARSONS:	No, this is the chair, sir.
HOLMES:	Don't I know where I want to sit?
DRIVER:	(Impatiently.) You'll sit 'ere. (They lead him up to operating chair.)
DRIVER:	(As they lead him up.) Now, the doctor'll have a look at ye. 'Ere's the doctor.
HOLMES:	That isn't a doctor.
DRIVER:	It is a doctor. (Seeing WATSON.) 'Ere, doctor, will you just come and have a look at this old gent? (HOLMES trying to stop him.) He's hurt 'isself a little, an' — an' —
HOLMES:	(Trying to stop DRIVER.) Wait, wait, wait!
DRIVER:	Well, well?

HOLMES: (Still standing back to audience and turned to DRIVER.)
Are you the driver?

DRIVER: Yes, I'm the driver.

HOLMES: Well, I'll have you arrested for this.

DRIVER: Arrested?

HOLMES: Arrested, arrested, arrested!

DRIVER: You cawn't arrest me.

HOLMES: I can't, but somebody else can.

DRIVER: 'Ere, 'ere.
(Trying to urge HOLMES to chair.)

HOLMES: You are a very disagreeable man! You are totally uninformed on every subject! I wonder you are able to live in the same house with yourself.

The DRIVER is trying to talk back and make HOLMES sit down. HOLMES turns suddenly on PARSONS. WATSON is trying to attract PARSONS' attention.

HOLMES: Are you a driver?

PARSONS: No, sir!

HOLMES: Well, what are you?

PARSONS: I'm the butler, sir.

HOLMES: Butler! Butler!

DRIVER: He's the doctor's servant.

HOLMES: Who'd have such a looking butler as you!
What fool would —

DRIVER: (Turning HOLMES toward him roughly.)
                         He is the doctor's servant!

HOLMES: Who asked you who he was?

DRIVER: Never mind who asked me—I'm telling you.

HOLMES: Well, go and tell somebody else.

DRIVER: (Trying to push HOLMES into chair.)
                         Sit down here. Sit down and be quiet.

WATSON: (To PARSONS.)
                         Have a cab ready for me. I must see if he's
                         badly hurt.

PARSONS: Yes, sir.
                         (Goes.)

HOLMES: (Resisting.)
                         Quiet! quiet! Where's my hat? My hat! My
                         hat!

DRIVER: Never mind your 'at.

HOLMES: I will mind my hat! and I hold you
                         responsible—

DRIVER: There's your hat in your 'and.

HOLMES: (Looks at hat.)
                         That isn't my hat! Here!
                         (DRIVER trying to push him into chair.)
                         You're responsible.
                         (In chair.)
                         I'll have you arrested.
                         (Clinging to DRIVER'S coat tail as he tries to
                         get away to door.)
                         Here come back.
                         (Choking with rage.)

DRIVER: (First wrenching away coat from HOLMES' grasp at door.)
I cawn't stay around 'ere, you know! Some one'll pinching my cab.
(Exit.)

HOLMES: (Screaming after him.)
Then bring your cab in here. I want —
(Lapses into groans and remonstrances.)
Why didn't somebody stop him? These cabmen! What did he bring me in for? I know where I am, it's a conspiracy. I won't stay in this place. If I ever get out of here alive —
(Etc.)

WATSON: (Steps quickly to door, speaking off.)
Parsons — that man's number.
(Quickly to old gent.)
Now sir if you'll be quiet for one moment, I'll have a look at you!
(Crosses to end of cabinet as if to look for instrument.)

MADGE advances near to the old gentleman, looking at him closely. She suddenly seems to be satisfied of something, backs away, and reaching out as if to get to the window and give signal, then coming face to face with WATSON as he turns, and smiling pleasantly at him. Business with glove. She begins to glide down stage, making a sweep around toward door as if to get out. She shows by her expression that she has recognized HOLMES, but is instantly herself again, thinking possibly that HOLMES is watch her, and she wishes to evade suspicion regarding her determination to get off at door. Quick as a flash the old gentleman springs to the door and stands facing her. She stops suddenly on finding him facing her, then wheels quickly about and goes rapidly across toward window.

HOLMES: (Sharp.)
Don't let her get to that window.

WATSON, who had moved up a little above windows, instantly springs before the windows. MADGE stops on being headed off in that direction.

WATSON: Is that you, Holmes?

MADGE stands motionless.

HOLMES: Quite so.
                    (Takes off his wig, etc.)

WATSON: What do you want me to do?

HOLMES: (Easily.)
                    That's all, you've done it. Don't do anything
                    more just now.

MADGE gives a sharp look at them, then goes very slowly for a few
steps and suddenly turns and makes a dash for centre door.

WATSON: Look out, Holmes! She can get out that way.
                    (A step or two up.)

MADGE runs off. HOLMES is unmoved.

HOLMES: I don't think so.
                    (Saunters over to above WATSON'S desk.)
                    Well, well, what remarkable weather we're
                    having, doctor, eh?
                    (Suddenly seeing cigarettes on desk.)
                    Ah! I'm glad to see that you keep a few
                    prescriptions carefully done up.
                    (Picks up a cigarette and sits on desk.)
                    Good for the nerves!
                    (HOLMES finds matches and lights cigarette.)
                    Have you ever observed, Watson, that those
                    people are always making—

Enter the DRIVER.

FORMAN: (Speaking at once — so as to break in on
                    HOLMES.)
                    I've got her, sir!

Very brief pause.

WATSON: Good heavens! Is that Forman?

HOLMES nods "Yes.".

HOLMES: Yes, that's Forman all right. Has Inspector
                    Bradstreet Come with his men?

FORMAN: Yes, sir. One of 'em's in the hall there 'olding
                    her. The others are in the kitchen garden. They
                    came in over the back Wall from Mortimer
                    Street.

HOLMES: One moment.
                    (Sits in thought.)
                    Watson, my dear fellow —
                    (WATSON moves toward HOLMES at desk.)
                    As you doubtless gather from the little episode
                    that has just taken place we are making the
                    arrests. The scoundrels are hot on my track. To
                    get me out of the way is the one chance left to
                    them — and I taking advantage of their mad
                    pursuit to draw them where we quietly lay our
                    hands on them —one by one. We've made a
                    pretty good haul already — four last night in
                    the gas chamber — seven this afternoon in
                    various places, and one more just now, but I
                    regret to say that up to this time the Professor
                    himself has so far not risen to the bait.

WATSON: Where do you think he is now?

HOLMES: In the open streets — under some clever
                    disguise — watching for a chance to get at me.

WATSON: And was this woman sent in here to—

HOLMES: Quite so. A spy — to let them know by some
                    signal, probably at that window —
                    (Pointing.)
                    — if she found me in the house. And it has Just
                    occurred to me that it might not be such a bad
                    idea to try the Professor with that bait. Forman!
                    (Motions him to come down.)

FORMAN: Yes, sir!

HOLMES   (Voice lower.)
                One moment.
                (Business.)
                Bring that Larrabee woman back here for a
                moment, and when I light a fresh cigarette —
                let go your hold on her — carelessly — as if
                your attention was attracted to something else.
                Get hold of her again when I tell you.

FORMAN: Very well sir.

Goes quickly to re-enter bringing in MADGE LARRABEE. They
stop. MADGE calm, but looks at HOLMES with the utmost hatred.
Brief pause.

HOLMES: My dear Mrs. Larrabee —
                (MADGE, who has looked away, turns to him
                angrily.)
                — I took the liberty of having you brought in
                for a moment —
                (Puffs cigarette, which he has nearly finished.)
                —in order to convey to you in a few fitting
                words — my sincere sympathy in your rather
                — unpleasant — predicament,

MADGE: (Hissing it out angrily between her teeth.)
                It's a lie! It's a lie! There's no predicament.

HOLMES: Ah — I'm charmed to gather — from your
                rather forcible observation — that you do not
                regard it as such. Quite right, too. Our prisons
                are so well conducted now. Many consider
                them quite as comfortable as most of the
                hotels. Quieter and more orderly.

MADGE: How the prisons are conducted is no concern of
                mine! There is nothing they can hold me for—
                nothing.

HOLMES: Oh — to be sure.
                (Putting fresh cigarette in mouth.)

(CONT/)

There may be something in that. Still — it
occurred to me that you might prefer to be near
your unfortunate husband — eh?
(Rises from table and goes to gas burner. Slight
good-natured chuckle.)
We hear a great deal about the heroic devotion
of wives, and all that —
(Lights cigarette at gas.)
— rubbish. You know, Mrs. Larrabee, when
we come right down to it —
(FORMAN carelessly relinquishes his hold on
MADGE'S arm, seems to have his
attention called to door. Stands as if listening
to something outside. MADGE gives a quick
glance about and at HOLMES who is lighting
a cigarette at the gas, and apparently not
noticing anything. She makes a sudden dash
for the window, quickly snaps up blind and
makes a rapid motion up and down before
window with right hand — then turns quickly,
facing HOLMES with triumphant defiance.
HOLMES is still lighting cigarette.)
Many thanks.
(To FORMAN.)
That's all, Forman. Pick her up again.

FORMAN at once goes to MADGE and turns her and waits in front of
window — holding her right wrist.

HOLMES: Doctor, would you kindly pull the blind down
               once more. I don't care to be shot from the
               street.

WATSON instantly pulls down blind.

NOTE — Special care must be exercised regarding these window
blinds. They must be made specially strong and solid, so that no
failure to operate is possible.

MADGE: (In triumph.)
               Ah! It's too late.

HOLMES: Too late, eh?
(Strolling a little.)

MADGE: The signal is given. You will hear from him soon.

HOLMES: It wouldn't surprise me at all.

Door bell rings.

Voices of BILLY and PARSONS outside. Door at once opened, BILLY on a little way, but held back by PARSONS for an instant. He breaks away from PARSONS. All very quick, BILLY dressed as a street gamin and carrying a bunch of evening papers

HOLMES: (As BILLY comes.)
I think I shall hear from him now.
(Shout.)
Let —
(BILLY stands panting)
— him go, Parsons. Quick, Billy.

BILLY comes close to HOLMES.

BILLY: He's just come sir.

HOLMES: From where?

BILLY: The house across the street; he was in there a-watchin' these windows. He must 'ave seen something for he's just come out—
(Breathlessly.)
There was a cab waitin' in the street for the doctor — and he's changed places with the driver.

HOLMES: Where did the driver go?

BILLY: He slunk away in the dark, sir, but he ain't gone far, there's two or three more 'angin' about.

Sir Arthur Conan Doyle

HOLMES: (Slight motion of the head towards FORMAN.)
                   Another driver to-night.

BILLY: They're all in it, sir, an' they're a-layin' to get
                   you in that cab w'en you come out, sir! But
                   don't you do it, sir!

HOLMES: On the contrary, sir, I'll have that new driver in
                   here sir! Get out again quick, Billy, and keep
                   your eyes on him!

BILLY: Yes, sir — thank you, sir!
                   (Goes.)

HOLMES: Yes, sir! Watson, can you let me have a heavy
                   portmanteau for a few moments—?

MADGE now watching for another chance to get at the window.

WATSON: Parsons — my large Gladstone — bring it
                   here!

PARSONS: Yes, sir.
                   (Goes out.)

WATSON: I'm afraid it's a pretty shabby looking—

MADGE suddenly tries to break loose from FORMAN and attempt to
make a dash for window. FORMAN turns and pulls her a step or two
away. Slight pause.

HOLMES: Many thanks, Mrs. Larrabee, but your first
                   signal is all that we require. By it you informed
                   your friend Moriarty that I was here in the
                   house. You are now aware of the fact that he is
                   impersonating a driver, and that it is my
                   intention to have him in here. You wish to
                   signal that there is danger. There is danger,
                   Mrs. Larrabee, but we don't care to have you
                   let him know it. Take her out, Forman, and
                   make her comfortable and happy.

FORMAN leads MADGE up to centre door as if to take her out. She pulls him to a stop and gives HOLMES a look of the most violent hatred.

HOLMES: And by the way, you might tell the inspector to
                     wait a few moments. I may send him another
                     lot. You can't tell!

FORMAN: Come along now!
                     (Takes her off.)

As MADGE is pulled up, she snaps her fingers in HOLMES'S face and goes off laughing hysterically.

HOLMES: Fine woman!

Enter PARSONS, carrying a large portmanteau or Gladstone valise.

HOLMES: Put it down there.
                     (Pointing down before him at floor.)
                     Thank you so much.

PARSONS puts portmanteau down as indicated.

HOLMES: Parsons, you ordered a cab for the doctor a
                     short time ago. It has been waiting, I believe.

PARSONS: Yes, sir, I think it 'as.

HOLMES: Be so good as to tell the driver, the one you'll
                     now find there, to come in here and get a
                     valise. See that he comes in himself When he
                     comes tell him that's the one.

PARSONS goes.

WATSON: But surely he won't come in.

HOLMES: Surely he will! It's his only chance to get me
                     into that cab! He'll take almost any risk for
                     that.
                     (Goes to above desk.)
                                   (CONT/)

169

	In times like this you should tell your man never to take the first cab that comes on a call— (Smokes.) — nor yet the second — the third may be safe!
WATSON:	But in this case—
HOLMES:	My dear fellow, I admit that in this case I have it to my advantage, but I speak for your future guidance.

Music Melodramatic danger agitato very subdued.

Door opens. PARSONS enters, pointing the portmanteau out to some one who is following.

PARSONS:	'Ere it is — right in, this way.
HOLMES:	(Goes to WATSON above table. In rather a loud voice to WATSON) Well, good-bye, old fellow! (Shakes hands with him warmly and bringing him down left a little.) I'll write you from Paris and I hope you'll keep me fully informed of the progress of events.

MORIARTY enters in the disguise of a cabman and goes at once to valise which PARSONS points out, trying to hurry it through and keeping face away from HOLMES but fidgeting about, not touching valise. PARSONS goes out.

| HOLMES: | (Speaks right on, apparently paying no attention to MORIARTY.)
As for these papers I'll attend to them personally. Here my man —
(To MORIARTY.)
— just help me to tighten up these straps and bit —
(He slides over to valise and kneels, pulling at strap, and MORIARTY bending over and doing same.)
(CONT/) |

170

> There are a few little things in this bag —
> (Business.)
> — that I wouldn't like to lose —
> (Business.)
> — and its Just as well to — Eh —
> (Looking round for instant.)
> — who's that at the window?

MORIARTY quickly looks up without lifting hands from valise and at the same instant the snap of handcuffs is heard, and he springs up with the irons on his wrists, making two or three violent efforts to break loose. He then stands motionless. HOLMES drops into chair, a cigarette in his mouth. MORIARTY in rising knocks his hat off and stands facing audience.

Music stops.

HOLMES: (In a very quiet tone.)
                 Doctor, will you kindly strike the bell two or
                 three times in rapid succession.

WATSON steps to desk and gives several rapid strokes of the bell.

HOLMES: Thanks!

Enter FORMAN. FORMAN goes down to MORIARTY and fastens handcuffs which he has on his own wrists to chain attached to that of MORIARTY'S. This is held an instant — the two men looking at each other.

HOLMES: Forman!

FORMAN: Yes, sir.

HOLMES: Got a man there with you?

FORMAN: Yes, sir, the inspector came in himself.

HOLMES: Ah — the inspector himself. We shall read
                 graphic accounts in to-morrow's papers of a
                 very difficult arrest he succeeded in making at
                 Dr. Watson's house in Kensington.
                          (CONT/)

171

Take him out, Forman, and introduce him to the inspector — they'll be pleased to meet.

FORMAN starts to force MORIARTY off. MORIARTY hangs back and endeavours to get at HOLMES — a very slight struggle.

HOLMES: Here! Wait! Let's see what he wants!

MORIARTY: (Low voice to HOLMES.)
                 Do you imagine, Sherlock Holmes, that this is the end.

HOLMES: I ventured to dream that it might be.

MORIARTY: Are you quite sure the police will be able to hold me?

HOLMES: I am quite sure of nothing.

MORIARTY: Ah!
                 (Slight pause.)
                 I have heard that you are planning to take a little trip — you and your friend here — a little trip on the Continent.

HOLMES: And if I do?

MORIARTY: (A step to HOLMES.)
                 I shall meet you there.
                 (Slight pause.)

HOLMES: That's all, Forman.

FORMAN moves up to door, quietly with MORIARTY.

MORIARTY: (Stopping at door.)
                 I shall meet you there. You will Change your course — you will try to elude me — but whichever way you turn— there will be eyes that see and wires that tell. I shall meet you there — and you know it. You know it! — and you know it.
                 (CONT/)

172

(Goes with FORMAN.)

Pause.

HOLMES: Did you hear that, Watson?

WATSON: Yes—but surely you don't place any
                        importance on such—

HOLMES: (stopping him with wave of hand)
                        Oh! no importance. But I have a fancy that he
                        spoke the truth.

WATSON: We'll give up the trip.

HOLMES: (a negative wave of the hand at WATSON)
                        It would be quite the same. What matters it
                        here or there—if it must come.
                        (Sits meditative)

WATSON: (Calling.)
                        Parsons!

PARSONS comes in WATSON points to the valise PARSONS
removes it and goes.

HOLMES: Watson, my dear fellow—
                        (Smokes.)
                        — it's too bad. Now that this is all over, I
                        suppose you imagine that your room will no
                        longer be required. Let me assure — let me
                        assure you—
                        (Voice trembles.)
                        — that the worst is yet to come.

WATSON: (Stands in front of desk.)
                        The worst to —
                        (Suddenly thinks of something. Pulls out watch
                        hurriedly.)
                        Why, heavens Holmes we have barely five
                        minutes.

173

HOLMES:　　　　　　(Looks up innocently at him.)
　　　　　　　　　　For what?

WATSON:　　　　　　To get to Baker Street — your rooms!

HOLMES still looks at him.

WATSON:　　　　　　Your appointment with Sir Edward and the
　　　　　　　　　　Count! They were to receive that packet of
　　　　　　　　　　letters from you.

HOLMES:　　　　　　(Nods assent.)
　　　　　　　　　　They're coming here.

Pause. WATSON looking at HOLMES.

WATSON:　　　　　　Here!

HOLMES:　　　　　　That is — if you will be so good as to permit it.

WATSON:　　　　　　Certainly — but why not there?

HOLMES:　　　　　　The police wouldn't allow us inside the ropes.

WATSON:　　　　　　Police! Ropes!

HOLMES:　　　　　　Police — ropes — ladders — hose — crowds
　　　　　　　　　　— engines —

WATSON:　　　　　　Why, you don't mean that —

HOLMES:　　　　　　(Nods.)
　　　　　　　　　　Quite so — the devils have burned me out.

WATSON:　　　　　　Good heavens — burned you —

Pause. HOLMES nods.

WATSON:　　　　　　Oh, that's too bad. What did you lose?

HOLMES:　　　　　　Everything! — everything! I'm so glad of it!
　　　　　　　　　　I've had enough. This one thing —
　　　　　　　　　　　　　　　(CONT/)

(Right hand strong gesture of emphasis — he
stops in midst of sentence — a frown upon his
face as he thinks — then in a lower voice)
— ends it! This one thing — that I shall do —
here in a few moments — is the finish.
(HOLMES rises.)

WATSON: You mean—Miss Faulkner?

HOLMES nods slightly in affirmative without turning to WATSON.

Love music. Very pp.

HOLMES: (Turning suddenly to WATSON.)
Watson — she trusted me! She — clung to me!
There were four to one against me! They said
"Come here," I said "Stay close to me," and
she did! She clung to me — I could feel her
heart beating against mine — and I was
playing a game! —
(Lower — parenthetical.)
— a dangerous game — but I was playing it!
— It will be the same to-night! She'll be there
— I'll be here! She'll listen — she'll believe
— and she'll trust me — and I'll—be playing
— a game. No more — I've had enough! It's
my last case!

WATSON has been watching him narrowly.

HOLMES: Oh well! what does it matter? Life is a small
affair at the most — a little while — a few
sunrises and sunsets — the warm breath of a
few summers — the cold chill of a few
winters—
(Looking down on floor a little way before him
in meditation.)
And then —
(Pause.)

WATSON: And then —?

HOLMES glances up at him. Upward toss of hand before speaking.

175

HOLMES: And then.

The music stops.

WATSON: (Going to HOLMES.)
        My dear Holmes — I'm afraid that plan of —
        gaining her confidence and regard went a little
        further than you intended —

HOLMES nods assent slightly.

HOLMES: (Mutters after nodding.):
        A trifle!

WATSON: For — her — or for you?

HOLMES: For her —
        (looks up at WATSON slowly)
        — and for me.

WATSON: (Astonished. After an instant's pause.)
        But — if you both love each other —

HOLMES: (Putting hand on WATSON to stop him
        sharply.)
        Sh — ! Don't say it!
        (Pause.)
        You mustn't tempt me — with such a thought.
        That girl! — young — exquisite — just
        beginning her sweet life — I — seared,
        drugged, poisoned, almost at an end! No! no! I
        must cure her! I must stop it, now — while
        there's time!
        (Pause.)
        She's coming here.

WATSON: She won't come alone?

HOLMES: No, Térèse will be with her.

HOLMES turns and goes to door to surgery, getting a book on the
way, and placing it in the way of door closing. Turns to WATSON.

HOLMES: When she comes let her wait in that room. You can manage that, I'm quite sure.

WATSON: Certainly — Do you intend to leave that book there

HOLMES: (Nods "Yes".)
To keep that door from closing. She is to overhear.

WATSON: I see.

HOLMES: Sir Edward and the Count are very likely to become excited. I shall endeavour to make them so. You must not be alarmed old fellow.

Bell of outside door rings off HOLMES and WATSON look at one another.

HOLMES: (Going to centre door.)
She may be there now. I'll go to your dressing-room, if you'll allow me, and brush away some of this dust.

WATSON: By all means!
(Goes to door.)
My wife is in the drawing-room. Do look in on her a moment — it will please her so much.

HOLMES: (At door.)
My dear fellow, it will more than please me!
(Opens door. Piano heard off when the door is opened.)
Mrs. Watson! Home! Love! Life! Ah, Watson!
(Eyes glance about thinking. He sighs a little absently, suddenly turns and goes out.)

WATSON turns and goes to his desk — not to sit. Enter PARSONS.

PARSONS: A lady sir, wants to know if she can speak to you. If there's anyone 'ere she won't come in.

WATSON: Any-name?

177

PARSONS: No, sir. I asked her and she said it was
                        unnecessary — as you wouldn't know 'er. She
                        'as 'er maid with 'er, sir.

WATSON: Then it must be — Show her in.

PARSONS turns to go.

WATSON: And Parsons —

PARSONS stops and turns.

WATSON: (Lower voice.)
                        Two gentlemen, Count von Stalburg and Sir
                        Edward Leighton will call. Bring them here to
                        this room at once, and then tell Mr. Holmes.
                        You'll find him in my dressing-room.

PARSONS: Yes, sir.

WATSON: Send everybody else away — I'll see that lady.

PARSONS: Yes, sir.

He goes, leaving door open. Brief pause. PARSONS appears outside
door, showing some one to the room. Enter ALICE FAULKNER.
ALICE glances apprehensively about, fearing she will see HOLMES.
Seeing that WATSON is alone, she is much relieved and goes towards
him. PARSONS closes door from outside.

ALICE: (With some timidity.)
                        Is this — is this Doctor Watson's room?

WATSON: (Encouragingly — and advancing a step or
                        two.)
                        Yes, and I am Doctor Watson.

ALICE: Is — would you mind telling me if Mr. Holmes
                        — Mr. — Sherlock Holmes — is here?

WATSON: He will be before long, Miss — er —

ALICE: My name is Alice Faulkner.

WATSON: Miss Faulkner. He came a short time ago, but
          has gone upstairs for a few moments.

ALICE: Oh! —
          (With an apprehensive look.)
          — and is he coming down — soon?

WATSON: Well the fact is Miss Faulkner he has an
          appointment with two gentlemen here and I
          was to let him know as soon as they arrived.

ALICE: Do you suppose I could wait — without
          troubling you too much — and see him —
          afterwards?

WATSON: Why certainly.

ALICE: Thank you — and I — I don't want him to
          know —that — I —that I came.

WATSON: Of course, if you wish, there's no need of my
          telling him.

ALICE: It's — very important indeed that you don't,
          Dr Watson. I can explain it all to you
          afterwards.

WATSON: No explanation is necessary Miss Faulkner.

ALICE: Thank you.
          (Glances about.)
          I suppose there is a waiting room for patients?

WATSON: Yes or you could sit in there.
          (Indicating surgery door.)
          You'll be less likely to be disturbed.

ALICE: Yes, thank you.
          (ALICE glances toward door.)
          I think I would rather be — where its entirely
          quiet.

Bell of front door outside rings.

179

WATSON: (Going to surgery door.)
                     Then step this way. I think the gentlemen have
                     arrived.

ALICE: (Goes to door and turns.)
                     And when the business between the gentlemen
                     is over would you please have some one tell
                     me?

WATSON: I'll tell you myself Miss Faulkner.

ALICE: Thank you.
                     (She goes.)

PARSONS enters.

PARSONS: Count von Stalburg. Sir Edward Leighton.

Enter SIR EDWARD and COUNT VON STALBURG. PARSONS
goes, closing door after him.

WATSON: Count — Sir Edward —
                     (Bowing and coming forward.)

SIR EDWARD: Dr Watson.
                     (Bows.)
                     Good evening.
                     (Placing hat on pedestal.)

VON STALBURG bows slightly and stands.

SIR EDWARD: Our appointment with Mr. Holmes was
                     changed to your house, I believe

WATSON: Quite right, Sir Edward. Pray be seated,
                     gentlemen.

SIR EDWARD and WATSON sit.

VON STALBURG: Mr. Holmes is a trifle late.
                     (Sits.)

WATSON: He has already arrived, Count. I have sent for
                 him.

VON STALBURG: Ugh!

Slight pause.

SIR EDWARD: It was quite a surprise to receive his message
                 an hour ago changing the place of meeting. We
                 should otherwise have gone to his house in
                 Baker Street.

WATSON: You would have found it in ashes, Sir Edward.

SIR EDWARD: What! Really!

VON STALBURG: Ugh!

Both looking at WATSON.

SIR EDWARD: The — the house burnt!

WATSON: Burning now, probably.

SIR EDWARD: I'm very sorry to hear this. It must be a severe
                 blow to him.

WATSON: No, he minds it very little.

SIR EDWARD: (Surprised.)
                 Really! I should hardly have thought it.

VON STALBURG: Did I understand you to say, doctor, that you
                 had sent for Mr. Holmes?

WATSON: Yes, Count, and he'll be here shortly. Indeed, I
                 think I hear him on the stairs now.

Pause. Enter HOLMES at centre door. He is very pale. His clothing is
re-arranged and cleansed, though he still, of course, wears the clerical
suit, white tie, etc. He stands near door a moment. SIR EDWARD and
COUNT rise and turn to him.

(CONT/)

WATSON rises and goes to desk, where he soon seats himself in chair behind desk. SIR EDWARD and the COUNT stand looking at HOLMES. Brief Pause.

HOLMES: (Coming forward and speaking in a low clear
                           voice, entirely calm, but showing some
                           suppressed feeling or anxiety at the back of it.)
                           Gentlemen, be seated again, I beg.

Brief pause. SIR EDWARD and the COUNT reseat themselves. HOLMES remains standing. He stands looking down before him for quite a while, others looking at him. He finally begins to speak in a low voice without first looking up.

HOLMES: Our business to-night can be quickly disposed
                           of. I need not tell you, gentlemen — for I have
                           already told you — that the part I play in it is
                           more than painful to me. But business is
                           business — and the sooner it is over the better.
                           You were notified to come here this evening in
                           order that I might —
                           (Pause.)
                           — deliver into your hands the packet which
                           you engaged me — on behalf of your exalted
                           client —

COUNT and SIR EDWARD bow slightly at "exalted client.".

HOLMES: — to recover. Let me say, in justice to myself,
                           that but for that agreement on my part, and the
                           consequent steps which you took upon the
                           basis of it, I would never have continued with
                           the work. As it was, however, I felt bound to
                           do so, and therefore pursued the matter — to
                           the very end — and I now have the honor to
                           deliver it into your hands.

HOLMES goes toward SIR EDWARD with the packet. SIR EDWARD rises and meets him. HOLMES places the packet in his hands, COUNT VON STALBURG rises and stands at his chair.

SIR EDWARD: (Formally.)
                     Permit me to congratulate you, Holmes, upon
                     the marvellous skill you have displayed, and
                     the promptness with which you have fulfilled
                     your agreement.

HOLMES bows slightly and turns away. SIR EDWARD at once
breaks the seals of the packet and looks at the contents. He begins to
show some surprise as he glances at one or two letters or papers and at
once looks closer. He quickly motions to COUNT, who goes at once
to him. He whispers something to him, and they both look at two or
three things together.

VON STALBURG: Oh! No! No!

SIR EDWARD: (Stopping examination and looking across to
                     HOLMES.)
                     What does this mean?
                     (Pause.)

HOLMES turns to SIR EDWARD in apparent surprise.

SIR EDWARD: These letters! And these — other things.
                     Where did you get them?

HOLMES: I purchased them — last night.

SIR EDWARD: Purchased them?

HOLMES: Quite so — quite so.

VON STALBURG: From whom — if I may ask?

HOLMES: From whom? From the parties interested — by
                     consent of Miss Faulkner.

SIR EDWARD: You have been deceived.

HOLMES: What!

WATSON rises and stands at his desk.

Sir Arthur Conan Doyle

SIR EDWARD: (Excitedly.)
                     This packet contains nothing — not a single
                     letter or paper that we wanted. All clever
                     imitations! The photographs are of another
                     person! You have been duped. With all your
                     supposed cleverness, they have tricked you!
                     Ha! ha! ha!

VON STALBURG: Most decidedly duped, Mr. Holmes!

HOLMES turns quickly to SIR EDWARD.

HOLMES: Why, this is terrible!
                     (Turns back to WATSON. Stands looking in
                     his face.)

SIR EDWARD: (Astonished.)
                     Terrible! Surely, sir, you do not mean by that,
                     that there is a possibility you may not be able
                     to recover them!

Enter ALICE and stands listening.

HOLMES: It's quite true!

SIR EDWARD: After your positive assurance! After the steps
                     we have taken in the matter by your advice!
                     Why — why, this is —
                     (Turns to COUNT, too indignant to speak.)

VON STALBURG: (Indignantly.)
                     Surely, sir, you don't mean there is no hope of
                     it?

HOLMES: None whatever, Count. It is too late now! I
                     can't begin all over again!

SIR EDWARD: Why, this is scandalous! It is criminal, sir! You
                     had no right to mislead us in this way, and you
                     shall certainly suffer the consequences. I shall
                     see that you are brought into court to answer
                     for it, Mr. Holmes. It will be such a blow to
                     your reputation that you —

184

HOLMES: There is nothing to do, Sir Edward — I am
          ruined — ruined —

ALICE: (Coming forward.)
          He is not ruined, Sir Edward.
          (Quiet voice, perfectly calm and self-
          possessed; she draws the genuine packet from
          her dress.)
          It is entirely owing to him and what he said to
          me that I now wish to give you the —
          (Starting toward SIR EDWARD as if to hand
          him the packet.)

HOLMES steps forward and intercepts her with left hand extended.
She stops surprised.

HOLMES: One moment —
          (Pause.)
          Allow me.
          (He takes packet from her hand.)

WATSON stands looking at the scene. Pause. HOLMES stands with
the package in his hand looking down for a moment. He raises his
head, as if he overcame weakness — glances at his watch, and turns to
SIR EDWARD and the COUNT. He speaks quietly as if the climax of
the tragedy were passed — the deed done. ALICE'S questioning gaze
he plainly avoids.

HOLMES: Gentlemen—
          (putting watch back in pocket)
          — I notified you in my letter of this morning
          that the package should be produced at a
          quarter-past nine. It is barely fourteen past —
          and this is it. The one you have there, as you
          have already discovered, is a counterfeit.

Love music.

HOLMES turns a little, sees ALICE, stands looking at her. ALICE is
looking at HOLMES with astonishment and horror. She moves back a
little involuntarily.

SIR EDWARD and VON STALBURG:
                              (Staring up with admiration and delight as they
                              perceive the trick.)
                              Ah! excellent!
                              Admirable, Mr. Holmes!
                              It is all clear now!
                              Really marvellous!
                              (To one another, etc.)
                              Yes—upon my word!

On SIR EDWARD and COUNT breaking into expressions of
admiration, WATSON quickly moves up to them, and stops them with
a quick "Sh!" All stand motionless. HOLMES and ALICE looking at
one another. HOLMES goes quickly to ALICE and puts the package
into her hands.

HOLMES: (As he does this)
                              Take this, Miss Faulkner. Take it away from
                              me, quick! It is yours. Never give it up. Use it
                              only for what you wish!

Stop music.

SIR EDWARD: (Springing forward with a mild exclamation.)
                              What! We are not to have it?
                              (Throwing other package up stage.)

VON STALBURG gives an exclamation or look with foregoing.

HOLMES: (Turning from ALICE —but keeping left hand
                              back upon her hands into which he put the
                              package —as if to make her keep it. Strong —
                              breathless — not loud — with emphatic shake
                              of head.)
                              No, you are not to have it.

SIR EDWARD: After all this?

HOLMES: After all this.

VON STALBURG: But, my dear sir—

SIR EDWARD: This is outrageous! Your agreement?

HOLMES: I break it! Do what you please — warrants —
                     summons — arrests — will find me here!
                     (Turns up and says under his breath to
                     WATSON.)
                     Get them out! Get them away!
                     (Stands by WATSON'S desk, his back to the
                     audience.)

Brief pause. WATSON moves toward SIR EDWARD and the
COUNT at the back of HOLMES.

WATSON: I'm sure, gentlemen, that you will appreciate
                     the fact —

ALICE: (Stepping forward — interrupting.)
                     Wait a moment, Doctor Watson!
                     (Going to SIR EDWARD.)
                     Here is the package, Sir Edward!
                     (Hands it to SIR EDWARD at once.)

WATSON motions to PARSONS, off to come on.

HOLMES: (Turning to ALICE.)
                     No!

ALICE: (To HOLMES.)
                     Yes —
                     (Turning to HOLMES. Pause.)
                     I much prefer that he should have them. Since
                     you last came that night and asked me to give
                     them to you, I have thought of what you said.
                     You were right — it was revenge.
                     (She looks down a moment, then suddenly
                     turns away.)

HOLMES stands motionless, near corner of desk, his eyes down.
PARSONS enters and stands waiting with SIR EDWARD'S hat in his
hand, which he took from off pedestal.

SIR EDWARD: We are greatly indebted to you, Miss
                     Faulkner—

Looks at VON STALBURG.

187

VON STALBURG: To be sure!

SIR EDWARD: And to you, too, Mr. Holmes — if this was a
                  part of the game.
                  (Motionless pause all round. Examining papers
                  carefully. COUNT looking at them also.)
                  It was certainly an extraordinary method of
                  obtaining possession of valuable papers — but
                  we won't quarrel with the method as long as it
                  accomplished the desired result! Eh, Count?
                  (Placing package in breast pocket and
                  buttoning coat.)

VON STALBURG: Certainly not, Sir Edward.

SIR EDWARD: (Turning to HOLMES.)
                  You have only to notify me of the charge for
                  your services —
                  (ALICE gives a little look of bitterness at the
                  word "charge".)
                  — Mr. Holmes, and you will receive a cheque
                  I have the honour to wish you —good night.

Music till end of Act

SIR EDWARD: (Bowing punctiliously.)
                  Dr. Watson.
                  (Bowing at WATSON.)
                  This way, Count.

WATSON bows and follows them to door. HOLMES does not move.
COUNT VON STALBURG bows to HOLMES and to WATSON and
goes, followed by SIR EDWARD. PARSONS exits. WATSON
quietly turns and sees HOLMES beckoning to him. WATSON goes to
HOLMES, who whispers to him after which he quietly goes.
HOLMES after a moment's pause, looks at ALICE.

HOLMES: (Speaks hurriedly.)
                  Now that you think it over, Miss Faulkner, you
                  are doubtless beginning to realize the series of
                  tricks by which I sought to deprive you of your
                  property.
                                  (CONT/)

I couldn't take it out of the house that night
like a straightforward thief — because it could
have been recovered at law, and for that reason
I resorted to a cruel and cowardly device which
should induce you to relinquish it.

ALICE:
(Not looking at him.)
But you — you did not give it to them —

Pause.

HOLMES:
(In a forced cynical hard voice.)
No — I preferred that you should do as you
did.

ALICE looks suddenly up at him in surprise and pain, with a
breathless " What?" scarcely audible. HOLMES meets her look
without a tremor.

HOLMES:
(Slowly, distinctly.)
You see, Miss Faulkner, it was a trick — a
deception — to the very — end.

ALICE looks in his face a moment longer and then down.

HOLMES:
Your maid is waiting.

ALICE:
(Stopping him by speech — no action.)
And was it — a trick last night — when they
tried to kill you?

HOLMES:
(Hearing ALICE, stops dead.)
I went there to purchase the counterfeit
package — to use as you have seen.

ALICE:
And — did you know I would come?

Pause.

HOLMES:
No.

ALICE gives a subdued breath of relief

189

HOLMES: But it fell in with my plans notwithstanding. Now that you see me in my true light, Miss Faulkner, we have nothing left to say but good night — and good-bye — which you ought to be very glad to do. Believe me, I meant no harm to you — it was purely business — with me. For that you see I would sacrifice everything. Even my supposed — friendship for you — was a pretense — a sham — everything that you —

She has slowly turned away to the front during his speech. She turns and looks him in the face.

ALICE: (Quietly but distinctly.)
I don't believe it.

They look at one another.

HOLMES: (After a while.)
Why not?

ALICE: From the way you speak — from the way you — look — from all sorts of things! —
(With a very slight smile.)
You're not the only one — who can tell things — from small details.

HOLMES: (Coming a step closer to her,)
Your faculty — of observation is — is somewhat remarkable, Miss Faulkner — and your deduction is quite correct! I suppose — indeed I know — that I love you. I love you. But I know as well what I am — and what you are —

ALICE begins to draw nearer to him gradually, but with her face turned front.

HOLMES: I know that no such person as I should ever dream of being a part of your sweet life!

(CONT/)

> It would be a crime for me to think of such a
> thing! There is every reason why I should say
> good-bye and farewell! There is every
> reason—

ALICE gently places her right hand on HOLMES' breast, which stops him from continuing speech. He suddenly stops. After an instant he begins slowly to look down into her face. His left arm gradually steals about her. He presses her head close to him and the lights fade away with ALICE resting in HOLMES' arms, her head on his breast.

Music swells gradually.

CURTAIN

Notes

Sherlock Holmes: A Drama In Four Acts had a protracted birth. Arthur Conan Doyle had long harboured a wish to write for the stage but while his creation, Sherlock Holmes, was a hit, Conan Doyle had yet to achieve any success in seeing his work on stage. American theatrical producer Charles Frohman approached Conan Doyle with the ambition of acquiring the rights to stage a Sherlock Holmes play. Conan Doyle himself had been working on a five act play pitting Holmes against Professor Moriarty. Upon reading Conan Doyle's script, Frohman felt it was not yet ready for production and suggested that William Gillette would be not only be the ideal author to rewrite the script but would be the perfect actor to play Holmes.

The rewritten play lifted material and dialogue directly from Conan Doyle's Holmes stories, including *A Study In Scarlet*, *The Final Problem* and most noticeably *A Scandal In Bohemia*, and Conan Doyle was credited as co-author, though the play was ultimately written by Gillette. Conan Doyle was, in truth, deeply uncomfortable by many of the liberties taken by the American writer-actor with Holmes, particularly with the changes to Holmes' character, softening him and making him far more emotionally open than he ever appeared in print. The character of Irene Adler in *A Scandal In Bohemia* had been replaced by the less scheming Alice Faulkner and Holmes' relationship with her was far more conventionally romantic than Holmes admirers then or since were used to. There is some evidence in the tone of Conan Doyle's correspondence with Gillette suggesting that the alterations to Holmes' character caused Conan Doyle to lose some interest in the project. However, the play's success softened Conan Doyle's objections.

Initially the play opened in New York on November 6, 1899 and ran for over two hundred performances before embarking upon a tour of America and then decanting across the Atlantic for a run in London's Lyceum Theatre in 1901, during which a young London actor named Charlie Chaplin played Billy. The play was a considerable success and Gillette revived it on a number of subsequent occasions.

The play has been staged in countless theatres since it was first written and continues to appear in stages across the globe. John Neville, Frank Langella, Leonard Nimoy and Robert Stephens are just a few of the actors to have taken the lead role in productions. The Royal Shakespeare Company's 1970s production starring John Wood was particularly well received.

The play has also been filmed on a number of occasions. The first, in 1916 featured Gillette himself as Holmes. Considered lost for decades, a print of the film was discovered in 2014 and will be made available after restoration. It was filmed again in 1922 with John Barrymore as Holmes and in 1932 Clive Brook wore the deerstalker. In 1981, Frank Langella returned to the role for a stage production filmed by HBO.

The Painful Predicament
of Sherlock Holmes
A Fantasy in about One-Tenth of an Act

William Gillette
1905

Cast of Characterrs

Gwendolyn Cobb
Sherlock Holmes
Billy
And two valuable assistants are the people most concerned

It all transpires in Sherlock Holmes's Baker Street apartments somewhere about the date of day before yesterday.

The time of day is not stated.

DARK CURTAIN

SHERLOCK HOLMES is discovered seated on the floor before the fire, smoking. There is a table with various things on it, an arm chair right of it. A high upholstered stool is at its left. Firelight from fire. Moonlight from window.

Strange lights from door when it is open. After the curtain is up and the firelight on, there is a pause.

Sudden loud ringing at front door bell outside in distance continuing impatiently. After time for opening of door, loud talking and protestations heard, GWENDOLYN pouring forth a steady stream in a high key insisting that she must see Mr. Holmes, that it is very important, a matter of life and death, etc., BILLY trying to tell her she cannot come up and shouting louder and louder in his efforts to make her hear. This continues a moment and then suddenly grows louder as the two come running up the stairs and approach the door; BILLY leading and the voice after him.

Enter BILLY, very excited. He pulls the door shut after him, and holds it while he turns to speak to HOLMES.

BILLY: I beg your pardon, sir—
                    (The door is pulled from outside and BILLY
                    turns to hold it, but turns again quickly to
                    HOLMES.)

Same business.

BILLY: I beg your pardon, sir— If you please, sir!—
                    It's a young lady 'as just came in, an' says she
                    must see you — she's 'ere now, sir, a-tryin' to
                    pull the door open — but I don't like 'er eye,
                    sir! … I don't it at all, sir!

HOLMES rises and turns up lamp. Lights on.

BILLY: 'Er eye is certainly bad, sir! An' she — she
                        don't seem to be able to leave off talkin' long
                        enough fer me to tell 'er as 'ow she can't see
                        you, sir!

HOLMES watches BILLY and the door with interest.

BILLY: I tried to tell 'er as you give orders not to see
                        no one. I shouted it out tremendous — but she
                        was talkin' so loud it never got to 'er — so I
                        run up to warn you — an' she come runnin'
                        after me — an' — an' —

Door suddenly pulled upon from outside while BILLY is talking to
HOLMES.

BILLY: An' ... an' 'ere she is, sir!

Enter GWENDOLYN COBB with unrestricted enthusiasm.

GWENDOLYN: (Entering joyously.)
                        Oh! There you are! This is Mr. Holmes, I
                        know! Oh — I've heard so much about you!
                        You really can't imagine!
                        (Going toward HOLMES.)
                        And I've simply longed to see you myself and
                        see if ... oh, do shake hands with me. (They
                        shake hands.)
                        Isn't it wonderful to realize I'm shaking hands
                        with Sherlock Holmes! It's simply ripping! To
                        think that I've lived to see this day!
                        (Looks at him.)
                        Of course, I suppose you're the real one —
                        detectives have so many disguises and things
                        that it might be you were only pretending —
                        but still, why should you?

He motions her to seat, she does not pause an instant for any business.

GWENDOLYN: Oh, thank you. Yes — I will sit down.

She moves to chair beside table and sits on arm of it.

HOLMES motions BILLY to go.

Exit BILLY.

GWENDOLYN: Because I came to ask your advise about
              something! Oh yes, it wasn't just curiosity that
              brought me here — I'm in a dreadful
              predicament — that's what you like, isn't it?
              — predicaments! Well, this is one — it is a
              lolla! It's simply awful! You've no idea! I
              don't suppose you ever had such a frightful
              affair to unravel. It isn't a murder or anything
              like that — it's a thousand times worse! Oh —
              millions of times worse. There are worse things
              than murder — aren't there, Mr. Holmes?

HOLMES nods again to indicate that he thinks so too.

GWENDOLYN: Oh, how nice of you to agree with me about it
              — few would do it so soon. But you can
              fathom my inmost soul — I feel that you are
              doing it now — and it gives me strength to go
              on — indeed it does, Mr. Holmes! Just your
              presence and your sympathy encourages me!
              (Looking at him admiringly.) And it's really
              you. And there's the fire.

GWENDOLYN jumps up and runs to it, going around the table.

HOLMES stands regarding her.

GWENDOLYN: I suppose it's a real fire, isn't it? You know can
              never tell in these days when everything seems
              to be adulterated — you don't know what
              you're getting, do you?

HOLMES shakes head emphatically.

GWENDOLYN: No, you don't! There you go again agreeing
              with me. How nice of you! It's inspiring!
              (Looking at him in rapture.)
              And it's so perfectly ripping to see you there
              before my eyes! But you're not smoking. Oh, I

199

do wish you'd smoke. I always think of you
that way! It doesn't seem right! Do smoke!

HOLMES lights pipe.

GWENDOLYN: Where's the tobacco?
(Looking on mantel, takes jar.)
HERE!
(Smells.)
It is true you smoke that terrible shag tobacco?
What is it like?
(Drops jar.)
Oh, I'm so sorry!
(Steps back and breaks violin.)
Oh! Isn't that too bad!

Stamps about on violin trying to extricate herself. Continues talking
and apologizing all the while. Suddenly sits on lounge to get loose
from violin and breaks bow which lies across the arm of lounge.

GWENDOLYN: Oh, dear me! I'm so sorry! Mercy, what was
that?

Takes out broken violin bow.

GWENDOLYN: I'm afraid you won't want me to come again
— if I go on like this! Oh!
(Springs to her feet.)
What have you got there cooking over that
lamp — I would so like a cup of tea!

Goes up to retort, etc.

GWENDOLYN: But I suppose —
(Smells of thing.)
No — it isn't tea! What a funny thing you're
boiling in it! It looks like a soap bubble with a
handle! I'm going to see what—
(Takes up retort and instantly drops it on
floor.)
Oh! it was hot! Why didn't you tell me it was
hot?
(CONT/)

(Gesturing excitedly.)
How could I know — I've never been here
before — one can't know everything about
things, alone and unprotected.

Backing up in her excitement upsets lamp, etc. which goes over with a
crash.

Lights off firelights again. Moonlight from window.

GWENDOLYN: There goes something else! It does seem to me
                you have more loose truck lying about — oh
                — I see! It's to trap people! What a splendid
                idea! They break the glass and you have them.
                (Moving toward him admiringly.)
                And you can tell from the kind of glass they
                break where they were born and why they
                murdered the man! Oh, it's perfectly thrilling!
                Now I suppose you know just from the few
                little things I've done since I've been here
                exactly what sort of a person I am — do you?

HOLMES nods quietly. He lights a candle.

Lights on.

GWENDOLYN: Oh, how wonderful! Everything seems
                wonderful! All the things about here … only
                it's so … oh! Why that looks just like a friend
                of mine!

Turning up papers on wall.

GWENDOLYN: And there's another! What a handsome man!
                But what has he got all those lines running
                across his face for? I should think it would hurt
                —and here's — oh, this is beautiful!
                (Tears it off.)
                You must let me keep this — it looks so much
                like a young man I know.

The other sketches fall down.

201

GWENDOLYN: Oh, dear, there go the rest of them. But you've
                        got plenty more, haven't you?
                        (Looks about.)
                        See that lady's foot? Why do you have such an
                        ugly foot hung up here! It isn't nice at all!

Pulls it down. Other sketches hung up fall with it.

GWENDOLYN: I'll send you a pretty water-colour of cows
                        drinking at a stream— it'll look so much
                        better! Mercy — did that man's fingers grow
                        together like that? How it must have hurt …
                        What did you do for him? I suppose Dr.
                        Watson attended to him — oh, if I could only
                        see him! And I want him to help you about this
                        dread affair of mine! It needs you both! And if
                        Dr. Watson wasn't with you it wouldn't seem
                        as if you were detecting at all. It's a terrible
                        thing — I'm in such trouble.

HOLMES motions her to sit.

GWENDOLYN: Oh thank you. I suppose I'd better tell you
                        about it now— and—

She is sitting on stool by table HOLMES remains standing.

GWENDOLYN: —then you can talk it over with Dr. Watson
                        and ask him what his idea is and then it'll turn
                        out that he was wrong and you knew all the
                        time oh — that's so wonderful — it gives me
                        that delicious crawly, creepy feeling as if mice
                        were running up and down my spine — oh!
                        (Facing toward front)
                        Oh!

HOLMES has edged round on the upper side of table and as she
shudders, etc. he quietly takes a handkerchief out of her dress or
pocket and moves quietly to other side of table and sits. He examines
the handkerchief while she is not looking, using a magnifying glass
etc.

202

GWENDOLYN: Now this is what I came to ask you about —
I'm sure you've never had such a painful case
to attend to — because it affects two human
souls ... not bodies ... pah ... what are bodies
... merely mud ... But souls ... they are
immortal — they live forever ... His name is
Levi Lichenstein He's what they call a Yankee.
Of course you know, without my telling you,
that we adore each other! Mr. Holmes, we
adore each other. It couldn't be expressed in
words! Poets couldn't do it! What are poets?
Pooh!
(Snaps fingers.)
We adore each other Do I need to say more?

HOLMES shakes head.

GWENDOLYN: No! Of course I don't ... ah, how you
understand! It's perfectly wonderful! Now
listen — I want to tell you my troubles.

HOLMES quietly scribbles on a pad of paper.

GWENDOLYN: That's right — take down what I say. Every
word is important. He's in jail! Put that down!
It's outrageous. And my own father did it. I'm
not ashamed of it — but if—
(Affected.)
—if — Oh, my God!

GWENDOLYN: (Grabs for handkerchief to weep but is unable
to find it.)
There!
(Springs to her feet.)
It's been stolen. I knew I should lose
something if I came here ... where the air
seems simply charged with thugs and
pickpockets.

HOLMES rises and politely passes her handkerchief to her and sits
again as before.

GWENDOLYN: Oh, thank you!
       (Sits.)
       My father put him there!
       (She sobs.)

HOLMES rings bell on table.

GWENDOLYN gives a convulsive sob on ringing of bell. But she goes right on talking, not paying any attention to the business and going on excitedly through her sobs and eye-wipings.

Enter BILLY. HOLMES motions him. He comes down back of HOLMES. HOLMES hands him the paper he has been scribbling upon and motions him off.

Exit BILLY.

GWENDOLYN: Oh, Mr. Holmes — think of one's own father
       being the one to bring disgrace upon one!
       Think of one's own father doing these cruel
       and shameful things. But it's always one's own
       father — he is the one out of the world who
       jumps headlong at the chance to be heartless
       and cruel and — and —
       (Three heavy and resounding thuds heard in
       distance, as if someone were pounding a heavy
       beam on the floor.)

GWENDOLYN springs to her feet with a scream.

Melodramatic music.

GWENDOLYN: Oh! … There it is … those awful three knocks!
       Something is going to happen. Is there any
       danger — do tell me …

HOLMES scribbles on piece of paper.

GWENDOLYN: Oh, don't keep me in this dreadful suspense —
       I have dreamt of those three awful knocks …
       but why should they come to me? Oh, heaven
       … you're not going to let them …

HOLMES pushes the paper across to her. She snatches it up and reads it in a loud voice.

GWENDOLYN: "Plumbers — in — the — house."

Stop music.

GWENDOLYN: Oh, I see! Plumbers!
(She sits again.)
And you knew it … could tell it was the plumbers without once leaving your chair! Oh, how wonderful … do you know, Levi is a little that way. He really is, Mr. Holmes. That's the reason I adore him so! Perhaps he can see too much! Do you think there's any danger of that? Oh, Mr. Holmes — tell me — do you think we'll be happy together? Oh — I'm sure you know — and you will tell me, won't you?

HOLMES scribbles on piece of paper.

GWENDOLYN: It's perfectly clear to you without even seeing him. I know it is and so much depends upon it when two souls seem drawn to each other. Tell me … I can bear anything and I'd so like to know if we shall be happy together or not.

HOLMES pushes piece of paper toward her. She picks it up quickly and reads it in a slow loud distinct voice.

GWENDOLYN: Has — he — ever —spoken —to —you? Oh yes? Indeed he has … He once told me …

Melodramatic music

GWENDOLYN: Oh, heavens … And he's in jail. He'll never speak again. I haven't told you yet … take down all these things … my father put him there. Yes — my own father! Levi has lent a friend of mine some money —a mere pittance — scarcely as much as that — say half a pittance.

(CONT/)

205

> My friend gave him a mortgage on some
> furniture his grandmother had left him and
> when he couldn't pay, the furniture came to
> Levi. Then they found another will and it left
> all this furniture to a distant aunt out in
> America and the lawyers issued a writ of
> replevin and then Levi sued out a habeas
> corpus and signed a bond so that he was
> responsible — and my father went on this bond
> — and the furniture was taken back! Levi had
> to get another bond, and while he was swearing
> it the distant aunt arrived from America and
> had him arrested for obtaining a habeas corpus
> under false pretenses and he brought suit
> against her for defamation of character — and
> he was right — she said the most frightful
> things. Why —
> (Rising.)
> — she stood there — in the office of his own
> barristers and spoke of him as a reprobate and
> a right angle triable!

Raises voice in excitement and moves about wildly.

GWENDOLYN: That miserable woman — with painted face
               and horrible American accent actually accused
               him of having falsified some of the furniture.
               And my father, hearing that we loved each
               other, swore out a warrant and he is in jail!
               (Screams, etc.)

Enter two uniformed men, followed by BILLY. They stop an instant,
looking at GWENDOLYN. In the height of her excitement she sees
them and stops dead with a wild moan. They go down to her at once
and get her quickly off at door. She goes without resistance.

BILLY: It was the right asylum, sir!
               (Exits.)

HOLMES rises. Takes an injection of cocaine. Lights pipe with candle
which he then blows out.

Lights off except red light of fire, etc.

HOLMES goes to lounge before fire, and sinks down upon it, leaning back on the cushions.

Lights gradually off.

Stop music.

CURTAIN

The Crown Diamond
An Evening with Sherlock Holmes

Sir Arthur Conan Doyle
1910

Cast of Characters

MR. SHERLOCK HOLMES
The famous Detective.

DR. WATSON
His Friend.

BILLY
Page to MR. HOLMES.

COL. SEBASTIAN MORAN
An intellectual Criminal.

SAM MERTON
A Boxer.

SCENE. — MR. HOLMES'S room in Baker Street. It presents the usual features, but there is a deep bow window to it, and across there is drawn a curtain running upon a brass rod fastened across eight feet above the ground and enclosing the recess of the window.

Enter WATSON and BILLY

WATSON:	Well, Billy, when will he be back?
BILLY:	I'm sure I couldn't say sir.
WATSON:	When did you see him last?
BILLY:	I really couldn't tell you.
WATSON:	What, you couldn't tell me?
BILLY:	No sir. There was a clergyman looked in yesterday and there was an old bookmaker and there was a workman.
WATSON:	Well?
BILLY:	But I'm not sure they weren't all Mr. Holmes. You see he's very hot on a chase just now.
WATSON:	Oh!
BILLY:	He neither eats nor sleeps. Well you've lived with him same as me. You know what he's like when he's after some one.
WATSON:	I know.
BILLY:	He's a responsibility sir, that he is. It's a real worry to me sometimes. When I asked him if he would order dinner, he said. "Yes, I'll have chops and mashed potatoes at 7:30 the day after to morrow." "Won't you eat before then sir?" I asked. "I haven't time, Billy. I'm busy," said he. He gets thinner and paler and his eyes get brighter. It's awful to see him.

WATSON:	Tut, tut, this will never do. I must certainly stop and see him.
BILLY:	Yes sir, it will ease my mind.
WATSON:	But what is he after?
BILLY:	It's this case of the Crown Diamond.
WATSON:	What the hundred thousand pound burglary?
BILLY:	Yes, sir. They must get it back sir. Why we had the Prime Minister and the Home Secretary both sitting on that very sofa. Mr. Holmes promised he'd do his very best for them. Quite nice he was to them. Put them at their ease in a moment.
WATSON:	Dear me! I've read about it in the paper. But I say, Billy, what have you been doing to the room? What's this curtain?
BILLY:	I don't know, sir. Mr. Holmes had it put there three days ago. But we've got something funny behind it.
WATSON:	Something funny?
BILLY:	(Laughing.) Yes, sir. He had it made.

BILLY goes to the curtain and draws it across, disclosing a wax image of Holmes seated in a chair, back to the audience.

WATSON:	Good heavens, Billy!
BILLY:	Yes, sir. It's like him, sir. (Picks the head off and exhibits it.)
WATSON:	It's wonderful! But what's it for, Billy?
BILLY:	You see, sir, he's anxious that those who watch him should think he's at home sometimes

when he isn't. There's the bell, sir.
(Replaces head, draws curtain.)
I must go.

BILLY goes out.

WATSON sits down, lights a cigarette, and opens a paper. Enter a tall, bent OLD WOMAN in black with veil and side-curls.

WATSON:	(Rising.) Good day, Ma'm.
WOMAN:	You're not Mr. Holmes?
WATSON:	No, Ma'm. I'm his friend, Dr. Watson.
WOMAN:	I knew you couldn't be Mr. Holmes. I'd always heard he was a handsome man.
WATSON:	(Aside.) Upon my word!
WOMAN:	But I must see him at once.
WATSON:	I assure you he is not in.
WOMAN:	I don't believe you.
WATSON:	What!
WOMAN:	You have a sly, deceitful face—oh, yes, a wicked, scheming face. Come, young man, where is he?
WATSON:	Really, Madam ... !
WOMAN:	Very well, I'll find him for myself. He's in there, I believe. (Walks toward bedroom door.)
WATSON:	(Rising and crossing.) That is his bedroom. Really, Madam, this is outrageous!

WOMAN: I wonder what he keeps in this safe.

She approaches it, and as she does so the lights go out, and the room is in darkness save for "DON'T TOUCH" in red fire over the safe. Four red lights spring up, and between them the inscription "DON'T TOUCH!" After a few seconds the lights go on again, and HOLMES is standing beside WATSON.

WATSON: Good heavens, Holmes!

HOLMES: Neat little alarm, is it not, Watson? My own
                          invention. You tread on a loose plank and so
                          connect the circuit, or I can turn it on myself. It
                          prevents inquisitive people becoming too
                          inquisitive. When I come back I know if any
                          one has been fooling with my things. It
                          switches off again automatically, as you saw.

WATSON: But my dear fellow, why this disguise?

HOLMES: A little comic relief, Watson. When I saw you
                          sitting there looking so solemn, I really
                          couldn't help it. But I assure you there is
                          nothing comic in the business I am engaged
                          upon. Good heavens!
                          (Rushes across room, and draws curtain, which
                          has been left partly open.)

WATSON: Why, what is it?

HOLMES: Danger, Watson. Airguns, Watson. I'm
                          expecting something this evening.

WATSON: Expecting what, Holmes?

HOLMES: (Lighting pipe.)
                          Expecting to be murdered, Watson.

WATSON: No, no, you are joking, Holmes!

HOLMES: Even my limited sense of humour could evolve
                          a better joke than that, Watson. No, it is a fact.
                                        (CONT/)

> And in case it should come off—it's about a
> two to one chance—it would perhaps be as
> well that you should burden your memory with
> the name and address of the murderer.

WATSON: Holmes!

HOLMES: You can give it to Scotland Yard with my love
                  and a parting blessing. Moran is the name.
                  Colonel Sebastian Moran. Write it down,
                  Watson, write it down! 136, Moorside
                  Gardens, N.W. Got it?

WATSON: But surely something can be done, Holmes.
                  Couldn't you have this fellow arrested?

HOLMES: Yes, Watson, I could. That's what's worrying
                  him so.

WATSON: But why don't you?

HOLMES: Because I don't know where the diamond is.

WATSON: What diamond?

HOLMES: Yes, yes, the great yellow Crown Diamond,
                  seventy seven carats, lad, and without flaw. I
                  have two fish in the net. But I haven't got the
                  stone there. And what's the use of taking
                  them? It's the stone I'm after.

WATSON: Is this Colonel Moran one of the fish in the
                  net?

HOLMES: Yes, and he's a shark. He bites. The other is
                  Sam Merton the boxer. Not a bad fellow, Sam,
                  but the Colonel has used him. Sam's not a
                  shark. He's a big silly gudgeon. But he's
                  flopping about in my net, all the same.

WATSON: Where is this Colonel Moran?

HOLMES:	I've been at his elbow all morning. Once he picked up my parasol. "By your leave, Ma'm," said he. Life is full of whimsical happenings. I followed him to old Straubenzee's workshop in the Minories. Straubenzee made the airgun — fine bit of work, I understand.
WATSON:	An airgun?
HOLMES:	The idea was to shoot me through the window. I had to put up that curtain. By the way, have you seen the dummy? (Draws curtain.)

WATSON nods.

Ah! Billy has been showing you the sights. It may get a bullet through its beautiful wax head at any moment.

Enter BILLY.

HOLMES:	Well, Billy?
BILLY:	Colonel Sebastian Moran, sir.
HOLMES:	Ah! the man himself. I rather expected it. Grasp the nettle, Watson. A man of nerve! He felt my toe on his heels. (Looks out of window.) And there is Sam Merton in the street— the faithful but fatuous Sam. Where is the Colonel, Billy?
BILLY:	Waiting-room, sir.
HOLMES:	Show him up when I ring.
BILLY:	Yes, sir.
HOLMES:	Oh, by the way, Billy, if I am not in the room show him in just the same.
BILLY:	Very good, sir.

BILLY goes out.

WATSON: I'll stay with you, Holmes.

HOLMES: No, my dear fellow, you would be horribly in the way.
(Goes to the table and scribbles a note.)

WATSON: He may murder you.

HOLMES: I shouldn't be surprised.

WATSON: I can't possibly leave you.

HOLMES: Yes, you can, my dear Watson, for you've always played the game, and I am very sure that you will play it to end. Take this note to Scotland Yard. Come back with the police. The fellow's arrest will follow.

WATSON: I'll do that with joy.

HOLMES: And before you return I have just time to find where the diamond is.
(Rings bell.)
This way, Watson. We'll go together. I rather want to see my shark without his seeing me.

WATSON and HOLMES go into the bedroom.

Enter BILLY and COLONEL SEBASTIAN MORAN, who is a fierce big man, flashily dressed, with a heavy cudgel.

BILLY: Colonel Sebastian Moran.

BILLY goes out.

COLONEL MORAN looks round, advances slowly into the room and starts as he sees the dummy figure sitting in the window. He stares at it, then crouches, grips his stick, and advances on tip-toe. When close to the figure he raises his stick. HOLMES comes quickly out of the bedroom door.

HOLMES: Don't break it, Colonel, don't break it.

COLONEL: (Staggering back.)
        Good Lord!

HOLMES: It's such a pretty little thing. Tavernier, the
        French modeller, made it. He is as good at
        waxwork as Straubenzee is at airguns.
        (Shuts curtains.)

COLONEL: Airguns, sir. Airguns! What do you mean?

HOLMES: Put your hat and stick on the side table. Thank
        you. Pray take a seat. Would you care to put
        your revolver out also? Oh, very good, if you
        prefer to sit upon it.

The COLONEL sits down.

HOLMES: I wanted to have five minutes' chat with you.

COLONEL: I wanted to have five minutes' chat with you.

HOLMES sits down near him and crosses his leg.

COLONEL: I won't deny that I intended to assault you just
        now.

HOLMES: It struck me that some idea of that sort had
        crossed your mind.

COLONEL: And with reason, sir, with reason.

HOLMES: But why this attention?

COLONEL: Because you have gone out of your way to
        annoy me. Because you have put your
        creatures on my track.

HOLMES: My creatures?

COLONEL: I have had them followed. I know that they
        come to report to you here.

HOLMES: No, I assure you.

COLONEL: Tut, sir! Other people can observe as well as
                 you. Yesterday there was an old sporting man;
                 to-day it was an elderly lady. They held me in
                 view all day.

HOLMES: Really, sir, you compliment me! Old Baron
                 Dowson, before he was hanged at Newgate,
                 was good enough to say that in my case what
                 the law had gained the stage had lost. And now
                 you come along with your kindly words. In the
                 name of the elderly lady and of the sporting
                 gentleman I thank you. There was also an out-
                 of-work plumber who was an artistic dream—
                 you seem to have overlooked him.

COLONEL: It was you. . . you!

HOLMES: Your humble servant! If you doubt it, you can
                 see the parasol upon the settee which you so
                 politely handed to me this morning down in the
                 Minories.

COLONEL: If I had known you might never—

HOLMES: Never have seen this humble home again. I
                 was well aware of it. But it happens you didn't
                 know, and here we are, quite chatty and
                 comfortable.

COLONEL: What you say only makes matters worse. It
                 was not your agents, but you yourself, who
                 have dogged me. Why have you done this?

HOLMES: You used to shoot tigers?

COLONEL: Yes, sir.

HOLMES: But why?

COLONEL: Pshaw! Why does any man shoot a tiger? excitement. The danger.

HOLMES: And no doubt the satisfaction of freeing the country from a pest, which devastates it and lives on the population.

COLONEL: Exactly.

HOLMES: My reasons in a nutshell.

COLONEL: (Springing to his feet.)
Insolent!

HOLMES: Sit down, sir, sit down! There was another more practical reason.

COLONEL: Well?

HOLMES: I want that yellow Crown Diamond.

COLONEL: Upon my word! Well, go on.

HOLMES: You knew that I was after you for that. The reason why you are here to-night is to find out how much I know about the matter. Well, you can take it that I know all about it, save one thing, which you are about to tell me.

COLONEL: (Sneering.)
And, pray, what is that?

HOLMES: Where the diamond is.

COLONEL: Oh, you want to know that, do you? How the devil should I know where it is?

HOLMES: You not only know, but you are about to tell me.

COLONEL: Oh, indeed!

HOLMES: You can't bluff me, Colonel. You're absolute
                 plate glass. I see to the very back of your mind.

COLONEL: Then of course you see where the diamond is.

HOLMES: Ah! then you do know. You have admitted it.

COLONEL: I admit nothing.

HOLMES: Now, Colonel, if you will be reasonable we can
                 do business together. If not you may get hurt.

COLONEL: And you talk about bluff!

HOLMES: (Raising a book from the table.)
                 Do you know what I keep inside this book?

COLONEL: No, sir, I do not.

HOLMES: You.

COLONEL: Me!

HOLMES: Yes, sir, you. You're all here, every action of
                 your vile and dangerous life.

COLONEL: Damn you, Holmes! Don't go too far.

HOLMES: Some interesting details, Colonel. The real
                 facts as to the death of Miss Minnie Warrender
                 of Laburnum Grove. All here, Colonel.

COLONEL: You—you devil!

HOLMES: And the story of young Arbothnot, who was
                 found drowned in the Regents Canal just
                 before his intended exposure of you for
                 cheating at cards.

COLONEL: I—I never hurt the boy.

HOLMES: But he died at a very seasonable time.
                                 (CONT/)

221

Do you want some more, Colonel? Plenty of it here. How about the robbery in the train deluxe to the Riviera, February 13th, 1892? How about the forged cheque on the Credit Lyonnais the same year?

COLONEL: No, you're wrong there.

HOLMES: Then I'm right on the others. Now, Colonel, you are a card-player. When the other fellow holds all the trumps it saves time to throw down your hand.

COLONEL: If there was a word of truth in all this, would I have been a free man all these years?

HOLMES: I was not consulted. There were missing links in the police case. But I have a way of finding missing links. You may take it from me that I could do so.

COLONEL: Bluff! Mr. Holmes, bluff!

HOLMES: Oh, you wish me to prove my words! Well, if I touch this bell it means the police, and from that instant the matter is out of my hands. Shall I?

COLONEL: What has all this to do with the jewel you speak of?

HOLMES: Gently, Colonel! Restrain that eager mind. Let me get to the point in my own hum-drum way. I have all this against you, and I also have a clear case against both you and your fighting bully in this case of the Crown Diamond.

COLONEL: Indeed!

HOLMES: I have the cabman who took you to Whitehall, and the cabman who brought you away.

(CONT/)

	I have the commissionaire who saw you beside the case. I have Ikey Cohen who refused to cut it up for you. Ikey has peached, and the game is up.
COLONEL:	Hell!
HOLMES:	That's the hand I play from. But there's one card missing. I don't know where this king of diamonds is.
COLONEL:	You never shall know.
HOLMES:	Tut! tut! don't turn nasty. Now, consider. You're going to be locked up for twenty years. So is Sam Merton. What good are you going to get out of your diamond? None in world. But if you let me know where it is. . . well, I'll compound a felony. We don't want you or Sam. We want the stone. Give up, and so far as I am concerned you can go free so long as you behave yourself in the future. If you make another slip, then God help you. But this time my commission is to get the stone, not you. (Rings bell.)
COLONEL:	But if I refuse?
HOLMES:	Then, alas, it must be you, not the stone.

Enter BILLY.

BILLY:	Yes, sir.
HOLMES:	(To the COLONEL.) I think we had better have your friend Sam at this conference. Billy, you will see a large and very ugly gentleman outside the front door. Ask him to come up, will you?
BILLY:	Yes, sir. Suppose he won't come, sir?

HOLMES: No force, Billy! Don't be rough with him. If you tell him Colonel Moran wants him, he will come.

BILLY: Yes, sir.

BILLY goes out.

COLONEL: What's the meaning of this, then?

HOLMES: My friend Watson was with me just now. I told him that I had a shark and a gudgeon in my net. Now, I'm drawing the net and up they come together.

COLONEL: (Leaning forward.)
You won't die in your bed Holmes!

HOLMES: D'you know, I have often had the same idea. For that matter, your own finish is more likely to be perpendicular than horizontal. But these anticipations are morbid. Let us give ourselves up to the unrestrained enjoyment of the present. No good fingering your revolver, my friend, for you know perfectly well that you dare not use it. Nasty, noisy things, revolvers. Better stick to airguns, Colonel Moran. Ah! … I think I hear the footsteps of your estimable partner.

Enter BILLY.

BILLY: Mr. Sam Merton.

Enter SAM MERTON, in check suit and loud necktie, yellow overcoat.

HOLMES: Good day, Mr. Merton. Rather damp in the street, is it not?

BILLY goes out.

MERTON: (To the COLONEL.)
                 What's the game? What's up?

HOLMES: If I may put it in a nutshell, Mr. Merton, I
                 should say it is all up.

MERTON: (To the COLONEL.)
                 Is this cove tryin' to be funny—or what? I'm
                 not in the funny mood myself.

HOLMES: You'll feel even less humourous as the evening
                 advances, I think I can promise you that. Now,
                 look here, Colonel. I'm a busy man and I can't
                 waste time. I'm going into the bedroom. Pray
                 make yourselves entirely at home in my
                 absence. You can explain to your friend how
                 the matter lies. I shall try over the Barcarolle
                 upon my violin.
                 (Looks at watch.)
                 In five minutes I shall return for your final
                 answer. You quite grasp the alternative, don't
                 you? Shall we take you, or shall we have the
                 stone?

HOLMES goes into his bedroom, taking his violin with him.

MERTON: What's that? He knows about the stone!

COLONEL: Yes, he knows a dashed sight too much about
                 it. I'm not sure that he doesn't know all about
                 it.

MERTON: Good Lord!

COLONEL: Ikey Cohen has split.

MERTON: He has, has he? I'll do him down a thick 'un
                 for that.

COLONEL: But that won't help us. We've got to make up
                 our minds what to do.

MERTON: Half a mo'. He's not listening, is he?
(Approaches bedroom door.)
No, it's shut. Look to me as if it was locked.

Music begins.

MERTON: Ah! there he is, safe enough.
(Goes to curtain.)
Here, I say!
(Draws it back, disclosing the figure.)
Here's that cove again, blast him!

COLONEL: Tut! it's a dummy. Never mind it.

MERTON: A fake, is it?
(Examines it, and turns the head.)
By Gosh, I wish I could twist his own as easy.
Well, strike me! Madame Tussaud ain't in it!

As MERTON returns towards the COLONEL, the lights suddenly go out, and the red "DON'T TOUCH" signal goes up. After a few seconds the lights readjust themselves. Figures must transpose at that moment.

MERTON: Well, dash my buttons! Look 'ere, Guv'nor, this is gettin' on ny nerves. Is it unsweetened gin, or what?

COLONEL: Tut! it is some childish hanky-panky of this fellow Holmes, a spring or an alarm or something. Look here, there's no time to lose. He can lag us for the diamond.

MERTON: The hell he can!

COLONEL: But he'll let us slip if we only tell him where the stone is.

MERTON: What, give up the swag! Give up a hundred thousand!

COLONEL: It's one or the other.

MERTON: No way out? You've got the brains, Guv'nor.
                  Surely you can think a way out of it.

COLONEL: Wait a bit! I've fooled better men than he.
                  Here's the stone in my secret pocket. It can be
                  out of England tonight, cut into four pieces in
                  Amsterdam before Saturday. He knows
                  nothing of Van Seddor.

MERTON: I thought Van Seddor was to wait till next
                  week.

COLONEL: Yes, he was. But now he must get the next
                  boat. One or other of us must slip round with
                  the stone to the "Excelsior" and tell him.

MERTON: But the false bottom ain't in the hat-box yet!

COLONEL: Well, he must take it as it is and chance it.
                  There's not a moment to lose. As to Holmes,
                  we can fool him enough. You see, he won't
                  arrest us if he thinks he can get the stone. We'll
                  put him on the wrong track about it, and before
                  he finds it is the wrong track, the stone will be
                  in Amsterdam, and we out of the country.

MERTON: That's prime.

COLONEL: You go off now, and tell Van Seddor to get a
                  move on him. I'll see this sucker and fill him
                  up with a bogus confession. The stone's in
                  Liverpool—that's what I'll tell him. By the
                  time he finds it isn't, there won't be much of it
                  left, and we'll be on blue water.
                  (He looks carefully round him, then draws a
                  small leather box from his pocket, and holds it
                  out.)
                  Here is the Crown Diamond.

HOLMES: (taking it, as he rises from his chair)
                  I thank you.

COLONEL: (Staggering back.)
               Curse you, Holmes!
               (Puts hand in pocket.)

MERTON: To hell with him!

HOLMES: No violence, gentlemen; no violence, I beg of
               you. It must be very clear to you that your
               position is an impossible one. The police are
               waiting below.

COLONEL: You — you devil! How did you get there?

HOLMES: The device is obvious but effective; lights off
               for a moment and the rest is common sense. It
               gave me a chance of listening to your racy
               conversation which would have been painfully
               constrained by a knowledge of my presence.
               No, Colonel, no. I am covering you with a .450
               Derringer through the pocket of my dressing-
               gown.
               (Rings bell.)

Enter BILLY.

HOLMES: Send them up, Billy.

BILLY goes out.

COLONEL: Well, you've got us, damn you!

MERTON: A fair cop … But I say, what about that
               bloomin' fiddle?

HOLMES: Ah, yes, these modern gramophones!
               Wonderful invention. Wonderful!

CURTAIN

The Speckled Band
An Adventure of Sherlock Holmes

Sir Arthur Conan Doyle
1910

Cast of Characters

MR. SHERLOCK HOLMES: The great Detective
MR. SCOTT WILSON: Engaged to ENID'S sister
DR. WATSON: Sherlock Holmes' Friend
MR. LONGBRACE: Coroner
BILLY: Page to SHERLOCK HOLMES
MR. BREWER: Foreman of the jury
DR. GRIMESBY RYLOTT: A retired Anglo-Indian Surgeon
and owner of Stoke Moran Manor
MR. ARMITAGE: A juror
ENID STONOR: His Step-daughter
MR. HOLT LOAMING
ALI: An Indian, valet to DR. RYLOTT
MR. MILVERTON
RODGERS: Butler to DR. RYLOTT
MR. JAMES B. MONTAGUE: Client of Mr. SHERLOCK
HOLMES
MRS. STAUNTON: Housekeeper to DR. RYLOTT
CORONER'S OFFICER
INSPECTOR DOWNING

Act I

The Hall of Stoke Place, Stoke Moran

Two years elapse between Acts I and II

SCENE. —Stoke Place at Stoke Moran. A large, oak-lined, gloomy hall, with everything in disrepair. At the back, centre, is a big double door which leads into the morning-room. To its right, but also facing the audience, is another door which leads to the outside entrance hall. A little down, right, is the door to DR. RYLOTT'S study. Farther down, right, a large opening gives access to the passageway of the bedroom wing. A fifth entrance, up left, leads to the servants' hall. There is a long table in the middle of the room, with chairs round.

ENID STONOR sits on a couch at one side, her face buried in the cushion, sobbing. RODGERS also discovered, the butler, a broken old man. He looks timidly about him and then approaches ENID.

RODGERS:	Don't cry, my dear young lady. You're so good and kind to others that it just goes to my heart to see such trouble to you. Things will all change for the better now.
ENID:	Thank you, Rodgers, you are very kind.
RODGERS:	Life can't be all trouble, Miss Enid. There must surely be some sunshine somewhere, though I've waited a weary time for it.
ENID:	Poor old Rodgers!
RODGERS:	Yes, it used to be poor young Rodgers, and now it's poor old Rodgers; and there's the story of my life.

Enter ALI, an Indian servant, from the servants' hall.

ALl:	Mrs. Staunton says you are to have beer and sandwiches for the jury, and tiffin for the coroner.
RODGERS:	Very good.
ALl:	Go at once.

RODGERS: You mind your own business. You think you
                are the master.

ALl: I carry the housekeeper's order.

RODGERS: Well, I've got my orders.

ALI: And I see they are done.

RODGERS: You're only the valet, a servant — same as me;
                as Mrs. Staunton for that matter.

ALl: Shall I tell master? Shall I say you will not take
                the order?

RODGERS: There, there, I'll do it.

Enter DR. GRIMESBY RYLOTT from his study.

RYLOTT: Well, what's the matter? What are you doing
                Rodgers?

RODGERS: Nothing, sir, nothing.

ALl: I tell him to set out tiffin.

RYLOTT: Go this instant! What do you mean?

RODGERS exits into servants' hall.

RYLOTT: Ali, stand at the door and show people in.
                (To ENID.)
                Oh! for God's sake stop your snivelling! Have
                I not enough to worry me without that?
                (Shakes her.)
                Stop it, I say! I'll have no more. They'll all be
                in here in a moment.

ENID: Oh? Don't be so harsh with me.

RYLOTT: Hark! I think I hear them.
                (Crossing toward bedroom passage.)
                        (CONT/)

234

| | What can they be loitering for? They won't learn much by looking at the body. I suppose that consequential ass of a coroner is giving them a lecture. If Professor Van Donop and Doctor Watson are satisfied, surely that is good enough for him. Ali! |

ALl: Yes, Sahib.

RYLOTT: How many witnesses have come?

ALI: Seven, Sahib.

RYLOTT: All in the morning room?

ALl: Yes, Sahib.

RYLOTT: Then put any others in there also.

ALl salaams.

RYLOTT: Woman will you dry your eyes and try for once to think of other people besides yourself? Learn to stamp down your private emotions. Look at me. I was as fond of your sister Violet as if she had really been my daughter, and yet I face the situation now like a man. Get up and do your duty.

ENID: (Drying her eyes.)
                What can I do?

RYLOTT: (Sitting on the settee beside her.)
                There's a brave girl. I did not mean to be harsh. Thirty years of India sends a man home with a cayenne pepper temper. Did I ever tell you the funny story of the Indian judge and the cabman?

ENID: Oh, how can you?

RYLOTT: Well, well, I'll tell it some other time.
                                (CONT/)

Don't look so shocked. I meant well, I was
trying to cheer you up. Now look here, Enid!
be a sensible girl and pull yourself together—
and I say! be careful what you tell them. We
may have had our little disagreements— every
family has—but don't wash our linen in public.
It is a time to forgive and forget. I always
loved Violet in my heart.

ENID: Oh! if I could only think so!

RYLOTT: Since your mother died you have both been to
                         me as my own daughters; in every way the
                         same; mind you say so. D'you hear?

ENID: Yes, I hear.

RYLOTT: Don't forget it.
                         (Rising, turns her face.)
                         Don't forget it. Curse them! are they never
                         coming, the carrion crows! I'll see what they
                         are after.

Exits into bedroom passage.

SCOTT WILSON enters at the hall door and is shown by ALl into the
morning-room. While he is showing him in, DR. WATSON enters,
and, seeing ENID with her face in the cushions, he comes across to
her.

WATSON: Let me say how sorry I am, Miss Stonor.
                         (Shaking hands.)

ENID: (Rises to meet him.)
                         I am so glad to see you, Dr. Watson.
                         (Sinks on stool and sobs.)
                         I fear I am a weak, cowardly creature, unfit to
                         meet the shocks of life. It is all like some
                         horrible nightmare.

WATSON: I think you have been splendidly brave. What
                         woman could fail to feel such a shock?

ENID: Your kindness has been the one gleam of light
                in these dark days. There is such bad feeling
                between my stepfather and the country doctor
                that I am sure he would not have come to us.
                But I remembered the kind letter you wrote
                when we came home, and I telegraphed on the
                chance. I could hardly dare hope that you
                would come from London so promptly.

WATSON: Why, I knew your mother well in India, and I
                remember you and your poor sister when you
                were schoolgirls. I was only too glad to be of
                any use—if indeed I was of any use. Where is
                your stepfather?

ENID: He has gone in to speak with the coroner.

WATSON: I trust that he does not visit you with any of
                that violence of which I hear so much in the
                village. Excuse me if I take a liberty; it is only
                that I am interested. You are very lonely and
                defenceless.

ENID: Thank you. I am sure you mean well, but
                indeed I would rather not discuss this matter.

All: (Advancing.)
                This way, sir.

WATSON: In a minute.

ALl: Master's orders, sir.
                (Coming down.)

WATSON: In a minute, I say.

ALI: Very sorry, sir. Must go now.

WATSON: (Pushing him away.)
                Stand back, you rascal. I will go in my own
                time. Don't you dare to interfere with me.

ALl shrugs shoulders and withdraws.

237

WATSON: Just one last word. It is a true friend who speaks, and you will not resent it. If you should be in any trouble, if anything should come which made you uneasy — which worried you—

ENID: What should come? You frighten me.

WATSON: You have no one in this lonely place to whom you can go. If by chance you should want a friend you will turn to me, will you not?

ENID: How good you are! But you mean more than you say. What is it that you fear?

WATSON: It is a gloomy atmosphere for a young girl. Your stepfather is a strange man. You would come to me, would you not?

ENID: I promise you I will.
(Rising.)

WATSON: I can do little enough. But I have a singular friend — a man with strange powers and a very masterful personality. We used to live together, and I came to know him well. Holmes is his name—Mr. Sherlock Holmes. It is to him I should turn if things looked black for you. If any man in England could help it is he.

ENID: But I shall need no help. And yet it is good to think that I am not all alone. Hush! they are coming. Don't delay! Oh! I beg to go.

WATSON: I take your promise with me.
(He goes into the morning-room.)

DR. RYLOTT enters from the bedroom wing, conversing with the CORONER. The JURY, in a confused crowd, come behind. There are a CORONER'S OFFICER and a police INSPECTOR.

CORONER:	Very proper sentiments, sir; very proper sentiments. I can entirely understand your feelings.
RYLOTT:	At my age it is a great thing to have a soothing female influence around one. I shall miss it at every turn. She had the sweet temperament of her dear mother. Enid, my dear, have you been introduced to Mr. Longbrace, the Coroner?
CORONER:	How do you do, Miss Stonor? You have my sympathy, I am sure. Well, well, we must get to business. Mr. Brewer, I understand that you have been elected as foreman. Is that so, gentlemen?
ALL:	Yes, yes.
CORONER:	Then perhaps you would sit here. (Looks at watch.) Dear me! it is later than I thought. Now, Dr. Rylott— (Sits at table.) —both you and your stepdaughter are witnesses in this inquiry, so your presence here is irregular.
RYLOTT:	I thought, sir, that under my own roof—
CORONER:	Not at all, sir, not at all. The procedure is entirely unaffected by such a consideration.
RYLOTT:	I am quite in your hands.
CORONER:	Then you will kindly withdraw.
RYLOTT:	Come, Enid.
CORONER:	Possibly the young lady would wish to be free, so we Could take her evidence first.
RYLOTT:	That would be most considerate. (CONT/)

239

You can understand, sir, that I would wish her spared in this ordeal. I leave you, dear girl. (Aside.) Remember!

RYLOTT is about to go into his study but is directed by the INSPECTOR into the morning-room.

CORONER: Put a chair, there, officer.

OFFICER places chair.

CORONER: That will do. Now, Miss Stonor! Thank you. The officer will swear you—

ENID is sworn by the OFFICER.

OFFICER: —The truth and nothing but the truth. Thank you.

ENID kisses the Book.

CORONER: Now, gentlemen, before I take the evidence, I will remind you of the general circumstances connected with the sudden decease of this unhappy young lady. She was Miss Violet Stonor, the elder of the stepdaughters of Dr. Grimesby Rylott, a retired Anglo-Indian doctor, who has lived for several years at this ancient house of Stoke Place, in Stoke Moran. She was born and educated in India, and her health was never robust. There was, however, no actual physical lesion, nor has any been discovered by the doctors. You have seen the room on the ground floor at the end of this passage, and you realize that the young lady was well guarded, having her sister's bedroom on one side of her and her stepfather's on the other. We will now take the evidence of the sister of the deceased as to what actually occurred. Miss Stonor, do you identify the body of the deceased as that of your sister, Violet Stonor?

ENID: Yes.

CORONER: Might I ask you to tell us what happened upon
                 the night of April 14? I understand that your
                 sister was in her ordinary health when you said
                 good-night to her?

ENID: Yes, she seemed as usual. She was never
                 strong.

CORONER: Had she some mental trouble?

ENID: (Hesitating.)
                 She was not very happy in her mind.

CORONER: I beg that you will have no reserves. I am sure
                 you appreciate the solemnity of this occasion.
                 Why was your sister unhappy in her mind?

ENID: There were obstacles to her engagement.

CORONER: Yes, yes, I understand that this will be dealt
                 with by another witness. Your sister was
                 unhappy in her mind because she was engaged
                 to be married and there were obstacles.
                 Proceed.

ENID: I was awakened shortly after midnight by a
                 scream. I ran into the passage. As I reached her
                 door I heard a sound like low music, then the
                 key turn in the lock, and she rushed out in her
                 nightdress. Her face was convulsed with terror.
                 She screamed out a few words and fell into my
                 arms, and then slipped down upon the floor.
                 When I tried to raise her I found that she was
                 dead. Then — then I fainted myself, and I
                 knew no more.

CORONER: When you came to yourself—?

ENID: When I came to myself I had been carried by
                 my stepfather and Rodgers, the butler, back to
                 my bed.

CORONER: You mentioned music. What sort of music?

ENID: It was a low, sweet sound.

CORONER: Where did this music come from?

ENID: I could not tell. I may say that once or twice I thought that I heard music at night.

CORONER: You say that your sister screamed out some words. What were the words?

ENID: It was incoherent raving. She was wild with terror.

CORONER: But could you distinguish nothing?

ENID: I heard the word "band"—I also heard the word "speckled." I cannot say more. I was myself almost as terrified as she.

CORONER: Dear me. Band — speckled — it sounds like delirium. She mentioned no name?

ENID: None.

CORONER: What light was in the passage?

ENID: A lamp against the wall.

CORONER: You could distinctly see your sister?

ENID: Oh, yes.

CORONER: And there was at that time no trace of violence upon her?

ENID: No, no!

CORONER: You are quite clear that she unlocked her door before she appeared?

ENID: Yes, I can swear it.

CORONER:	And her window? Did she ever sleep with her window open?
ENID:	No, it was always fastened at night.
CORONER:	Did you examine it after her death?
ENID:	I saw it next morning; it was fastened then.
CORONER:	One other point, Miss Stonor. You have no reason to believe that your sister contemplated suicide?
ENID:	Certainly not.
CORONER:	At the same time when a young lady— admittedly of a nervous, highly-strung disposition — is crossed in her love affairs, such a possibility cannot be excluded. You can throw no light upon such a supposition?
ENID:	No.
FOREMAN:	Don t you think Mr. Coroner if the young lady had designs upon herself she would have stayed in her room and not rushed out into the passage?
CORONER:	Well that is for your consideration and judgement. You have heard this young lady's evidence. Have any of you any questions to put?
ARMITAGE:	(Rising.) Well I'm a plain man, a Methodist and the son of a Methodist —
CORONER:	What is your name sir?
ARMITAGE:	I'm Mr. Armitage sir. I own the big shop in the village.
CORONER:	Well sir?

243

ARMITAGE: I'm a Methodist and the son of a Methodist —

CORONER: Your religious opinions are not under
                discussion, Mr. Armitage.

ARMITAGE: But I speaks my mind as man to man I pays my
                taxes the same as the rest of them.

CORONER: Have you any questions to ask?

ARMITAGE: I would like to ask this young lady whether her
                stepfather uses her ill for there are some queer
                stories got about in the village.

CORONER: The question would be out of order. It does not
                bear upon the death of the deceased.

FOREMAN: Well sir I will put Mr. Armitage's question in
                another shape. Can you tell us Miss, whether
                your stepfather ill-used the deceased young
                lady?

ENID: He—he was not always gentle.

ARMITAGE: Does he lay hands on you?—that's what I want
                to know.

CORONER: Really, Mr. Armitage.

ARMITAGE: Excuse me, Mr. Coroner. I've lived in this
                village, boy and man for fifty years and I can
                look any man in the face.

ARMITAGE sits.

CORONER: You have heard the question, Miss Stonor. I
                don't know that we could insist upon your
                answering it.

ENID: Gentlemen, my stepfather has spent his life in
                the tropics. It has affected his health.
                                (CONT/)

There are times—there are times— when he loses control over his temper. At such times he is liable to be violent. My sister and I thought — hoped — that he was not really responsible for it. He is sorry for it afterwards.

CORONER: Well, Miss Stonor, I am sure I voice the sentiments of the Jury when I express our profound sympathy for the sorrow which has come upon you.

JURY all murmur, "Certainly," "Quite so," etc.

CORONER: Call Mr. Scott Wilson. We need not detain you any longer.

ENID rises and goes into the morning-room.

OFFICER: (At door.)
Mr. Scott Wilson.

Enter SCOTT WILSON—a commonplace young gentleman.

CORONER: Swear him, officer—

SCOTT WILSON mumbles and kisses the Book.

CORONER: I understand, Mr. Scott Wilson, that you were engaged to be married to the deceased.

WILSON: Yes, sir.

CORONER: Since how long?

WILSON: Six weeks.

CORONER: Was there any quarrel between you?

WILSON: None.

CORONER: Were you in a position to marry?

WILSON: Yes.

245

CORONER: Was there any talk of an immediate marriage?

WILSON: Well, sir, we hoped before the summer was
              over.

CORONER: We hear of obstacles. What were the obstacles?

WILSON: Dr. Rylott. He would not hear of the marriage.

CORONER: Why not?

WILSON: He gave no reason, sir.

CORONER: There was some scandal, was there not?

WILSON: Yes, sir, he assaulted me.

CORONER: What happened?

WILSON: He met me in the village. He was like a raving
              madman. He struck me several times with his
              cane, and he set his boar-hound upon me.

CORONER: What did you do?

WILSON: I took refuge in one of the little village shops.

ARMITAGE: (Jumping up.)
              I beg your pardon, young gentleman, you took
              refuge in my shop.

WILSON: Yes, sir, I took refuge in Mr. Armitage's shop.

ARMITAGE sits.

CORONER: And a police charge resulted?

WILSON: I withdrew it, sir, out of consideration for my
              fiancée.

CORONER: But you continued your engagement?

WILSON: I would not be bullied out of that.

CORONER: Quite so. But this opposition, and her fears as to your safety, caused Miss Stonor great anxiety?

WILSON: Yes.

CORONER: Apart from that, you can say nothing which throws any light on this sad event?

WILSON: No. I had not seen her for a week before her death.

CORONER: She never expressed any particular apprehension to you?

WILSON: She was always nervous and unhappy.

CORONER: But nothing definite?

WILSON: No.

CORONER: Any questions, gentlemen.
(Pause.)
Very good. Call Dr. Watson! You may go.

SCOTT WILSON goes out through the entrance hall.

OFFICER: (At morning-room door.)
Dr. Watson!

Enter DR. WATSON.

CORONER: You will kindly take the oath. Gentlemen, at the opening of this Court, and before you viewed the body, you had read to you the evidence of Professor Van Donop, the pathologist who is unable to be present to-day. Dr. Watson's evidence is supplementary to that. You are not in practice, I understand, Dr. Watson?

WATSON: No, sir.

CORONER: A retired Army Surgeon, I understand?

WATSON: Yes.

CORONER: Dear me! you retired young.

WATSON: I was wounded in the Afghan Campaign.

CORONER: I see, I see. You knew Dr. Rylott before this
                tragedy?

WATSON: No, sir. I knew Mrs. Stonor when she was a
                widow, and I knew her two daughters. That
                was in India. I heard of her re-marriage and her
                death. When I heard that the children, with
                their stepfather, had come to England, I wrote
                and reminded them that they had at least one
                friend.

CORONER: Well, what then?

WATSON: I heard no more until I received a wire from
                Miss Enid Stonor. I at once came down to
                Stoke Moran.

CORONER: You were the first medical man to see the
                body?

WATSON: Dr. Rylott is himself a medical man.

CORONER: Exactly. You were the first independent
                medical man?

WATSON: Oh, yes, sir.

CORONER: Without going too far into painful details, I
                take it that you are in agreement with Professor
                Van Donop's report and analysis?

WATSON: Yes, sir.

CORONER: You found no physical lesion?

WATSON:	No.
CORONER:	Nothing to account for death?
WATSON:	No.
CORONER:	No signs of violence?
WATSON:	No.
CORONER:	Nor of poison?
WATSON:	No.
CORONER:	Yet there must be a cause?
WATSON:	There are many causes of death which leave no sign.
CORONER:	For instance—?
WATSON:	Well, for instance, the subtler poisons. There are many poisons for which we have no test.
CORONER:	No doubt. But you will remember, Dr. Watson, that this young lady died some five or six hours after her last meal. So far as the evidence goes it was only then that she could have taken Poison, unless she took it of her own free will; in which case we Should have expected to find some paper or bottle in her room. But it would indeed be a strange poison which could strike her down so suddenly many hours after it was taken. You perceive difficulty?
WATSON:	Yes sir.
CORONER:	You could name no such poison?
WATSON:	No.
CORONER:	Then what remains?

WATSON: There are other causes. One may die of
               nervous shock or one may die of a broken
               heart.

CORONER: Had you any reason to think that the deceased
               had undergone nervous shock?

WATSON: Only the narrative of her sister.

CORONER: You have formed no conjecture as to the nature
               of the shock?

WATSON: No sir.

CORONER: You spoke of a broken heart. Have you any
               reason for using such an expression?

WATSON: Only my general impression that she was not
               happy.

CORONER: I fear we cannot deal with general impressions.

Murmurs of acquiescence from the JURY.

CORONER: You have no definite reason?

WATSON: None that I can put into words.

CORONER: Has any juror any question to ask?

ARMITAGE: (Rising.)
               I'm a plain downright man and I want to get to
               the bottom of this thing.

CORONER: We all share your desire Mr. Armitage.

ARMITAGE: Look here Doctor you examined this lady. Did
               you find any signs of violence?

WATSON: I have already said I did not.

ARMITAGE: I mean bruises, or the like.

WATSON: No sir.

CORONER: Any questions?

ARMITAGE: I would like to ask the Doctor whether he
                   wrote to these young ladies because he had any
                   reason to think they were ill-used.

WATSON: No, sir. I wrote because I knew their mother.

ARMITAGE: What did their mother die of?

WATSON: I have no idea.

CORONER: Really Mr. Armitage you go too far!

ARMITAGE sits.

CORONER: Anything else?

FOREMAN: May I ask, Dr. Watson, whether you examined
                   the window of the room to see if any one from
                   outside could have molested the lady?

WATSON: The window was bolted.

FOREMAN: Yes, but had it been bolted all night?

WATSON: Yes, it had.

CORONER: How do you know?

WATSON: By the dust on the window-latch.

CORONER: Dear me, Doctor, you are very observant!

WATSON: I have a friend, sir, who trained me in such
                   matters.

CORONER: Well, your evidence seems final on that point.
                   We are all obliged to you, Dr. Watson, and will
                   detain you no longer.

Exit DR. WATSON into the morning-room.

OFFICER: (At door.)
                    Mr. Rodgers!

Enter RODGERS.

CORONER: Swear him!

Business of swearing.

CORONER: Well, Mr. Rodgers, how long have you been in
                    the service of Dr. Rylott?

RODGERS: For many years, sir.

CORONER: Ever since the family settled here?

RODGERS: Yes, sir. I'm an old man, sir, too old to change.
                    I don't suppose I'd get another place if I lost
                    this one. He tells me it would be the gutter or
                    the workhouse.

CORONER: Who tells you?

RODGERS: Him, sir — the master. But I am not saying
                    anything against him, sir. No, no, don't think
                    that — not a word against the master. You
                    won't misunderstand me?

CORONER: You seem nervous?

RODGERS: Well, I'm an old man, sir, and things like
                    this—

CORONER: Quite so, we can understand. Now, Rodgers,
                    upon the night of April 14, you helped to carry
                    the deceased to her room.

RODGERS: Did I, sir? Who said that?

CORONER: We had it in Miss Stonor's evidence. Was it
                    not so?

RODGERS:	Yes, yes, if Miss Enid said it. What Miss Enid says is true. And what the master says is true. It's all true.
CORONER:	I suppose you came when you heard the scream?
RODGERS:	Yes, yes, the scream in the night; I came to it.
CORONER:	And what did you see?
RODGERS:	I saw—I saw— (Puts his hands up as if about to faint.)
CORONER:	Come, come, man, speak out.
RODGERS:	I'm—I'm frightened.
CORONER:	You have nothing to fear. You are under protection of the law. Who are you afraid of? Your master?
RODGERS:	(Rising.) No, no, gentlemen, don't think that! No, no!
CORONER:	Well, then—what did you see?
RODGERS:	She was on the ground, sir, and Miss Enid beside her —both in white night clothes. My master was standing near them.
CORONER:	Well?
RODGERS:	We carried the young lady to her room and laid her on her couch. She never spoke nor moved. I know no more indeed I know no more.

Sinking into his chair.

CORONER:	Any questions, gentlemen?
ARMITAGE:	You live in the house all the time?

RODGERS: Yes, sir.

ARMITAGE: Does your master ever knock you about?

RODGERS: No, sir, no.

ARMITAGE: Well, Mr. Scott Wilson told us what happened
                    to him, and I know he laid the gardener up for
                    a week and paid ten pound to keep out of court.
                    You know that yourself.

RODGERS: No, no, sir, I know nothing of the kind.

ARMITAGE: Well, every one else in the village knows.
                    What I want to ask is — was he ever violent to
                    these young ladies?

FOREMAN: Yes, that's it. Was he violent?

RODGERS: No, not to say violent. No, he's a kind man, the
                    master.

Pause.

CORONER: Call Mrs. Staunton, the housekeeper. That will
                    do.

Exit RODGERS into the servant's hall.

Enter MRS. STAUNTON from the morning-room.

CORONER: You are housekeeper here?

MRS. STAUNTON: Yes, sir.
                    (Standing.)

CORONER: How long have you been here?

MRS. STAUNTON: Ever since the family settled here.

CORONER: Can you tell us anything of this matter?

MRS. STAUNTON: I knew nothing of it, sir, till after the poor young lady had been laid upon the bed. After that it was I who took charge of things, for Dr. Rylott was so dreadfully upset that he could do nothing.

CORONER: Oh! he was very upset, was he?

MRS. STAUNTON: I never saw a man in such a state of grief.

CORONER: Living in the house you had numerous opportunities of seeing the relations between Dr. Rylott and his two stepdaughters.

MRS. STAUNTON: Yes, sir.

CORONER: How would you describe them?

MRS. STAUNTON: He was kindness itself to them. No two young ladies could be better treated than they have been.

CORONER: It has been suggested that he was sometimes violent to them.

MRS. STAUNTON: Never, sir. He was like a tender father.

ARMITAGE: How about that riding switch? We've heard tales about that.

MRS. STAUNTON: Oh, it's you, Mr. Armitage? There are good reasons why you should make mischief against the Doctor. He told you what he thought of you and your canting ways.

CORONER: Now, then, I cannot have these recriminations. If I had known, Mr. Armitage, that there was personal feeling between the Doctor and you—

ARMITAGE: Nothing of the sort, sir. I'm doing my public duty.

CORONER: Well, the evidence of the witness seems very
                  clear in combating your assertion of ill-
                  treatment. Any other Juror? Very good, Mrs.
                  Staunton.

Exit MRS. STAUNTON into the servants' hall.

CORONER: Call Dr. Grimesby Rylott.

OFFICER: (Calls at morning-room door.)
                  Dr. Rylott.

Enter DR. RYLOTT.

CORONER: Dr. Rylott, do you identify the body of the
                  deceased as that of your stepdaughter, Violet
                  Stonor?

RYLOTT: Yes, sir.

CORONER: Can you say anything which will throw any
                  light upon this unhappy business?

RYLOTT: You may well say unhappy, sir. It has
                  completely unnerved me.

CORONER: No doubt.

RYLOTT: She was the ray of sunshine in the house. She
                  knew my ways. I am lost without her.

CORONER: No doubt. But we must confine ourselves to
                  the facts. Have you any explanation which will
                  cover the facts of your stepdaughter's death?

RYLOTT: I know just as much of the matter as you do It
                  is a complete and absolute mystery to me.

CORONER: Speaking as a doctor, you had no misgivings as
                  to her health?

RYLOTT: She was never robust, but I had no reason for
                  uneasiness.

CORONER: It has come out in evidence that her happiness had been affected by your interference with her engagement?

RYLOTT: (Rising.)
             That is entirely a misunderstanding sir. As a matter of fact I interfered in order to protect her from a man I had every reason to believe was a mere fortune hunter. She saw it herself in that light and was relieved to see the last of him.

CORONER: Excuse me sir but this introduces a new element into the case. Then the young lady had separate means?

RYLOTT: An annuity under her mother's will.
             (Sits.)

CORONER: And to whom does it now go?

RYLOTT: I believe that I might have a claim upon it but I am waiving it in favour of her sister.

CORONER: Very handsome I am sure.

Murmurs from the JURY.

ARMITAGE: (Rising.)
             I expect sir so long as she lives under your roof you have the spending of it.

CORONER: Well, well, we can hardly go into that.

ARMITAGE: Had the young lady her own cheque book?

CORONER: Really Mr. Armitage you get away from the subject.

ARMITAGE: It is the subject.

RYLOTT: (Rising.)
                       I am not here, sir, to submit to impertinence.

CORONER: I must ask you, Mr. Armitage—
                       (Holds up hand.)

ARMITAGE sits.

CORONER: Now, Dr. Rylott, the medical evidence, as you
                       are aware, gives us no cause of death. You can
                       suggest none?

RYLOTT: No, sir.

CORONER: Your stepdaughter has affirmed that her sister
                       unlocked her door before appearing in the
                       passage. Can you confirm this?

RYLOTT: Yes, I heard her unlock the door.

CORONER: You arrived in the passage simultaneously with
                       the lady?

RYLOTT: Yes.

CORONER: You had been aroused by the scream?

RYLOTT: Yes.

CORONER: And naturally you came at once?

RYLOTT: Quite so. I was just in time to see her rush from
                       her room and fall into her sister's arms. I can
                       only imagine that she had some nightmare or
                       hideous dream which had been too much for
                       her heart. That is my own theory of her death.

CORONER: We have it on record that she said some
                       incoherent words before she died.

RYLOTT: I heard nothing of the sort.

CORONER: She said nothing so far as you know?

RYLOTT: Nothing.

CORONER: Did you hear any music?

RYLOTT: Music, sir? No, I heard none.

CORONER: Well, what happened next?

RYLOTT: I satisfied myself that the poor girl was dead.
                 Rodgers, my butler, had arrived, and together
                 we laid her on her couch. I can really tell you
                 nothing more.

CORONER: You did not at once send for a doctor?

RYLOTT: Well, sir, I was a doctor myself. To satisfy
                 Enid I Consented in the morning to telegraph
                 for Dr. Watson, who had been the girls' friend
                 in India. I really could do no more.

CORONER: Looking back, you have nothing with which to
                 reproach yourself in your treatment of this
                 lady?

RYLOTT: She was the apple of my eye, I would have
                 given my life for her.

CORONER: Well, gentlemen, any questions?

ARMITAGE: Yes, a good many.
                 (Rising.)

The other JURYMEN show some impatience.

ARMITAGE: Well, I pay my way, the same as the rest of
                 you, and I claim my rights. Mr. Coroner, I
                 claim my rights.

CORONER: Well, well, Mr. Armitage, be as short as you
                 can.
                 (Looks at his watch.)
                 It is nearly two.

259

ARMITAGE: See here, Dr. Rylott, what about that great hound of yours? What about that whip you carry. What about the tales we hear down in the village of your bully-raggin' them young ladies?

RYLOTT: (Rising.)
Really, Mr. Coroner, I must claim your protection. This fellow's impertinence is intolerable.

CORONER: You go rather far, Mr. Armitage. You must confine yourself to definite questions upon matters of fact.

RYLOTT sits.

ARMITAGE: Well, then, do you sleep with a light in your room?

RYLOTT: No, I do not.

ARMITAGE: How was you dressed in the passage?

RYLOTT: In my dressing-gown.

ARMITAGE: How did you get it?

RYLOTT: I struck a light, of course, and took it from a hook.

ARMITAGE: Well, if you did all that, how did you come into the passage as quick as the young lady who ran out just as she was?

RYLOTT: I can only tell you it was so.

ARMITAGE: Well, I can only tell you I don't believe it.

CORONER: You must withdraw that, Mr. Armitage.

ARMITAGE: I says what I mean, Mr. Coroner, and I say it again, I don't believe it. I've got common sense if I haven't got education.

RYLOTT: (Rising.)
I can afford to disregard his remarks, Coroner.

CORONER: Anything else, Mr. Armitage?

ARMITAGE: I've said my say, and I stick to it.

CORONER: Then that will do, Dr. Rylott.

Pause. DR. RYLOTT is going up towards the morning door.

CORONER: By the way, can your Indian servant help us at all in the matter?

RYLOTT: (Coming down again.)
Ali sleeps in a garret and knew nothing till next morning. He is my personal valet.

CORONER: Then we need not call him. Very good, Dr. Rylott. you can remain if you wish.
(To JURY.)
Well, gentlemen, you have heard the evidence relating to this very painful case. There are several conceivable alternatives. There is death by murder. Of this I need not say there is not a shadow or tittle of evidence. There is death by suicide. Here, again, the presumption is absolutely against it. Then there is death by accident. We have nothing to lead us to believe that there has been an accident. Finally, we come to death by natural causes. It must be admitted that these natural causes are obscure, but the processes of nature are often mysterious, and we cannot claim to have such an exact knowledge of them that we can always define them. You have read the evidence of Professor Van Donop and you have heard that of Dr. Watson.
(CONT/)

> If you are not satisfied it is always within your
> competence to declare that death arose from
> unknown causes. It is for you to form your own
> conclusions.

The JURY buzz together for a moment. The CORONER looks at his
watch, rises, and goes over to DR. RYLOTT.

CORONER: We are later than I intended.

RYLOTT: These absurd interruptions—!

CORONER: Yes, at these country inquests we generally
                have some queer fellows on the jury.

RYLOTT: Lunch must be ready. Won't you join us.

CORONER: Well, well, I shall be delighted.

FOREMAN: We are all ready, sir.

CORONER returns to table.

CORONER: Well, gentlemen?
                (Sits.)

FOREMAN: We are for unknown causes.

CORONER: Quite so. Unanimous?

ARMITAGE: No, sir. I am for further investigation. I don't
                say it's unknown and I won't say it's unknown.

CORONER: I entirely agree with the majority finding. Well,
                gentlemen that will finish our labours.
                Officer—

The OFFICER comes to him. ARMITAGE sits.

CORONER: You will all sign the inquisition before you
                leave this room officer will take your
                signatures as you pass out

The JURY rise—sign book as they go out into the entrance hall.

Crossing to ARMITAGE.

CORONER: Mr. Armitage One moment. Mr. Armitage I
               am sorry that you are not yet satisfied.

ARMITAGE: No sir I am not.

CORONER: You are a little exacting.
               (Turns away.)

RYLOTT: (Touching ARMITAGE on the shoulder.)
               I have only one thing to say to you sir. Get out
               of my house. Do you hear?

ARMITAGE: Yes Dr Rylott I hear. And I seem to hear
               something else. Something crying from the
               ground, Dr. Rylott, from the ground.

Exits slowly into the entrance hall.

RYLOTT: Impertinent rascal!
               (Turns away.)

Enter WATSON, ENID and the other witnesses from the morning
room. They all file out towards the entrance hail.

ENID has come down stage. DR WATSON comes back from door.

WATSON: Good bye Miss Enid.
               (Shakes hands. Then in a lower voice.)
               Don t forget that you have a friend.

He goes out.

Business of CORONER and RYLOTT lighting cigarettes— ENID
catches RYLOTT'S eye across CORONER and shrinks down onto a
chair.

CURTAIN

Act II

Two years elapse between Acts I and II.

Scene 1

DR. RYLOTT'S study at Stoke Place.
The door at one side, a pair of French windows on the other.
It is two years later.

Enter MRS. STAUNTON, showing in ARMITAGE.

MRS. STAUNTON:	I can't tell how long the Doctor may be. It's not long since he went out.
ARMITAGE:	Well, I'll wait for him, however long it is.
MRS. STAUNTON:	It's nothing I could do for you, I suppose.
ARMITAGE:	No, it is not.
MRS. STAUNTON:	Well, you need not be so short. Perhaps, after you've seen the Doctor, you may be sorry.
ARMITAGE:	There's the law of England watching over me, Mrs. Staunton. I advise you not to forget it— nor your master either. I fear no man so long as I am doing my duty.

Enter ENID.

ARMITAGE:	Ah, Miss Stonor, I am very glad to see you.
ENID:	(Bewildered.) Good-day, Mr. Armitage. What brings you up here?
ARMITAGE:	I had a little business with the Doctor. But I should be very glad to have a chat with you also.
MRS. STAUNTON:	I don't think the Doctor would like it, Miss Enid.

ARMITAGE: A pretty state of things. Isn't this young lady able to speak with whoever she likes? Do you call this a prison, or a private asylum, or what? These are fine doings in a free country.

MRS. STAUNTON: I am sure the Doctor would not like it.

ARMITAGE: Look here, Mrs. Staunton, two is company and three is none. If I'm not afraid of your master, I'm not afraid of you. You're a bit beyond your station, you are. Get to the other side of that door and leave us alone, or else—

MRS. STAUNTON: Or what, Mr. Armitage?

ARMITAGE: As sure as my father was a Methodist I'll go down to the J.P. and swear out an information that this young lady is under constraint.

MRS. STAUNTON: Oh—well, you need not be so hot about it. It's nothing to me what you say to Miss Enid. But the Doctor won't like it.

She goes out.

ARMITAGE: (Looking at the door.)
You haven't such a thing as a hatpin?
(Crossing over to door.)

ENID: No.

ARMITAGE: If I were to jab it through that keyhole —

ENID: Mr. Armitage please don't.

ARMITAGE: You'd hear Sister Jane's top note. But we'll speak low for I don't mean she shall hear. First of all Miss Enid are they using you? Are you all right?

ENID: Mr. Armitage I know you mean it all for kindness but I cannot discuss my personal affairs with you. I hardly know you.

ARMITAGE: Only the village grocer. I know all about that.
             But I've taken an interest in you Miss Stonor
             and I'm not the kind of man that can't leave go
             his hold. I came here not to see you, but your
             stepfather.

ENID: Oh, Mr. Armitage, I beg you to go away at
             once. You have no idea how violent he is if
             any one thwarts him. Please, please go at once.

ARMITAGE: Well Miss Stonor your only chance of getting
             to go is to answer my questions. When my
             conscience is clear, I'll go and not before. My
             conscience tells me that it is my duty to stay
             here till I have some satisfaction.

ENID: (Crossing to settee and sitting.)
             What is it, Mr. Armitage. Let's sit down.

ARMITAGE: (Bringing chair over to settee.)
             Well I'll tell you. I make it my business to
             know what is going on in this house. It may be
             that I like you or it may be that I dislike your
             stepfather. Or it may be that it is just my nature
             but so it is I've got my own ways of finding
             out, and I find out.

ENID: What have you found out?

ARMITAGE: Now look here, Miss. Cast your mind back to
             that inquest two years ago.

ENID: Oh!
             (Turning away.)

ARMITAGE: I'm sorry if it hurts you, but I must speak plain.
             When did your sister meet her death? It was
             shortly after her engagement was it not?

ENID: Yes, it was.

ARMITAGE: Well, you're engaged now, are you not?

ENID: Yes, I am.

ARMITAGE: Point number one. Well, now, have there not
               been repairs lately, and are you not forced to
               sleep in the very room your sister died in?

ENID: Only for a few nights.

ARMITAGE: Point number two. In your evidence you said
               you heard music in the house at night. Have
               you never heard music of late?

ENID: Good God! only last night I thought I heard it;
               and then persuaded myself that it was a dream.
               But how do you know these things, Mr.
               Armitage, and what do they mean?

ARMITAGE: Well, I won't tell you how I know them, and I
               can't tell you what they mean. But it's devilish,
               Miss Stonor, devilish!
               (Rising.)
               Now I've come up to see your stepfather and to
               tell him, as man to man, that I've got my eye
               on him, and that if anything happens to you it
               will be a bad day's work for him.

ENID: (Rising.)
               Oh, Mr. Armitage, he would beat you within
               an inch of your life. Mr. Armitage, you cannot
               think what he is like when the fury is on him.
               He is terrible.

ARMITAGE: The law will look after me.

ENID: It might avenge you, Mr. Armitage, but it
               could not protect you. Besides, there is no
               possible danger. You know of my engagement
               to Lieutenant Curtis?

ARMITAGE: I hear he leaves to-morrow.

267

ENID: That is true. But the next day I am going on a visit to his mother, at Fenton. Indeed, there is no danger.

ARMITAGE: Well, I won't deny that I am consoled by what you say, but there's just one condition on which I would leave this house.

ENID: What is that?

ARMITAGE: Well, I remember your friend, Dr. Watson, at the inquest — and we've heard of his connection with Mr. Sherlock Holmes. If you'll promise me that you'll slip away to London to-morrow, see those two gentlemen, and get their advice, I'll wash my hands of it. I should feel that some one stronger than me Was looking after you.

ENID: Oh, Mr. Armitage, I couldn't.

ARMITAGE: (Folding his arms.)
Then I stay here.

ENID: It is Lieutenant Curtis's last day in England.

ARMITAGE: When does he leave?

ENID: In the evening.

ARMITAGE: Well if you go in the morning you'd be back in time.

ENID: But how can I get away?

ARMITAGE: Who's to stop you? Have you money?

ENID: Yes, I have enough.

ARMITAGE: Then go.

ENID: It is really impossible.

ARMITAGE: (Sitting.)
                 Very good. Then I'll have it out with Doctor.

ENID: (Crossing to him.)
                 There, there! I'll promise. I'll go. I won't have
                 you hurt I'll write and arrange it all somehow.

ARMITAGE: Word of honour?

ENID: Yes, yes I'll write to Dr Watson. Oh do go.
                 This way.
                 (Goes to the French window.)
                 If you keep among the laurels you can get to
                 the high road and no one will meet you.

ARMITAGE: (Going up to the windows. Pause. Returning.)
                 That dog about?

ENID: It is with the Doctor. Oh do go! and thank
                 you— Thank you with all my heart.

ARMITAGE: My wife and I can always take you in. Don't
                 you forget it.

ARMITAGE goes out ENID stands looking after him. As she does so
Mrs Staunton enters the room.

MRS STAUNTON: I saw Mr. Armitage going off through the
                 shrubbery.
                 (Looks out of window.)

ENID: Yes he has gone.

MRS. STAUNTON: But why did he not wait to see the Doctor.

ENID: He's changed his mind.

MRS STAUNTON: He is the most impertinent busybody in the
                 whole village. Fancy the insolence of him
                 coming up here without a with-your-leave or
                 by-your-leave. What was it he wanted, Miss
                 Enid?

Sir Arthur Conan Doyle

ENID: It is not your place, Mrs. Staunton, to ask such questions.

MRS. STAUNTON: Oh, indeed! For that matter, Miss Enid, I should not have thought it was your place to have secrets with the village grocer. The Doctor will want to know all about it.

ENID: What my stepfather may do is another matter. I beg, Mrs. Staunton, that you will attend to your own affairs and leave me alone.

MRS. STAUNTON: (Putting her arms akimbo.)
High and mighty, indeed! I'm to do all the work of the house, but the grocer can come in and turn me out of the room. If you think I am nobody you may find yourself mistaken some of these days.

ENID: How dare you—
(She makes for the door, as RYLOTT enters.)

RYLOTT: Why, Enid, what's the matter? Anyone been upsetting you? What's all this, Mrs. Staunton?

ENID: Mrs. Staunton has been rude to me.

RYLOTT: Dear, dear! Here's a storm in a teacup. Well, now, come and tell me all about it. No one shall bother my little Enid. What would her sailor boy say?

MRS. STAUNTON: Mr. Armitage has been here. He would speak with Miss Enid alone. I didn't think it right. That is why Miss Enid is offended.

RYLOTT: Where is the fellow?

MRS. STAUNTON: He is gone. He went off through the shrubbery.

RYLOTT: Upon my word, he seems to make himself at home. What did he want, Enid?

ENID: He wanted to know how I was.

RYLOTT: This is too funny! You have made a conquest,
                   Enid. You have a rustic admirer.

ENID: I believe he is a true friend who means well to
                   me.

RYLOTT: Astounding! Perhaps it is as well for him that
                   he did not prolong his visit. But now, my dear
                   girl, go to your room until I send for you. I am
                   very sorry that you have been upset, and I will
                   see that such a thing does not happen again.
                   Tut, tut! my little girl shall not be worried.
                   Leave it to me.
                   (Goes up to door with ENID.)

ENID goes out.

RYLOTT: Well, what is it, then? Why have you upset
                   her?

MRS. STAUNTON: Why has she upset me? Why should I be
                   always the last to be considered?

RYLOTT: Why should you be considered at all?

MRS. STAUNTON: You dare to say that to me—you that promised
                   me marriage only a year ago. If I was what I
                   should be, then there would be no talk as to
                   who is the mistress of this house. I'll put up
                   with no more of her tantrums, talking to me as
                   if I were the kitchen-maid.
                   (Turning from him.)

RYLOTT: You forget yourself.

MRS STAUNTON: I forget nothing. I don t forget your promise
                   and it will be a bad day for you if you don't
                   keep it.

RYLOTT: I'll put you out on the roadside if you dare
                   speak so to me.

MRS STAUNTON: You will, will you? Try it and see. I saved you once. Maybe I could do the other thing if I tried.

RYLOTT: Saved me?

MRS STAUNTON: Yes saved you. If it hadn't been for my evidence at that inquest that fellow Armitage would have taken the Jury with him. Yes he would. I've had it from them since.

RYLOTT: Well you only spoke the truth.

MRS STAUNTON: The truth! Do you think I don't know?

RYLOTT: What do you know?

She is silent and looks hard at him.

RYLOTT: What do you know?

She is still silent

RYLOTT: Don't look at me like that woman. What do you know?

MRS STAUNTON: I know enough

Pause.

RYLOTT: Tell me then—how did she die?

MRS STAUNTON: Only you know that. I may not know how she died but I know very well —

RYLOTT: (Interrupting.)
                 You were always fanciful Kate but I know very well that you have only my own interests at heart. Put it out of your head if I have said anything unkind. Don't quarrel with this little fool, or you may interfere with my plans.
                                  (CONT/)

272

Just wait a little longer and things will come straight with us. You know that I have a hasty temper but it is soon over.

MRS. STAUNTON: You can always talk me round, and you know it. Now, listen to me, for I am the only friend you've got. Don't try it again. You've got clear once. But a second would be too dangerous.

RYLOTT: They would make no more of the second than of the first. No one in the world can tell. It's impossible, I tell you. If she marries, half my income is gone.

MRS. STAUNTON: Yes, I know. Couldn't she sign it to you?

RYLOTT: She can be strong enough when she likes. She would never sign it to me. I hinted at it once, and she talked of a lawyer.
(Pause.)
But if anything should happen to her—well, there's an end to all our trouble.

MRS. STAUNTON: They must suspect.

RYLOTT: Let them suspect. But they can prove nothing.

MRS. STAUNTON: Not yet.

RYLOTT: On Wednesday she goes a-visiting, and who knows when she may return? No, it's to-morrow or never.

MRS. STAUNTON: Then let it be never.

RYLOTT: And lose half my income without a struggle? No, Kate, it's all or nothing with me now.

MRS. STAUNTON: Well, look out for Armitage.

RYLOTT: What about him?

273

MRS. STAUNTON: He must have known something before he dared to come here.

RYLOTT: What can he know of our affairs?

MRS. STAUNTON: There's Rodgers. You think he's half-witted. So he is. But he may know more and say more than we think. He talks and Armitage talks. Maybe Armitage gets hold of him.

RYLOTT: We'll soon settle that.
(Crossing to bell-pull.)
I'll twist the old rogue's neck if he has dared to play me false. There's one thing—he can't hold anything in if I want it to come out. Did you ever see a snake and a white mouse? You just watch.

Enter RODGERS.

RYLOTT: Come here, Rodgers.

RODGERS: Yes, sir.

RYLOTT: Stand here, where the light falls on your face, Rodgers. I shall know then if you are telling me the truth.

RODGERS: The truth, sir. Surely I would tell that.

RYLOTT: (Takes chair from behind settee.)
Sit there! Don't move! Now look at me. That's right. You can't lie to me now. You've been down to see Mr. Armitage.

RODGERS: Sir—I hope—there was no harm in that.

RYLOTT: How often?

RODGERS: Two or three times.

RYLOTT: How often?

RODGERS: Two or three—

RYLOTT: How often?

RODGERS: When I go to the village I always see him.

MRS STAUNTON: That's nearly every day.

RYLOTT: What have you told him about me?

RODGERS: Oh, sir, nothing.

RYLOTT: What have you told him?

RODGERS: Just the news of the house sir.

RYLOTT: What news?

RODGERS: Well, about Miss Enid's engagement, and Siva biting the gardener and the cook giving notice and the like.

RYLOTT: Nothing more than this?

RODGERS: No sir.

RYLOTT: Nothing more about Miss Enid?

RODGERS: No sir.

RYLOTT You swear it?

RODGERS: No, sir, no. I said nothing more.

RYLOTT: (Springing up catching him by the neck shaking him.)
You doddering old rascal how came you to say anything at all? I kept you here out of charity and you dare to gossip about my affairs. I've had enough of you —
(Throwing him off.)
(CONT/)

275

I'll go to London tomorrow and get a younger man. You pack up your things and go. Do you hear?

RODGERS: Won't you look it over sir? I'm an old man sir. I have no place to go to. Where am I to go?

RYLOTT: You can go to the devil for all I care, or to your friend Armitage the grocer. There is no place for you here. Get out of the room.

RODGERS: Yes sir. You won't reconsider it?

RYLOTT: Get out. And tell Miss Enid I want her.

RODGERS: Yes, sir.

RODGERS goes out.

MRS. STAUNTON: You have done wisely. He was not safe.

RYLOTT: The old devil suited me too in a way. A younger man may give more trouble.

MRS STAUNTON: You'll soon break him in.

RYLOTT: Yes, I expect I will.
(Crossing to her.)
Now, make it right with Enid for my sake. You must play the game to the end.

MRS. STAUNTON: It's all right. I'm ready for her.

Enter ENID.

RYLOTT: My dear, Mrs. Staunton is very sorry if she has given you any annoyance. I hope you will accept her apology in the same spirit that it is offered.

MRS. STAUNTON: I meant no harm, Miss Enid, and I was only thinking of the master's interests. I hope you'll forgive me.

ENID: Certainly, I forgive you, Mrs. Staunton.

RYLOTT: There's a good little girl. Now, Mrs. Staunton,
                   you had better leave us.

MRS. STAUNTON goes out.

RYLOTT: Now, my dear, you must not be vexed with
                   poor Mrs. Staunton, for she is a very hard-
                   working woman and devoted to her duty,
                   though, of course, her manners are often
                   wanting in polish. Come now, dear, say that it
                   is All right.

ENID sits on settee.

ENID: I have said that I forgive her.

RYLOTT: You must tell me anything I can do, to make
                   you happier. Of course, you have some one
                   else now, but I would not like you to forget
                   your old stepfather altogether. Until the day
                   when you have to leave me, I wish to do the
                   very best for you.

ENID: You are very kind.

RYLOTT: Can you suggest anything that I can do?

ENID: No, no, there is nothing.

RYLOTT: I was a little too rough last week. I am sorry for
                   that. I should wish your future husband to like
                   me. You will tell him, when you see him, that I
                   have done what I could to make you happy?

ENID: Yes, yes.

RYLOTT: You see him to-morrow?

ENID: Yes.

277

RYLOTT: And he leaves us to-morrow evening?
            (Sitting beside her on settee.)

ENID: Yes.

RYLOTT: You have all my sympathy, dear. But he will
            soon back again, and then, of course, you will
            part no more. You will be sorry to hear that old
            Rodgers has been behaving badly, and that I
            must get rid of him.

ENID: (Rising.)
            Rodgers! What has he done?

RYLOTT: He grows more foolish and incompetent every
            day. I propose to go to London myself
            tomorrow to get a new butler. Would you send
            a line in my name to the agents to say that I
            shall call about two o clock?

ENID: I will do so.

RYLOTT: There's a good little girl.
            (Pause. Crossing to her and placing his hand on
            her shoulder.)
            There's nothing on your mind, is there?

ENID: Oh no.

RYLOTT: Well then run away and get your letter written.
            I dare bet you have another of your own to
            write. One a day — or two a day?—what is his
            allowance? Well, well, we have all done it at
            some time.

Enter ALI with milk jug glass and saucer on a tray.

ALI: I beg pardon Sahib, I go.

RYLOTT: Come in! Come in! Put my milk down on the
            table.

ALI does so.

RYLOTT: Now my dear please don't forget to write the
                   letter to the agents.

ENID goes out.

RYLOTT: You fool! Why did you not make sure I was
                   alone?

ALI: I thought no one here but Sahib.

RYLOTT: Well as it happens there's no harm done.
                   (Goes to door and locks it. Pulls down blind of
                   window.)

While he does so ALI opens a cupboard and takes out a square wicker
work basket. RYLOTT pours milk into saucer and puts it before
basket. Then he cracks his fingers and whistles while ALI plays on an
Eastern flute.

CURTAIN

Scene 2
MR. SHERLOCK HOLMES' room in Baker Street.

Enter BILLY, showing in DR. WATSON.

WATSON: I particularly want to see Mr. Holmes.

BILLY: Well, sir, I expect he will be back almost
                   immediately.

WATSON: Is he very busy just now?

BILLY: Yes, sir, we are very busy. We don't get much
                   time to ourselves these days.

WATSON: Any particular case?

BILLY: Quite a number of cases, sir. Two German
                   princes and the Duchess of Ferrers yesterday.
                   The Pope's been bothering us again.
                              (CONT/)

279

Wants us to go to Rome over the cameo robbery. We are very overworked.

WATSON: Well, I'll wait for Mr. Holmes.

BILLY: Very good, sir. Here is The Times. There's four for him in the waiting-room now.

WATSON: Any lady among them?

BILLY: Not what I would call a lady, sir.

WATSON: All right, I'll wait.
(Lights a cigarette and looks around him.)
Just the same as ever. There are the old chemicals! Heavens! what have I not endured from those chemicals in the old days? Pistol practice on the wall. Quite so. I wonder if he still keeps tobacco in that Persian slipper? Yes, here it is. And his pipes in the coal-scuttle—black clays. Full of them—the same as ever.
(Takes one out and smells it.)
Faugh! Bottle of cocaine—Billy, Billy!

BILLY: I've done my best to break him of it, sir.

WATSON: All right, Billy, you can go.

BILLY goes out.

WATSON: There's the old violin—the same old violin, with one string left.
(Sits on settee.)

Enter SHERLOCK HOLMES, disguised as a workman, with tools.

HOLMES: You sent for me, Mr. Sherlock Holmes.

WATSON: I am not Mr. Holmes.

HOLMES: Beg pardon, sir, it was to mend the gas-bracket.

WATSON: What's wrong with it?

HOLMES: Leaking sir.

WATSON: Well go on with your work.

HOLMES: Yes, sir.
                     (Goes to the bracket.)
                     Hope I won't disturb you sir?

WATSON: (Taking up The Times.)
                     That's all right Don't mind me.

HOLMES: Very untidy man Mr. Holmes sir.

WATSON: What do you mean by that?

HOLMES: Well, sir, you can't help noticing it. It's all
                     over the room. I've 'eard say he was as tidy as
                     any when he started, but he learned bad 'abits
                     from a cove what lived with him. Watson was
                     his name.

Slips into bedroom.

WATSON: (Rising.)
                     You impertinent fellow! How dare you talk in
                     such a fashion? What do you want?
                     (Looks round.)
                     Why! What the deuce has become of him?

The workman emerges as SHERLOCK HOLMES, in dressing-gown
with hands in pockets.

WATSON: Good Heavens Holmes! I should never have
                     recognized you.

HOLMES: My dear Watson when you begin to recognize
                     me it will indeed be the beginning of the end.
                     When your eagle eye penetrates my disguise I
                     shall retire to an eligible poultry farm.

WATSON: But why—?

HOLMES:

A case my dear Watson a case! One of those small conundrums which a trustful public occasionally confides to my investigation. To the British workman, Watson, all doors are open. His costume is unostentatious and his habits are sociable. A tool bag is an excellent passport and a tawny moustache will secure the co-operation of the maids. It may interest you to know that my humble double is courting a cook at Battersea.
(Strikes match and lights pipe.)

WATSON:

My dear Holmes! Is it fair to the girl?

HOLMES:

Chivalrous old Watson! It's a game of life and death, and every card must be played! But in this case I have a hated rival — the constable on the adjoining beat — so when I disappear, all will readjust itself. We walk out on Saturday evenings. Oh! those walks! But the honour of a Duchess is at stake. A mad world, my masters.
(Turns to survey Watson.)
Well, Watson, what is your news?

WATSON:

(Smiling.)
Well, Holmes, I came here to tell you what I am sure will please you.

HOLMES:

Engaged, Watson, engaged! Your coat, your hat, your gloves, your buttonhole, your smile, your blush! The successful suitor shines from you all over. What I had heard of you or perhaps what I had not heard of you, had already excited my worst suspicions.
(Looks fixedly at Watson.)
But this is better and better, for I begin to perceive that it is a young lady whom I know and respect.

WATSON:

But, Holmes, this is marvellous. The lady is Miss Morstan, whom you have indeed met and admired. But how could you tell —

HOLMES: By the same observation, my dear Watson,
           which assures me that you have seen the lady
           this morning.
           (Picks a hair off WATSON's breast, wraps it
           round his finger, and glances at it with his
           lens.)
           Charming, my dear fellow, charming. There is
           no mistaking the Titian tint. You lucky fellow!
           I envy you.

WATSON: Thank you, Holmes. Some of these days I may
           find myself congratulating you.

HOLMES: No marriage without love, Watson.

WATSON: Then why not love?
           (Placing his hand on HOLMES' shoulders.)

HOLMES: Absurd, Watson, absurd! I am not for love, nor
           love for me. It would disturb my reason,
           unbalance my faculties. Love is like a flaw in
           the crystal, sand in the clockwork, iron near the
           magnet. No, no, I have other work in the
           world.

WATSON: You have, indeed. Billy says you are very busy
           just now.

HOLMES: There are one or two small matters.

WATSON: Have you room to consider one other—the
           case of Miss Enid Stonor?

HOLMES: My dear fellow, if you have any personal
           interest in it.
           (Sitting on divan.)

WATSON: Yes, I feel keenly about it.

HOLMES: (Taking out note-book.)
           Let us see how I stand.
                    (CONT/)

There is the Baxter Square murder — I have put the police on the track. The Clerkenwell Jewel Robbery — that is now clearing. The case of the Duchess of Ferrers— I have my material. The Pope's cameos. His Holiness must wait. The Princess who is about to run from home—let her run. I must see one or two who are waiting for me —
(Rings bell.)
— then I am entirely at your disposal.

Enter BILLY.

BILLY: Yes, Mr. Holmes.

HOLMES: How many are waiting?

BILLY: Three, sir.

HOLMES: A light morning. Show them in now.

BILLY goes out.

WATSON: Well, I'll look in later.

HOLMES: (Striking match and lighting pipe.)
No, no, my dear fellow! I have always looked on you as a partner in the Firm — Holmes, Watson, Billy & Co. That's our brass plate when we raise one. If you'll sit there I shall soon be free.

Enter BILLY, with a card on tray. .MR HOLT LOAMING follows, a rich, dissipated-looking, middle-aged man in an astrakhan-collared coat. BILLY goes out.

HOLMES: (Reading.)
Mr. Holt Loaming. I remember the name. A racing man, I believe?

LOAMING: Yes, sir.

HOLMES: Pray take a seat.

284

LOAMING draws up near the table.

HOLMES: What can I do for you?

LOAMING: Time's money, Mr. Holmes, both yours and
               mine. I'm pretty quick off the mark, and you
               won't mind that. I'm not here on the advice
               gratis line. Don't you think it. I've my cheque
               book here—
               (Takes it out.)
               —and there's plenty behind it. I won't grudge
               you your fee, Mr. Holmes. I promise you that.

HOLMES: Well, Mr. Loaming, let us hear the business.

LOAMING: My wife, Mr. Holmes—damn her!—she's
               given me the slip. Got back to her own people
               and they've hid her. There's the law, of course,
               but she'd get out all kinds of lies about ill-
               treatment. She's mine, and I'll just take her
               when I know where to lay my hands on her.

HOLMES: How would you take her?

LOAMING: I just have to walk up to her and beckon. She's
               one of those wincing kind of nervous fillies
               that kick about in the paddock but give in when
               once the bridle's on them and they feel the
               whip. You show me where she is, and I'll do
               the rest.

HOLMES: She is with her own people, you say?

LOAMING: Well, there's no man in the case, if that's what
               you're driving at. Lord! if you knew how
               straight she is, and how she carries on when I
               have a fling. She's got a cluster of aunts, and
               she's lyin' low somewhere among them. It's
               for you to put her up.

HOLMES: I fancy not, Mr. Loaming.

LOAMING: Eh? What's that?

HOLMES: I rather like to think of her among that cluster of aunts.

LOAMING: But, damn it, sir, she's my wife.

HOLMES: That's why!

LOAMING;   (Getting up.)
Well, it's a rum start, this. Look here, you don't know what you're missing. I'd have gone to five hundred. Here's the cheque.

HOLMES: The case does not attract me.
(Rings bell.)

Enter BILLY.

HOLMES: Show Mr. Loaming out, Billy.

LOAMING: It's the last you'll see of me, Mr. Holmes.

HOLMES: Life is full of little consolations.

LOAMING: Damn!

He takes his hat and goes out with BILLY.

HOLMES: I'm afraid I shall never be a rich man, Watson.

Re-enter BILLY.

HOLMES: Well?

BILLY: Mr. James B. Montague, sir.

Enter MONTAGUE, as BILLY goes out.

HOLMES: Good morning, Mr. Montague. Pray take a chair.

MONTAGUE sits.

HOLMES: What can I do?

MONTAGUE: (A furtive-looking man with furtive ways.)
              Anything fresh about the sudden death of my
              brother, sir? The police said it was murder, and
              you said it was murder; but we don't get any
              further, do we?
              (Placing hat on floor.)

HOLMES: I have not lost sight of it.

MONTAGUE: That man Henderson was a bad man, Holmes,
              an evil liver and a corruption. Yes, sir, a
              corruption a danger. Who knows what passed
              between them? I've suspicions—I've always
              had my suspicions.

HOLMES: So you said.

MONTAGUE: Have you worked any further on that line, sir?
              Because, if you tell me from time to time how
              it is shaping, I may be able to give you a word
              in season.

HOLMES: I have my eye on him—a very cunning rascal,
              as you say. We have not enough to arrest him
              on, but we work away in the hope.

MONTAGUE: Good, Mr. Holmes, good! Watch him; you'll
              get him, as safe as Judgment.

HOLMES: I'll let you know if anything comes of it.
              (Rings bell.)

MONTAGUE: (Rising.)
              That's right, sir. Watch 'im. I'm his brother,
              sir. It's me that should know. It's never out of
              my mind.

Enter BILLY.

HOLMES: Very good, Mr. Montague. Good-morning.

MONTAGUE and BILLY go out.

HOLMES: Curious little murder, Watson; done for most inadequate motive. That was the murderer.

WATSON: Good Heavens!

HOLMES: My case is almost complete. Meanwhile I amuse him and myself by the pretended pursuit of the wrong man — an ancient device, Watson.

Re-enter BILLY.

HOLMES: Well, any more?

BILLY: Mr. Milverton is here, Mr. Holmes.

HOLMES: Show him in when I ring.

BILLY goes out.

HOLMES: I am sorry to delay the business upon which you wished to consult me; but this, I hope, will be the last. You remember Milverton?

WATSON: No.

HOLMES: Ah! it was after your time. The most crawling reptile in London — the King of the Blackmailers — a cunning, ruthless devil. I have traced seventeen suicides to that man's influence. It is he who is after the Duchess of Ferrers.

WATSON: The beautiful Duchess, whose re-marriage is announced?

HOLMES: Exactly. He has a letter which he thinks would break off the wedding.
(Rings.)
It is my task to regain it.

Enter MILVERTON.

HOLMES: Well, Mr. Milverton. Pray take a seat.

MILVERTON: Who is this?

HOLMES: My friend, Dr. Watson. Do you mind?

MILVERTON: (Sitting.)
Oh! I have no object in secrecy. It is your client's reputation, not mine, which is at stake.

HOLMES: Your reputation! Good Heavens!
(Crossing to fireplace and filling pipe from slipper.)

MILVERTON: Not much to lose there, is there, Mr. Holmes? I can't be hurt. But she can. Hardly a fair fight, is it?

HOLMES: What are the terms now?
(Filling pipe.)

MILVERTON: Steady at seven thousand. No money—no marriage.

HOLMES: Suppose she tells the whole story to the Marquis? Then your letter is not worth sixpence. He would condone all. Come, now, what harm is in the letter?

MILVERTON: (Sprightly — very sprightly.)
However, it is purely a matter of business. If you think it is in the best interests of your client that the Marquis should see the letter— why, you would be very foolish to pay a large sum to regain it.

HOLMES: The lady has no great resources.

MILVERTON: But her marriage is a most suitable time for her friends and relations to make some little effort. I can assure you that this envelope would give more joy than all the tiaras and bracelets in Regent Street.

HOLMES:	No, it is impossible!
MILVERTON:	Dear me! Dear me! How unfortunate.
HOLMES:	It can profit you in no way to push matters to an end.
MILVERTON:	There you mistake. I have other cases maturing. If it were known that I had been severe on the Duchess the others would be more open to reason.
HOLMES:	Well, well, you give us till noon to-morrow? (Rings.)
MILVERTON:	But not an hour longer.

Enter BILLY.

HOLMES:	We are at your mercy. Surely you won't treat us too harshly?
MILVERTON:	Not a minute longer. (Putting on hat.)

BILLY and MILVERTON go out.

HOLMES:	Terrible! Terrible! A fumigator would be useful, eh, Watson — Pah!
WATSON:	What can you do?
HOLMES:	My dear Watson—what have I done? It is this gentleman's cook who has honoured me. In the intervals of philandering, I have made an acquaintance with the lock on the safe. Mr. Milverton spent last night at his club; when he returns home he will find there has been a little burglary at The Battersea, and his precious letter is missing. (Rings bell.)
WATSON:	Holmes, you are splendid!

Enter BILLY.

HOLMES:	Tut, tut! (To BILLY.) Well, any more?
BILLY:	One lady, sir—just come—Miss Enid Stonor, of Stoke Moran.
WATSON:	Ah! this is the case. (Rising.)
HOLMES:	I'll ring, Billy.

BILLY goes out.

HOLMES:	Now, Watson! Stonor! Stonor! Surely I associate the name with something?
WATSON:	I told you of the case at the time. Sudden mysterious death of a girl at an old house in Stoke Moran, some two years ago.
HOLMES:	My dear fellow! it all comes back to me. An inquest was it not, with a string of most stupid and ineffectual witnesses.
WATSON:	I was one of them.
HOLMES:	Of course — so you were, so you were. I docketed the evidence. It introduced to my notice a gentleman of singular and most interesting personality. I have a few notes. (Takes down a scrapbook from a row.) Let's see—it's R—Ranter—Roma — Rylott! That's our man. Fifty-five years of age, killed his khitmutgar in India; once in a madhouse, married money—wife died — distinguished surgeon. Well, Watson, what has the distinguished surgeon been up to now? (Throwing scrapbook on divan.)
WATSON:	Devilry, I fear.

HOLMES: I have the case very clear in my mind.

WATSON: Then you may remember that the death of the lady followed close upon her engagement?

HOLMES: Exactly.

WATSON: Miss Enid Stonor in turn became engaged, about a month ago, to a neighbour, Lieutenant Curtis.

HOLMES: Ah!

WATSON: Unhappily, the young man leaves for the Mediterranean to-day. She will henceforward be alone at Stoke Moran.

HOLMES: I see.

WATSON: And some circumstances have excited her alarm.

HOLMES: I gather that the amiable stepfather stands to lose in case of a marriage.

WATSON: That is so. Of course, supposing that Rylott did the other girl to death, it seems unlikely, on the face of it, that he would try it on again, as two sudden deaths in the house could hardly pass the coroner —

HOLMES: No, no, Watson! you are making the mistake of putting your normal brain into Rylott's abnormal being. The born criminal is often a monstrous egotist. His mind is unhinged from the beginning. What he wants he must have. Because he thinks a thing, it is right. Because he does a thing, it will escape detection. You can't say a priori that he will take this view or that one. Perhaps we had best have the young lady in.
(Rings bell.)

                    (CONT/)

> My dear fellow, you'll get into trouble if you
> go about righting the wrongs of distressed
> damsels. It won't do, Watson, it really won't.

Enter ENID. WATSON gets up and meets her.

WATSON: How do you do, Miss Enid? This is my friend,
        Mr. Holmes, of whom I spoke.

HOLMES shakes hands with ENID.

HOLMES: How do you do, Miss Stonor? Dear me! you
        must find a dog-cart a cold conveyance in this
        weather.

ENID: A dog-cart, Mr. Holmes?

HOLMES: One can hardly fail to observe the tell-tale
        splashes on the left sleeve. A white horse and
        clay soil are indicated. But what is this? You
        are trembling. Do sit down.

ENID: (Looking round and sitting on settee.)
        Tell me, Mr. Holmes, my stepfather has not
        been here?

HOLMES: No.

ENID: He saw me in the street. I dashed past him in a
        cab. he saw me; our eyes met, and he waved
        me to stop.

HOLMES: Why is your stepfather in London?

ENID: He came up on business.

HOLMES: It would be interesting to know what the
        business was.

ENID: It was to get a new butler. Rodgers, our old
        one, left us, and a new butler is to come at
        once. I doubt if any servant would come to
        such a place.

HOLMES:	He may certainly find some difficulty. He would, no doubt, apply to an agent.
ENID:	At two o'clock, to Patterson and Green, of Cavendish Street.
HOLMES:	Exactly. I know them. But this is a digression, is it not? We get back to the fact that he saw you in the street?
ENID:	Yes, it was in Pall Mall. I fancy he followed me.
HOLMES:	Would he imagine you would come here?
ENID:	No, he would think I was going to Dr. Watson's. He knows that Dr. Watson is my only friend in London.
HOLMES:	What has been Dr. Ryolott's attitude towards you your engagement?
ENID:	He has been much kinder, because he knows I have one to protect me. But even so, there are moments — (Raises her arm.)
HOLMES:	Good Heavens!
ENID:	He does not realize his own strength. When he is angry he is like a fierce wild beast. Only last week he thrashed the blacksmith.
HOLMES:	He is welcome to the blacksmith, but not to my clients. This must not occur again. Does your fiancé know of this?
ENID:	I would not dare to tell him. He would do something dreadful. Besides, as I say, my stepfather has, on the whole, been kinder. But there is a look in his eyes, when I turn on him suddenly, that chills me to the bone. (CONT/)

His kindness is from his head, not from his heart. I feel as if he were waiting—waiting—

HOLMES: Waiting for what?

ENID: Waiting for my fiancé to leave. Waiting till he has me at his mercy. That room freezes my blood. Often I cannot sleep for horror.

WATSON: What? He has changed your room?
(Rising from armchair.)

ENID: My old room is under repair.

WATSON: You sleep, then, in the room where your sister died?

ENID: In the same room. And other things have happened. The music has come again.

HOLMES: The music? Tell me about this music.

ENID: It came before my sister's death. She spoke of it, and then I heard it myself the night she died. But it has come again. Oh, Mr. Holmes, I am terrified.

HOLMES: There, there! you've had enough to break any one's nerve. This—music—does it seem to be inside the house or outside?

ENID: Indeed, I could not say.

HOLMES: What is it like?

ENID: A sort of soft, droning sound.

HOLMES: Like a flute or pipe?

ENID: Yes. It reminds me of my childhood in India.

HOLMES: Ah—India?

ENID: And there's one other thing that puzzles me — my sister's dying words — as she lay in my arms she gasped out two words.

HOLMES: What were they?

ENID: "Band" and "Speckled."

HOLMES: Band—speckled—and Indian music. You sleep with your door and window fastened?

ENID: Yes, but so did poor Violet. It did not save her, and it may not save me.

HOLMES: Could there be anything in the nature of secret doors or panels?

ENID: No. I have searched again and again. There is nothing.

HOLMES: And nothing peculiar in the room?

ENID: No, I cannot say there is.

HOLMES: I must really drop in and have a look at this most interesting apartment. Suggestive—very suggestive.
(Pause.)
When did you hear this music last?

ENID: Last night.

HOLMES: And your fiancé leaves to-day?

ENID: He leaves to-day. What shall I do?

HOLMES: Well, Miss Stonor, I take up your case. It presents features which commend it to me. You must put yourself into my hands.

ENID: I do—unreservedly.
(Rising, and crossing to him.)

HOLMES: (To WATSON.)
            It is a question whether we are justified in
            letting her return at All to Stoke Moran.

ENID: I must return. At five o'clock my fiancé leaves,
            and I shall not see him again for months.

HOLMES: Ah! that is a complication. Where is the
            A.B.C.?
            (Finds it in umbrella stand.)
            Stonehouse—Stowell—Stoke—

ENID: I know my train, Mr. Holmes.

HOLMES: I was looking for mine.

ENID: You are coming down?

HOLMES: I shall not be content until I have seen this
            room of yours. Yes, that will do. I could get up
            to you between eleven and twelve, to-night.
            Would you have the goodness to leave your
            shutter open? The room is, I understand, upon
            the ground floor?

ENID: Oh! Mr. Holmes, it is not safe. You cannot
            think of the danger.

HOLMES: I have taken up your case, Miss Stonor, and
            this is part of it. Have you any friends in Stoke
            Moran?

ENID: Mr. Armitage and his wife.

HOLMES: That is most fortunate. Now, listen to me, Miss
            Stonor. When you have returned home certain
            circumstances may arise which will ensure
            your safety. In that case you will at Stoke Place
            until I come in the evening. On the other hand,
            things may miscarry, and you may not be safe.
            In that case I will so manage that a warning
            will reach you.
                            (CONT/)

297

	You will then break from home and take refuge with the Armitages. Is that clear?
ENID:	Who will bring me the warning?
HOLMES:	I cannot say. But you have my assurance that it will come.
ENID:	Then, until it does, I will stay at Stoke Place.
HOLMES:	And should any new development occur you could always send me a telegram, could you not?
ENID:	Yes, I could do that.
HOLMES:	Then it is not goodbye, but au revoir.

Enter BILLY.

HOLMES:	What is it?
BILLY:	Please, Mr. Holmes, a gentleman to see you, at once.
HOLMES:	Who is he?
BILLY:	A very impatient gentleman, sir. It was all I could do to get him to stay in the waiting-room.
ENID:	Is he tall, dark, with a black beard, and a long white scar on his cheek?
BILLY:	That's him, Miss.
ENID:	Oh, Mr. Holmes, what shall I do? He has followed me.
WATSON:	If he went to my rooms, my landlady had instructions to send any one on here.
HOLMES:	Exactly.

ENID:	Oh! I dare not meet him, I dare not. Can't I slip out somehow?
HOLMES:	I see no reason why you should stay. Billy, show the lady out by the side passage.
BILLY:	Don't be alarmed, Miss, I'll see you through.

BILLY and ENID go out.

WATSON:	This fellow is dangerous, Holmes. You may need a weapon.
HOLMES:	There's something of the kind in that drawer at your right.

Enter BILLY.

BILLY:	Shall I stay when I show him in, Mr. Holmes?
HOLMES:	Why so?
BILLY:	An ugly customer, Mr.. Holmes.
HOLMES:	Tut, tut! show him up.

BILLY goes out.

HOLMES:	Well, Watson I must thank you for a most interesting morning. You are certainly the stormy petrel of crime.

Enter DR RYLOTT.

RYLOTT:	This is Mr. Sherlock Holmes I believe.
HOLMES:	Your belief is justified.
RYLOTT:	I have reason to think that you have taken unsolicited interest in my affairs.
HOLMES:	Your name being—?

RYLOTT: My name, sir, is Grimesby Rylott—Doctor
             Grimesby Rylott, of Stoke Moran.
             (Throws down card.)

HOLMES: A pretty place, I hear! And obviously good for
             the lungs.

RYLOTT: Sir, you are trifling with me. I have come here
             to ask whether you have had a visit from my
             stepdaughter, Miss Enid Stonor —

HOLMES: The first law in my profession, Doctor, is never
             to answer questions.

RYLOTT: Sir, you shall answer me.

HOLMES: We could do with warmer weather.

RYLOTT: I insist upon an answer.

HOLMES: But I hear the crocuses are coming on.

RYLOTT: Curse your crocuses! I've heard of you, you
             meddling busybody. And you, Dr. Watson—I
             expected to find you here. What do you mean
             by interfering with my lawful affairs?

WATSON: So long as they are lawful, Dr. Rylott, no one
             is likely to interfere with them.

RYLOTT: Now look here, Mr. Holmes, perhaps I may
             seem to you a little hot-headed—

HOLMES: Dear me, Dr. Rylott, what put that idea into
             your head?

RYLOTT: I apologize if I have seemed rude —
             (Sitting.)

HOLMES: Robust — a little robust — nothing more.

RYLOTT: I wish to put the matter to you as man to man.
                         (CONT/)

	You know what girls are, how sudden and unreasonable their prejudices may be. Imagine, sir, how hurt I should feel to be distrusted by one whom I have loved.
HOLMES:	You have my deep sympathy, Dr. Rylott.
RYLOTT:	(Pleased.) Ah!
HOLMES:	You are a most unfortunate man. There was that tragedy two years ago—
RYLOTT:	Yes, indeed!
HOLMES:	I think I could help you in that matter.
RYLOTT:	How so?
HOLMES:	As a friend, and without a fee.
RYLOTT:	You are very good.
HOLMES:	I am very busy, but your case seems so hard that I will put everything aside to assist you.
RYLOTT:	In what way, sir?
HOLMES:	I will come down at once, examine the room in which the tragedy occurred, and see if such small faculties as I possess can throw any light upon the matter.
RYLOTT:	Sir, this is an intolerable liberty. (Rising.)
HOLMES:	What! you don't want help?
RYLOTT:	It is intolerable, I say. What I ask you to do— what I order you to do is to leave my affairs alone. Alone, sir—do you hear me?
HOLMES:	You are perfectly audible.

301

RYLOTT: I'll have no interference—none! Don't dare to meddle with me. D'you hear, the pair of you? You—Holmes, I'm warning you.

HOLMES: (Looking at his watch.)
I fear I must end this interview. Time flies when one is chatting. Life has its duties as well as its pleasures, Doctor.

RYLOTT: Insolent rascal! I'll—I'll—
(Turns to the grate and picks up the poker.)

WATSON jumps up.

HOLMES: No, Watson, no! It does need poking, but perhaps you would put on a few coals first.

RYLOTT: You laugh at me? You don't know the man you are dealing with. You think that my strength fails because my hair is turned. I was the strongest man in India once. See that!
(Bends the poker and throws it down at HOLMES' feet.)
I am not a safe man to play with, Mr. Holmes.

HOLMES: Nor am I a safe man to play with, Dr. Rylott. Let me see—what were we talking about before the Sandow performance?

RYLOTT: You shall not overcrow me with your insolence! I tell you now, and you, too, Dr. Watson, that you interfere with my affairs to your own danger. You have your warning.

HOLMES: I'll make a note of it.

RYLOTT: And you refuse to tell me if Miss Stonor has been here?

HOLMES: Don't we seem to be travelling just a little in a circle?

RYLOTT: (Picking up hat from table.)
                  Well, you can't prevent me from finding out
                  from her.

HOLMES: Ah! there I must talk a little seriously to you
                  Grimesby Rylott. You have mentioned this
                  young lady, and I know something of her
                  circumstances. I hold you responsible. My eye
                  is on you sir and the Lord help you — the Lord
                  help you if any harm befall her. Now leave this
                  room, and take my warning with you.

RYLOTT: You cursed fool! I may teach you both not to
                  meddle with what does not concern you. Keep
                  clear of Stoke Moran!

RYLOTT goes out slamming the door.

HOLMES: I had a presentiment he would slam the door.

WATSON rises.

HOLMES: Stoke Moran must be less dull than many
                  country villages. Quite a breezy old gentleman
                  Watson. Well I must thank you for a pretty
                  problem. What the exact danger may be which
                  destroyed one sister and now threatens the
                  other may be suspected, but cannot yet be
                  defined. That is why I must visit the room.

WATSON: I will come with you Holmes.

HOLMES: My dear fellow you are no longer an
                  unattached knight-errant. Dangerous quests are
                  forbidden. What would Morstan say?

WATSON: She would say that the man who would desert
                  his friend would never make a good husband.

HOLMES: Well, my dear Watson, it may be our last
                  adventure together, so I welcome your co-
                  operation.

WATSON: Well, I'll be off.

HOLMES: You will leave Victoria to night at eleven fifteen, for Stoke Moran.

WATSON: Good bye — I'll see you at the station.

HOLMES: Perhaps you will.

WATSON goes.

HOLMES: Perhaps you will!
(Rings bell.)
Perhaps you won't!
(Stands near fire.)

Enter BILLY.

BILLY: Yes, sir.

HOLMES: Ever been in love Billy?

BILLY: Not of late years, sir.

HOLMES: Too busy, eh?

BILLY: Yes, Mr. Holmes.

HOLMES: Same here. Got my bag there, Billy?

BILLY: Yes, sir.
(Puts it on table.)

HOLMES: Put in that revolver.

BILLY: Yes, sir.

HOLMES: And the pipe and pouch.

BILLY: (Takes it from table.)
Yes, sir.

HOLMES: Got the dark lantern?

BILLY: Yes, sir.

HOLMES: The lens and the tape?

BILLY: Yes, sir.

HOLMES: Plaster of Paris, for prints?

BILLY: Yes, sir.

HOLMES: Oh, and the cocaine.
                (Hands it.)

BILLY: Yes, sir.
                (Throws it down.)

HOLMES: You young villain! you've broken it.
                (Takes his ear and turns his head round.)
                You're a clever boy, Billy.

BILLY: Yes, Mr. Holmes.

CURTAIN

Act III

Scene 1
The Hall of Stoke Place

MRS STAUNTON is discovered at the back reading a telegram

MRS STAUNTON: Are you there Rodgers?

Enter RODGERS.

RODGERS: Well, Mrs. Staunton.

MRS STAUNTON: I've had a telegram from the master. He will be here presently. He is bringing the new butler with him so you can hand over to-night.

RODGERS: To-night, Mrs Staunton. It all seems very sudden.

MRS STAUNTON: Peters will need your room. That's his name, Peters. He brings a young girl with him, his daughter. The attic will do for her. That will do Rodgers.

RODGERS goes into the morning room.

Enter ENID from the entrance hall.

ENID: Oh, Mrs Staunton.

MRS STAUNTON: Yes, Miss.

ENID: Has any message come in my absence?

MRS STAUNTON: No, Miss.

ENID: Let me know at once if any comes.

ENID goes into the bedroom wing.

MRS STAUNTON: Yes Miss. A message! A message!

Enter ALI hurriedly.

MRS SAUNDERS: (To him.)
Well?

ALI: Has she come back?

MRS STAUNTON: Yes, she is in her room.

ALI: I see her meet Curtis Sahib. Then I lose her.

MRS. STAUNTON: Well, she has come back. I have heard from the master. She is not to go out any more. He will come soon. Until he does, we must hold her. She asked if there was a message for her. Who can she expect a message from? Ah—stand back, Ali, she's coming.

ALI stands at door to servants' hall.

Re-enter ENID, still dressed for walking.

MRS. STAUNTON: I beg pardon, Miss, but what are you going to do?

ENID: I am going down to the village.
(Crosses towards entrance hall.)

MRS. STAUNTON: What for?

ENID: How dare you ask me such a question? What do you mean by it?

MRS. STAUNTON: I thought it was something we could do for you.

ENID: It was not.

MRS. STAUNTON: Then I am sorry, Miss, but it can't be done. The Doctor didn't like you going to London to-day. His orders are that you should not go out again.

ENID: How dare you? I am going out now.

MRS. STAUNTON: Get to the door, Ali! It's no use, Miss, we must
                        obey our orders. You don't budge from here.

ENID: What is the meaning of this?

MRS. STAUNTON: It is not for the likes of us to ask the meaning.
                        The Doctor is a good master, but his servants
                        have to obey him.

ENID: I will go out.
                        (Tries to rush past.)

MRS. STAUNTON: Lock the door, Ali.

ALI locks the door to the entrance hall.

MRS STAUNTON   The other locks are locked as well. You
                        needn't try the windows, for Siva is loose. All
                        right, Ali, give me the key—you can go!

ALI goes into the servants' hall.

MRS STAUNTON: Now, Miss, do what the Doctor wishes. That's
                        my advice to you.

She exits into the servants' hall.

ENID waits until she has gone; then she rushes across to the writing-
table and scribbles a telegram.

RODGERS enters from the morning-room.

ENID: Oh, Rodgers—

RODGERS: Yes, Miss.

ENID: Come here, Rodgers!

RODGERS comes down.

ENID: I want to speak to you. I hear that you are
             leaving us. I wanted say how sorry I am.

RODGERS: God bless you, Miss Enid. My heart is sore to
             part with you. All the kindness I've ever had in
             this house has from poor Miss Violet and you.

ENID: Rodgers, if ever I have done anything for you,
             you can repay it now a hundredfold.

RODGERS: Nothing against the master, Miss Enid! Don't
             ask to do anything against the master.

ENID: How can you love him?

RODGERS: Love him! No, no, I don't love him, Miss Enid.
             But I fear him—oh! I fear him. One glance of
             his eyes seems to cut me — to pierce me like a
             sword. I wouldn't even listen to anything
             against him, for I feel it would come round to
             him, and then — then—!

ENID: What can he do to you?

RODGERS: Oh, I couldn't, Miss Enid—don't ask me. What
             a man! what a man! Has he a child in his room,
             Miss Enid?

ENID: A child?

RODGERS: Yes—the milk—who drinks the milk? He
             drinks no milk. Every morning I take up the
             jug of milk. And the music, who is it he plays
             the music to?

ENID: Music! You have heard it, too. I'm so
             frightened. I'm in danger. I know I'm in
             danger.
             (Rising.)

RODGERS: In danger, Miss Enid?

ENID: And you can save me.

RODGERS: Oh, Miss Enid, I couldn't—I couldn't—I have
            no nerve. I couldn't.

ENID: All I want you to do is to take a telegram.

RODGERS: A telegram, Miss Enid?

ENID: They won't let me out, and yet I must send it.

RODGERS: Perhaps they won't let me out.

ENID: You could wait a little, and then slip away to
            the office.

RODGERS: What is the telegram, Miss Enid? Say it slowly.
            My poor old head is not as clear as it used to
            be.

ENID: Give it to the clerk.

RODGERS: No, no, I must be sure it is nothing against the
            master.

ENID: It is my business—only mine. Your master's
            name is not even mentioned. See — it is to Mr.
            Sherlock Holmes — he is a friend of mine —
            Baker Street, London. "Come to me as soon as
            you can. Please hurry." That is All. Dear
            Rodgers, it means so much to me—please—
            please take it for me.

RODGERS: I can't understand things like I used.

ENID: Oh! Do take it, Rodgers! You said yourself that
            I had always been kind to you. You will take it,
            won't you?
            (Holds out telegram to RODGERS.)

RODGERS: Yes, yes, I will take it, Miss Enid.
            (Takes telegram and puts it in his pocket.)

ENID: Oh! You don't know what a service you are
                   doing. It may save me—it may save my going
                   all the way to town.

RODGERS: Well, well, of course I will take it. What's that?

Wheels heard outside.

Enter MRS. STAUNTON and ALI.

MRS. STAUNTON: Quick, Ali! get the door unlocked. He won't
                   like to be kept waiting. Rodgers, be ready to
                   receive your master.

ENID: (To RODGERS.)
                   Don't forget—as soon as you can.

She goes into the bedroom wing, followed by MRS. STAUNTON.

Wheels stop.

ALI throws open the hall door and salaams. Enter RYLOTT, followed
by HOLMES, disguised as Peters, the new butler, who is followed by
BILLY, disguised as a young girl, with a big hat-box.

RYLOTT: (Taking off things and handing them to ALI.)
                   Where is Miss Enid? Did she return?

ALI: Yes, sir, she is in her room.

RYLOTT: Ah!
                   (To RODGERS.)
                   What! still here.

RODGERS: I had some hopes, sir—

RYLOTT: Get away! Lay the supper! I'll deal with you
                   presently.

RODGERS goes into the servants' hall.

RYLOTT: Ali, you can go also.
                              (CONT/)

311

<table>
<tr><td></td><td>Show this young girl to the kitchen.
(To HOLMES.)
What is her name?</td></tr>
<tr><td>HOLMES:</td><td>Amelia—the same as her mother's.</td></tr>
<tr><td>RYLOTT:</td><td>Go to the kitchen, child, and make yourself useful.</td></tr>
</table>

ALI goes out, followed by BILLY.

RYLOTT:	(To HOLMES.) Now, my man, we may as well understand each other first as last. I'm a man who stands no nonsense in my own house. I give good pay, but I exact good service. Do you understand?
HOLMES:	Yes, sir.
RYLOTT:	I've had a man for some time, but he is old and useless. I want a younger man to keep the place in order. Rodgers will show you the cellar and the other things you should know. You take over from to-morrow morning.
HOLMES:	Very good, sir. I'm sure, sir, it was very good of you to take me with such an encumbrance as my poor little orphaned Amelia.
RYLOTT:	I've taken you not only with a useless encumbrance but without references and without a character. Why have I done that? Because I expect I shall get better service out of you. Where are you to find a place if you lose this one? Don't you forget it.
HOLMES:	I won't forget, sir. I'll do all I can. If I can speak to your late butler, sir, I have no doubt he will soon show me my duties.
RYLOTT:	Very good. (Rings bell.)

Enter MRS. STAUNTON from the bedroom wing.

RYLOTT: Mrs. Staunton, tell Rodgers I want him. By the
                    way, where is Siva?

MRS. STAUNTON: Loose in the park, sir.

She goes into the servants' hall.

RYLOTT: By the way, I had best warn you, Peters, not to
                    go out till my boar-hound comes to know you.
                    She's not safe with strangers — not very safe
                    with any one but myself.

HOLMES: I'll remember, sir.

RYLOTT: Warn that girl of yours.

Enter RODGERS.

HOLMES: Yes, I will.

RYLOTT: Ah, Rodgers, you will hand your keys over to
                    Peters. When you have done so, come to me in
                    the study.

RODGERS: Yes, sir.

RYLOTT goes into his study.

HOLMES: (After looking round.)
                    Well, I'm not so sure that I think so much of
                    this place. Maybe you are the lucky one after
                    all. I hope I am not doing you out of your job.
                    I'd chuck it for two pins. If it wasn't for
                    Amelia I'd chuck it now.

RODGERS: If it wasn't you it would be some one else. Old
                    Rodgers is finished—used up. But he said he
                    wanted to see me in the study. What do you
                    think he wants with me in the study?

HOLMES:	Maybe to thank you for your service; maybe to make you a parting present.
RODGERS:	His eyes were hard as steel. What can he want with me? I get nervous these days, Mr. Peters. What was it he told me to do?
HOLMES:	To hand over the keys. (Taking his overcoat off.)
RODGERS:	Yes, yes, the keys. (Taking out keys.) They are here, Mr. Peters. That's the cellar key, Mr. Peters. Be careful about the cellar. That was the first time he struck me — when I mistook the claret for the Burgundy. He's often hasty, but he always kept his hands off till then.
HOLMES:	But the more I see of this place the less I fancy it. I'd be off to-night, but it's not so easy these days to get a place if your papers ain't in order. See here, Mr. Rodgers, I'd like to know a little more about my duties. The study is there, ain't it?
RODGERS:	Yes, he is there now, waiting— waiting for me.
HOLMES:	Where is his room?
RODGERS:	You see the passage yonder. Well, the first room you come to is the master's bedroom; the next is Miss Enid's —
HOLMES:	I see. Well, now, could you take me along to the master's room and show me any duties I have there?
RODGERS:	The master's room? No one ever goes into the master's room. All the time I've been here I've never put my head inside the door.

HOLMES: (Surprised.)
                 What? no one at all?

RODGERS: Ali goes. Ali is the Indian valet. But no one
                 else.

HOLMES: I wonder you never mistook the door and just
                 walked in.

RODGERS: You couldn't do that for the door is locked.

HOLMES: Oh! he locks his door does he? Dear me! None
                 of the keys here any use, I suppose?

RODGERS: Don't think of such a thing. What are you
                 saying? Why should you wish to enter the
                 master's room?

HOLMES: I don't want to enter it. The fewer rooms the
                 less work. Why do you suppose he locks the
                 door?

RODGERS: It is not for me nor for you to ask why the
                 master does things. He chooses to do so. That
                 is enough for us.

HOLMES: Well Mr. Rodgers if you'll excuse my saying
                 so, this old 'ouse 'as taken some of the spirit
                 out of you. I'm sure I don't wonder. I don't see
                 myself staying here very long. Wasn't there
                 some one died here not so long ago?

RODGERS: I'd rather not talk of it, Mr. Peters.

HOLMES: A woman died in the room next the doctor's.
                 The cabman was telling me as we drove up.

RODGERS: Don't listen to them, Mr. Peters. The master
                 would not like it. Here is Miss Enid and the
                 Doctor wants me.

Enter ENID from the bedroom wing.

ENID: Rodgers can I have a word with you?

RODGERS: Very sorry Miss Enid, the master wants me.

RODGERS goes into the study.

ENID: (To HOLMES.)
                         Are you—?

HOLMES: I am Peters, Miss, the new butler

ENID: Oh!
                         (Sits down beside table and writes.)

HOLMES crosses and stands behind the table. Pause.

ENID: Why do you stand there? Are you a spy set to
                         watch me? Am I never to have one moment of
                         privacy?

HOLMES: I beg pardon, Miss.

ENID: I'm sorry if I have spoken bitterly. I have had
                         enough to make me bitter.

HOLMES: I'm very sorry. Miss. I'm new to the place and
                         don't quite know where I am yet. May I ask
                         Miss if your name is Stonor?

ENID: Yes. Why do you ask?

HOLMES: There was a lad at the station with a message
                         for you.

ENID: (Rising.)
                         A message for me! Oh! it is what I want of All
                         things on earth! Why did you not take it?

HOLMES: I did take it, Miss, it is here.
                         (Hands her a note.)

ENID: (Tears it open, reads.)
                 "Fear nothing, and stay where you are. All will
                 be right. Holmes." Oh! it is a ray of sunshine in
                 the darkness—such darkness. Tell me, Peters,
                 who was this boy?

HOLMES: I don't know, Miss—just a very ordinary
                 nipper. The Doctor had gone on to the cab, and
                 the boy touched my sleeve and asked me to
                 give you this note in your own hand.

ENID: You said nothing to the Doctor.

HOLMES: Well, Miss, it seemed to be your business, not
                 his. I just took it, and there it is.

ENID: God bless you for it.
                 (She conceals the note in her bosom.)

HOLMES: I'm only a servant, Miss, but if I can be of any
                 help to you, you must let me know.

HOLMES goes into the bedroom wing.

ENID takes the note out of her bosom, reads it again, then hurriedly
replaces it as RYLOTT and RODGERS re-enter.

RYLOTT: Very good. You can go and pack your box.

RODGERS: (Cringing.)
                 Yes, sir. You won't—

RYLOTT: That's enough. Get away!

RODGERS goes into the servants' hall.

ENID sits at the tea-table.

RYLOTT: (Comes over to ENID.)
                 There you are! I want a word or two with you.
                 What the devil do you mean by slipping off to
                 London the moment my back was turned? And
                 what did you do when you got there?

Sir Arthur Conan Doyle

ENID: I went there on my own business.

RYLOTT: Oh! on your own business, was it? Perhaps
                   what you call your own business may prove to
                   be my business also. Who did you see? Come,
                   woman, tell me!

ENID: It was my own business. I am of age. You have
                   no claim to control me.

RYLOTT: I know exactly where you went. You went to
                   the rooms of Mr. Sherlock Holmes, where you
                   met Dr. Watson, who had advised you to go
                   there. Was it not so?

ENID: I will answer no questions. If I did as you say, I
                   was within my rights.

RYLOTT: What have you been saying about me? What
                   did you go to consult Mr. Holmes about?

ENID remains silent.

RYLOTT: D'you hear? What did you go about? By God,
                   I'll find a way to make you speak!
                   (Seizes her by the arm.)
                   Come!

Enter HOLMES.

HOLMES: Yes, sir?

RYLOTT: I did not ring for you.

HOLMES: I thought you called.

RYLOTT: Get out of this! What do you mean?

HOLMES: I beg your pardon, sir.

He goes into the servants hall.

RYLOTT goes to the door of the servants hall, looks through, then returns.

RYLOTT: Look here Enid, let us be sensible. I was too hot now. But you must realize the situation. Your wisest and safest course is complete submission. If you do what I tell you, there be no friction between us.

ENID: What do you wish me to do?

RYLOTT: Your marriage will complicate the arrangement which was come to at your mother's death. I want you of own free will to bind yourself to respect it. Come Enid, you would not wish that your happiness should cause loss and even penury to me. I am an elderly man. I have had losses too, which make it the more necessary that I should preserve what is left. If you will sign a little deed it will be best for both of us.

ENID: I have promised to sign nothing until a lawyer has seen it.

RYLOTT: Promised? Promised whom?

ENID: I promised my fiancée.

RYLOTT: Oh! you did, did you? But why should lawyers come between you and me, Enid? I beg you — I urge you to do what I ask
(Opening out papers before her.)

ENID: No, no. I cannot. I will not.

RYLOTT: Very good! Tell me the truth, Enid. I won't be angry. What are your suspicions of me?

ENID: I have no suspicions.

RYLOTT: Did I not receive your fiancé with civility?

ENID: Yes, you did.

RYLOTT: Have I not, on the whole, been kind to you all this winter?

ENID: Yes, you have.

RYLOTT: Then, tell me, child, why do you suspect me?

ENID: I don't suspect you.

RYLOTT: Why do you send out messages to get help against me?

ENID: I don't understand you.

RYLOTT: Didn't you send out for help? Tell me the truth, child.

ENID: No.

RYLOTT: (With a yell.)
            You damned little liar!
            (Bangs the telegram down before her.)
            What was this telegram that you gave to Rodgers?

ENID sinks back, half fainting.

RYLOTT: Ah! you infernal young hypocrite. Shall I read it to you? "Come to me as soon as you can. Please hurry." What did you mean by that? What did you mean, I say?
            (Clutching her arm.)
            None of your lies —out with it.

ENID: Keep your hands off me, you coward!

RYLOTT: Answer me— answer me, then!

ENID: I will answer you! I believe that you murdered my mother by your neglect. I believe that in some way you drove my sister to her grave.
            (CONT/)

Now, I am certain that you mean to do the same to me. You're a murderer—a murderer! We were left to your care— helpless girls. You have ill-used us—you have tortured us—now you have murdered one of us, and you would do the same to me. You are a coward, a monster, a man fit only for the gallows!

RYLOTT: You'll pay for this, you little devil! Get to your room.

ENID: I will. I'm not without friends, as you may find.

RYLOTT: You've got some plot against me. What have you been arranging in London? What is it? (Clutches her.)

ENID: Let me go!

RYLOTT: What did you tell them? By God, I'll twist your head off your shoulders if you cross me! (Seizes her by the neck.)

ENID: Help! Help!

Enter HOLMES.

HOLMES: Hands off, Dr. Rylott.

RYLOTT releases ENID.

HOLMES: You had best go to your room, young lady. I'll see that you are not molested. Go at once, I tell you, go.

RYLOTT: You infernal villain. I'll soon settle you.

After ENID goes out, he runs to a rack at the side, gets a whip, opens the hall door, stands near it with his whip.

RYLOTT: Now, then, out you go! By George, you'll remember Stoke Moran.

HOLMES:	Excuse me, sir, but is that a whip?
RYLOTT:	You'll soon see what it is.
HOLMES:	I am afraid I must ask you to put it down.
RYLOTT:	Oh, indeed! must you? (Comes forward to him.)
HOLMES:	(Taking out a revolver.) Yes, sir! You'll please put down that whip.
RYLOTT:	(Falling back.) You villain!
HOLMES:	Stand right back, sir. I'll take no risks with a man like you. Right back, I say! Thank you, sir.
RYLOTT:	Rodgers! Ali! My gun!

He runs into his study.

| HOLMES: | Hurry up, Billy! No time to lose. |

Enter BILLY, as Amelia, from the servants' hall.

| BILLY: | Yes, Mr. Holmes. |

HOLMES and BILLY go out through the entrance hall.

Several shots are heard outside. RYLOTT rushes in from his study with his gun.

Enter ALl —running in from outside.

ALI:	Stop, Sahib, stop!
RYLOTT:	What were those shots?
ALI:	The new butler, sir. He shoot Siva!

RYLOTT:	Shot my dog! By God, I'll teach him! (Rushes toward door.)
ALI:	No, no, Sahib. He gone in darkness. What do you do? People come. Police come.
RYLOTT:	You're right. (Puts gun down.) We have another game; Ali, you will watch outside Miss Enid's window to-night.
ALI:	Yes, Sahib, shall I watch all night?
RYLOTT:	All night? No, not all night! You will learn when you may cease your watch.

CURTAIN

Scene 2
ENID'S Bedroom, Stoke Place

ENID is discovered seated near the lamp at a small table near a window. A knock is heard at the door.

ENID:	Who is there?
RYLOTT:	(Off.) It is I.
ENID:	What do you want?
RYLOTT:	Why is your light still burning?
ENID:	I have been reading.
RYLOTT:	You are not in bed then?
ENID:	Not yet.
RYLOTT:	Then I desire to come in.
ENID:	But it is so late.

RYLOTT: (Rattles door.)
               Come, come, let me in this instant.

ENID: No, no I cannot!

RYLOTT: Must I break the door in?

ENID: I will open it. I will open it.
               (Opens door.)
               Why do persecute me so?

RYLOTT enters in his dressing gown.

RYLOTT: Why are you so childish and so suspicious?
               Your mind has brooded upon your poor sister's
               death until you have built up these fantastic
               suspicions against me. Tell me now Enid —
               I'm not such a bad sort you know, if you only
               deal frankly with me. Tell me, have you any
               idea of your own about how your sister died?
               Was that what you went to Mr. Holmes about
               this morning? Couldn't you take me into your
               confidence as well as him? Is it not natural that
               I should feel hurt when I see you turn to a
               stranger for advice?

ENID: How my poor sister met her death only your
               own wicked heart can know. I am as sure that
               it came to her through you as if I had seen you
               strike her down. You may kill me if you like,
               but I will tell you what I think.

RYLOTT: My dear child, you are overwrought and
               hysterical. What can have put such wild ideas
               into your head? After all, I may have a hasty
               temper—I have often deplored it to you — but
               what excuse have I ever given you for such
               monstrous suspicions?

ENID: You think that by a few smooth words you can
               make me forget all your past looks, your acts.
               You cannot deceive me, I know the danger and
               I face it.

324

RYLOTT:	What, then, is the danger?
ENID:	It is near me to-night, whatever it is.
RYLOTT:	Why do you think so?
ENID:	Why is that Indian watching in the darkness? I opened my window just now, and there he was. Why is he there?
RYLOTT:	To prevent your making a public fool of yourself. You are capable of getting loose and making a scandal.
ENID:	He is there to keep me in my room until you come to murder me.
RYLOTT:	Upon my word, I think your brain is unhinged. Now, look here, Enid, be reasonable for a moment.
ENID:	What's that?
RYLOTT:	What is it, then?
ENID:	I thought I heard a cry.
RYLOTT:	It's the howling of the wind. Listen to me. If there is friction between us — and I don't for a moment deny that there is —why is it? You think I mean to hurt you. I could only have one possible motive for hurting you. Why not remove that motive? Then you could no longer work yourself into these terrors. Here is that legal paper I spoke of. Mrs. Staunton could witness it. All I want is your signature.
ENID:	No, never.
RYLOTT:	Never!
ENID:	Unless my lawyer advises it.

325

RYLOTT: Is that final?

ENID   (Springing up.)
                  Yes, it is. I will never sign it.

RYLOTT: Well, I have done my best for you. It was your
                  last chance.

ENID: Ah! then you do mean murder.

RYLOTT: The last chance of regaining my favour. You—
                  (Pause.)
                  Get to your bed and may you wake in a more
                  rational mood to-morrow. You will not be
                  permitted to make a scandal. Ali will be at his
                  post outside, and I shall sit in the hall; so you
                  may reconcile yourself to being quiet. Nothing
                  more to say to me?

He goes out.

When he has gone, ENID listens to his departing footsteps. Then she
locks the door once again, and looks round her.

ENID: What is that tapping? Surely I heard tapping!
                  Perhaps it is the pulse within my own brain?

Tapping.

ENID: Yes! there it is again! Where was it? Is it the
                  signal of death?
                  (Looks wildly round the walls.)
                  Ah! it grows louder. It is the window.
                  (Goes towards window.)
                  A man! a man crouching in the darkness. Still
                  tapping. It's not Ali! The face was white. Ah!

The window opens and HOLMES enters.

HOLMES: My dear young lady, I trust that I don't intrude.

ENID: Oh, Mr. Holmes, I'm so glad to see you!
                              (CONT/)

Save me! save me! Mr. Holmes, they mean to murder me.

HOLMES: Tut, tut! we mean that they shall do nothing of sort.

ENID: I had given up All hope of your coming.

HOLMES: These old-fashioned window-catches are most inefficient.

ENID: How did you pass the Indian and the dog?

HOLMES: Well, as to the Indian, we chloroformed him. Watson is busy tying him up in the arbour at the present moment. The dog I was compelled to shoot at an earlier stage of the proceeding.

ENID: You shot Siva!

HOLMES: I might have been forced to shoot her master also. It was after I sent you to your room. He threatened me with a whip.

ENID: You were — you were Peters, the butler.

HOLMES: (Feeling the walls.)
I wanted to be near you. So this is the famous room, is it? Dear me! Very much as I had pictured it. You will excuse me for not discovering myself to you, but any cry or agitation upon your part would have betrayed me.

ENID: But your daughter Amelia?

HOLMES: Ah, yes, I take Billy when I can. Billy as messenger is invaluable.

ENID: Then you intended to watch over me till night?

HOLMES: Exactly. But the man's brutality caused me to
                 show my hand too soon. However, I have
                 never been far from your window. I gather the
                 matter is pressing.

ENID: He means to murder me to-night.

HOLMES: He is certainly in an ugly humour. He is not in
                 his room at present.

ENID: No, he is in the hall.

HOLMES: So we can talk with safety. What has become
                 of the excellent Watson?
                 (Approaches window.)
                 Come in, Watson, come in!

Enter WATSON from window.

HOLMES: How is our Indian friend?

WATSON: He is coming out of the chloroform; but he can
                 neither move nor speak. Good evening, Miss
                 Stonor, what a night it is.

ENID: How can I thank you for coming?

HOLMES: You'll find Dr. Watson a useful companion on
                 such an occasion. He has a natural turn for
                 violence — some survival of his surgical
                 training. The wind is good. Its howling will
                 cover all sounds. Just sit in the window,
                 Watson, and see that our retreat is safe. With
                 your leave, I will inspect the room a little more
                 closely. Now, my dear young lady, I can see
                 that you are frightened to death, and no
                 wonder. Your courage, so far, has been
                 admirable. Sit over here by the fire.

ENID: If he should come—!

HOLMES: In that case answer him.
                          (CONT/)

	Say that you have gone to bed.
	(Takes lamp from table.)
	A most interesting old room — very quaint indeed! Old-fashioned comfort without modern luxury. The passage is, as I understand, immediately outside?
ENID:	Yes.
HOLMES:	Mr. Peters made two attempts to explore the ground, but without avail. By the way, I gather that you tried to send me a message, and that old Rodgers gave it to your stepfather.
ENID:	Yes, he did.
HOLMES:	He is not to be blamed. His master controls him. He had to betray you. (Placing lamp down.)
ENID:	It was my fault.
HOLMES:	Well, well, it was an indiscretion, but it didn't matter. Let me see now, on this side is the room under repair. Quite so. Only one door. This leads into the passage?
ENID:	Yes.
HOLMES:	And that passage to the hall?
ENID:	Yes.
HOLMES:	Here is where the genial old gentleman sleeps when he is so innocently employed. Where is his door?
ENID:	Down the passage.
HOLMES:	Surely I heard him— (A step is heard in the passage.)
ENID:	Yes, it's his step.

329

HOLMES holds his hat over the light. There is a knock at the door.

RYLOTT:	(Outside door.) Enid!
ENID:	What is it?
RYLOTT:	Are you in bed?
ENID:	Yes.
RYLOTT:	Are you still of the same mind?
ENID:	Yes, I am.

Pause. They all listen.

HOLMES:	(Whispering.) Has he gone into his room?
ENID:	(Crossing to door, listening.) No, he's gone down the passage again to the hall.
HOLMES:	Then we must make the most of the time. Might I trouble you, Watson, for the gimlet and the yard measure? Thank you! The lantern also. Thank you! You can turn up the lamp. I am interested in this partition wall. (Standing on the bed.) No little surprise, I suppose? No trap-doors and sliding panels? Funny folk, our ancestors, with a quaint taste in practical joking. (Gets on bed and fingers the wall.) No, it seems solid enough. Dear me! and yet you say your sister fastened both door and window. Remarkable. My lens, Watson. A perfectly respectable wall—in fact, a commonplace wall. Trap-door in the floor? (Kneels at one side of the bed, then the other.) No, nothing suspicious in that direction. Ancient carpeting — (CONT/)

(Crossing round bed.)
— oak wainscot—nothing more. Hullo!
(Pulling at bed-post.)

WATSON: Why, what is it?

HOLMES: Why is your bed clamped to the floor?

ENID: I really don't know.

HOLMES: Was the bed in your other room clamped?

ENID: No, I don't think it was.

HOLMES: Very interesting. Most interesting and
                 instructive. And this bell-pull—where does it
                 communicate with?

ENID: It does not work.

HOLMES: But if you want to ring?

ENID: There is another over here.

HOLMES: Then why this one?

ENID: I don't know. There were some changes after
                 we came here.

HOLMES: Quite a burst of activity, apparently. It took
                 some strange shapes.
                 (Standing on the bed.)
                 You may be interested to know that the bell-
                 rope ends in a brass hook. No wire attachment;
                 it is a dummy. Dear me! how very singular. I
                 see a small screen above it, which covers a
                 ventilator, I suppose?

ENID: Yes, Mr. Holmes, there is a ventilator.

HOLMES: Curious fad to ventilate one room into another
                 when one could as well get the open air.
                              (CONT/)

331

Most original man, the architect. Very singular indeed. There is no means of opening the flap from here; it must open on the other side.

WATSON: What do you make of it, Holmes?

HOLMES: Suggestive, my dear Watson, very suggestive. Might I trouble you for your knife? With your permission, Miss Stonor, I will make a slight alteration.
(Stands on bed-head and cuts the bell-pull.)

WATSON: Why do you do that, Holmes?

HOLMES: Dangerous, Watson, dangerous. Bear in mind that this opening, concealed by a flap of wood, leads into the room of our cheery Anglo-Indian neighbour. I repeat the adjective, Watson — Anglo-Indian.

WATSON: Well, Holmes?

HOLMES: The bed is clamped so that it cannot be shifted. He has a dummy bell-pull which leads to the bed. He has a hole above it which opens on his room. He is an Anglo-Indian doctor. Do you make nothing of all this? The music, too? The music. What is the music?

WATSON: A signal, Holmes.

HOLMES: A signal! A signal to whom?

WATSON: An accomplice.

HOLMES: Exactly. An accomplice who could enter a room with locked doors— an accomplice who could give a sure death which leaves no trace. An accomplice who can only be attracted back by music.

ENID: Hush! he is gone to his room.

A door is heard to close outside.

HOLMES:	Listen! The door is shut.
	(As Watson is about to take up lamp.)
	Keep the lamp covered, so that if the ventilator is opened no light will show. He must think the girl is asleep. Keep the dark lantern handy. We must wait in the dark. I fancy we shall not have long to wait.
ENID:	I am so frightened.
HOLMES:	It is too much for you.
WATSON:	Can I do anything, Holmes?
HOLMES:	You can hand me my hunting-crop. Hush! What's that?

Flute music is heard.

HOLMES:	My stick, Watson— quick, be quick! Now take the lantern. Have you got it? When I cry, "Now!" turn it full blaze upon the top of the bell-rope. Do you understand?
WATSON:	Yes.
HOLMES:	Down that bell-rope comes the messenger of death. It guides to the girl's pillow. Hush! the flap!

The flap opens, disclosing a small square of light. This light is obscured. Music a good deal louder.

HOLMES:	(Cries sharply.)
	Now

WATSON turns the lantern full on to the bell-rope. A snake is half through the hole. HOLMES lashes at it with his stick. It disappears backwards.

The flute music stops.

WATSON: It has gone.

HOLMES: Yes, it has gone, but we know the truth.

A loud cry is heard.

WATSON: What is that?

HOLMES: I believe the devil has turned on its master.

Another cry.

HOLMES: It is in the passage.
         (Throws open the door.)

In the doorway is seen DR. RYLOTT in shirt and trousers, the snake round his head and neck.

RYLOTT: Save me! save me!

RYLOTT rushes in and falls on the floor. WATSON strikes at the snake as it writhes across the room.

WATSON: (Looking at the snake.)
         The brute is dead.

HOLMES: (Looking at RYLOTT.)
         So is the other.

They both run to support the fainting lady.

HOLMES: Miss Stonor, there is no more danger for you
         under this roof.

CURTAIN

Notes

In 1909, Sir Arthur Conan Doyle 's production of *The House of Temperley* at the Adelphi Theatre was failing badly, with the already struggling show hit further by the death of King Edward VII. The play closed, leaving Conan Doyle with and empty theatre and in serious financial peril. Remembering the earlier success of William Gillette's Sherlock Holmes play a decade earlier, Conan Doyle decided to write a Holmes play of his own.

Conan Doyle wrote the play in a week, and within a fortnight of *The House of Temperley* closing, the theatre company was in rehearsal for the new Holmes play.

The writer selected *The Speckled Band*, one of his favourite Holmes short stories, as the basis for his production, adding a few incidents from elsewhere in the canon. H.A. Saintsbury was selected to play Holmes in the production with Lyn Harding cast as the villainous Roylott.

The play enjoyed a successful run at the Adelphi before transferring to The Globe. Later, the play would head out on a tour of the United Kingdom, with two companies touring the show to maximize income from the play.

Despite the show's success, reaction was not completely positive. While Saintsbury, who had earlier replaced William Gillette in the first Sherlock Holmes play, was given generally good notices, the real star was Lyn Harding, whose portrayal of Rylott dominated the stage, occasionally pushing Holmes and Watson into the shadows. The lack of exposition for Holmes' deductive processes is often criticized in revues of the play's script, as is the weak and abrupt ending. One of the more bizarre criticisms of the original production was that of the serpent in the play's final act, which was dismissed as terrible and obviously fake... despite the fact that a real snake was actually used.

In spite of any criticisms, the play was a huge financial success and rescued Conan Doyle's finances.

The Speckled Band has been adapted for countless radio and television productions in subsequent years and was again adapted for the stage in 2014, when Liam Tims took on the role of Holmes for a production which premiered at Treasurer's House in Ripley, North Yorkshire.

Holmes and Watson have taken to the board on numerous occasions in various subsequent productions over the years. One of the most intriguing was *The Secret of Sherlock Holmes*, which lifted Jeremy Brett and Edward Hardwick's definitive performances from their Granada TV series and put them into London's West End for a successful run. Tom Baker took the lead in the fascinating *Sherlock Holmes and The Mask of Moriarty* in 1985, which premiered in Dublin, while noted genre author Brian Clemens wrote *Sherlock Holmes And Jack The Ripper*, at least the third depiction of Holmes' investigation of the notorious Whitechapel murders. One of the best known productions has to be *The Crucifer of Blood*, a broad adaptation by Paul Giovanni of *The Sign of Four*.

There have been comedies, musicals and even a ballet based on Sherlock Holmes as well as more traditional mystery plays, which continue to be performed regularly. Would any of them have existed without the early productions reprinted in this volume? That's a question only Mr Holmes can answer.

72743981R00186

Made in the USA
Columbia, SC
27 June 2017